SPYBUS

BOB ADAMS

To Mary
lots of love

Bob

CHAPTER ONE

Jason fingered his bullet hole. He often did while sitting at his desk in the counter espionage unit thinking. He spent a lot of time thinking. Those who entered his office, and they were very few, would sit down on a chair right at the centre of the other side of the desk. The observant ones, and the staff here were paid to be observant, would notice a small hole three inches below the moulding of the desktop. The James Bond aficionados among them, and that meant every one of them, even those who didn't know what aficionado meant, realised that this was the hole through which a bullet would pass on its rapid way towards the entrails of any unwelcome visitor. They realised wrongly. Jason Jackson had no gun. He had that rank within the service, which entailed his signing for a replacement pencil under the reproachful eye of the buyer after handing back the used stump. He was licensed to fill - forms.

The aforementioned orifice was there to impress. The secrecy within the unit was such that no one member knew the rank, duties or powers of the others, at least at Jason's level. So his peers were duly impressed. The effect on his seniors would not have been quite the same. However persons from the upper rung never came to Jason. He went to them - at the double.

The internal phone on his desk vibrated into life. The upper rung was ringing. Jason pulled his finger out and dashed along the corridor, glanced to see that the green light was shining above the controller's door, ran straight into the solid mahogany and split open the almost healed cut on his nose. "Damn it. Not again." This was the second collision with the door this week, the fourth this month. He turned quickly, tears in his eyes, went back to his own room, put his electronic key card in his breast pocket and approached his boss's door warily. When he was precisely eighteen inches from it the door slid silently open.

Roger Stafford looked up at his bleeding colleague and sighed. If the quality of staff he was being allocated these days reflected the importance the government placed on security, he thought, they might as well post our troop dispositions on the front page of the Times. At this time of turmoil and change in Europe his section was fully extended which, he had found, seemed to mean only that their visits abroad were protracted and their travelling expenses inflated. He had also lost many of his best men to a new section whose remit was to ensure that the improving political situation in Europe did not work to Britain's disadvantage and to plot accordingly.

He sighed again. "Sit down, Jason - and don't bend over my desk. I had a hell of a job getting the bloodstains out last time. Winters of M19 asked if I did interrogations in here now."

"Sorry, Roger. Would forget my own head if it weren't stuck on."

"Well, if heads have to roll in this department, and roll they will if we don't get to the bottom of the Torow affair, you'll find yours is not stuck on too securely."

Jason had never heard of Torow so couldn't see what the bottom of his affair had to do with him. He looked suitably aware and concerned. His eyes ran round the plush, mahogany paneled, and deep carpeted office, which contrasted so painfully with his own upgraded cupboard. He had hoped that all this would be his one-day, but he had not done well since joining Roger's section. He had not become one of the boys. He had decided that he would have to cultivate Roger; ingratiate himself. He looked at the plump narrow eyed man and searched for a suitable topic.

On the wall opposite Roger was a photograph of the Prime Minister which was perhaps why Roger never looked relaxed. On one side wall was a photograph of the Head of the CIA. The wall opposite had been blank but Jason now noticed a bright new photograph.

"Who is that?" asked Jason more to defer the imminent discussion than from genuine curiosity; discussions with Roger were always bad news.

"That is Horrom, head of the KGK - the new set up. Been reading Montgomery's Memoirs. He kept a photograph of Rommel facing him in his battle caravan. Said it helped to remind him what sort of man he was up against. Looked into his eyes. That sort of thing"

"What a good idea. And who are those others with him?"

Roger hesitated as if to check whether this was confidential information. "His wife - and his four children."

Jason peered at the picture. It was a cheerful group photograph taken in a small colourful garden. "Lovely dog"

"That's Vido."

"You can't see his eyes very clearly."

Roger looked exasperated. "It's a Newfoundland. They are very hairy dogs."

"No, the man's eyes." Jason corrected, carefully hiding his own exasperation. "You can hardly see them."

"Look, I would rather have had a close up at his desk or in the questioning room but that is the only one I could get."

"It's a good photograph. Happy group. He looks a nice man.

"Yes, doesn't he? Devilish clever isn't it?"

"Yes, indeed". Jason brought a blood stained handkerchief from his pocket and gingerly dabbed his nose. He saw a look of scorn on the other man's face and decided he'd better come to the point of his visit. "You asked me to look at our set up in Tyrnia in view of the disappearance of a contact there."

"Torow," snapped Roger.

"Ah, Torow," Jason, who had never heard of him, nodded knowingly. "Well, we have very little in the way of organization in Tyrnia but I've thought of a way of getting to him." He waited for a look of curiosity and/or admiration. All he got was an impatient grunt.

"Well, get on with it," barked Roger, looking at his watch.

"We send in a whole bus load of spies."

"Go on," growled Roger with a show of even less interest.

Jason leaned forward like a child about to divulge some great secret about its parents' behaviour to an enthralled playground. "In the bus would be one of us - a real professional spy." Roger raised his eyes to heaven. "And lots of amateur spies. To confuse them."

Roger for the first time looked mildly interested. He hid this with a flat voice. "You mean use the make believe spies as decoys while our man gets through?"

"I was hoping you would say that." Jason kept all the gloating out of his voice

"Oh, were you. Now why that?"

"Well. I thought if someone as intelligent as you--" He paused for effect. It had no effect. "If someone as intelligent as you," he said, trying again, "would think that, then my plan might work."

"What plan? Get on with it, man."

"I thought the professional could be the decoy and the amateurs could go for it. Whatever it is."

"You mean prefer a newly recruited bunch of wallies straight off the street to our highly trained, carefully selected band of specialists?" Roger paused, stared at his new photograph, thought for a bit, then said, "You know there might just be something in this. Go on."

"We send a small bus load across as tourists, one regular and about a dozen casuals. The pro would be spotted in about five minutes, as usual, and taken away then the bus party could get on with the real work."

Roger thought for a minute and, desperately trying to hide his growing enthusiasm for the idea, snapped. "And where the hell would we get these casuals?"

"We could look at the list of nuts we get volunteering all the time. And I can get a note of people who have enquired about outlandish adventure holidays - the travel firm I use when we don't want the foreign office to know where we're going will help I'm sure. And everyone in the office could recommend someone. That would give us variety."

"They would have to look like a typical bus party. That means a pretty weird bunch. Yes, our staff would certainly know just the right sort of person. You know we might be onto something here."

"A sort of Trojan bus, I thought," ventured Jason, feeling pleased with himself.

"You save your mythology for your expenses claims, Jason. Right, have a list of prospective tourists on my desk this time tomorrow. A mixed list. And I'll interview them."

"Like the Dirty Dozen, isn't it, sir?"

"Well, I hope they don't make such a mess of my desk. Thank you, Jason. Now please remove all traces of your visit."

Jason wiped the desk with his handkerchief and rose to depart.

"Jason," shouted Roger as he was going out. "Not a word. Remember if this goes wrong a man might die."

CHAPTER TWO

Larry, the man who might die, hoped he looked a sorry sight lying on a soiled mattress in a prison cell in - he didn't know where. The painted on bruises had escaped detection.

The doctor finished his examination, straightened his thin back, took off his half spectacles and pronounced firmly, "I am afraid it will be some time before you can interrogate this man. He is in a bad way."

"How much time?" asked the interrogator as he reached for his jacket.

"Two weeks preferably, one at least. I can dress the wounds - they are not too serious. But some bad bruising. It looks as if he has been in a car crash or been badly beaten up. Had quite a shock. Heartbeat is very high. Overweight too. Could not stand much. He would just black out or - or pass on - not productive."

The doctor looked relieved that he had deferred the torment. Larry, who knew a bit of Tyrnian, was also relieved. The tattoo undercoat to the bruises had been a good touch.

"One week, no more. I've got somebody I can be getting on with in the meantime. Look after this one - he is important." The interrogator now spoke quietly in English with a heavy accent.

'To keep me in the picture,' thought Larry. 'A horror picture.'

The interrogator narrowing his already small eyes to turn his request into a command shrugged the jacket onto his broad shoulders and stalked out of the cell without a glance at Larry.

The doctor's eyes met Larry's momentarily. They hinted the faintest glimmer of sympathy dowsed by resignation. He's thinking, thought Hassall, this is just my job, don't blame me. Larry tried to convey by his expression that he accepted this but his genuinely bruised lips made this difficult. Roger had insisted on a few real wounds. No sacrifice for the cause was too great for Roger provided, Larry had noticed, someone else was making the sacrifice. The drug he had been given to get the old ticker racing was also timed well, he thought; did the trick beautifully. The doctor shuffled off, a tired man who had won a tiny victory.

Larry was left alone. One week was tight but would just fit in with the planned timing. He was under no illusions as to why he had been selected for this important task. He had a very high threshold of pain which had been a great help in his wrestling days. No one had ever really hurt him however good the hold or fall but the disadvantage was that often he had not submitted when he should. He was, therefore, a bit more punch drunk than most ex-wrestlers. He had the obligatory mat man's cauliflower ear; most people meeting him took him to be a retired boxer. He was intelligent but sometimes his mind wandered; away with the fairies you might have said in days gone by. These periods of pixilated thinking helped confuse his captors. Of course he had not been given up to date information on who was who or what was what in the rapidly changing political scene of Eastern Europe, which was helpful - not necessarily to him - but helpful. Roger held to the belief that information was best sucked into a vacuum.

Larry was not a regular member of the counter espionage unit. He was used for occasions when a bit of give and take was likely, particularly - he had learned - take; but was not just a punch bag. He had the skill to maximize dramatically the effect of an assault while minimizing the real damage and, when he really concentrated, could stay alert in the most dire of circumstances.

He had been the first person Roger had thought of when the Tyrnians made several vicious but unsuccessful attempts to kidnap a senior British diplomat and Roger wanted to know why. So a trap was set with Larry as the bait. The trap was now well and truly sprung.

Everything is going to plan, thought Larry, except that Torow, the linkman, hasn't made contact yet. Torow is a genius at this sort of thing. Everyone in the Service has a high regard for him. Torow will arrange the rescue - when the job is done.

'Listen to the question.' That was all he had to do.

He pulled around his body the soft paper blanket provided, no doubt, so that he would have nothing with which to take his own life. Not that he had the slightest intention of doing that. Unless! He felt again with the tip of his tongue the tooth with the jagged edge. He wished they had used a little more finesse when they had taken out the filling and replaced it with one of the kitmaster's pills. His tongue kept going to the sharp edge. It would be curtains if he knocked off the cap so, with a great effort of willpower, he kept pulling his tongue away. It was a routine precaution he told himself. Torow would get him out of this - just as soon as he had learned the question.

CHAPTER THREE

Jason looked at the list in his hand and chuckled. Mixed the man said, well - mixed it was. Jason had included twenty names knowing that only twelve would be required; eleven if you took out the pro. That would give Roger, who liked to be in control, the feeling he was making the choice. However Jason regarded this project as his own so he had included a few characters so outrageous that even Roger would not choose them. The remaining group would have a chance. He was becoming quite enthusiastic and would await their return with the tingle of confident anticipation. He laughed at the thought of moaning Monica in the team and he took a mental note to thank his friend Finlay for giving him one of his impossible choices. Finlay had a big party planned for his brother returning from the Middle East and he earnestly desired the absence of his nagging neighbour, Monica. No chance.

Jason felt like a card sharp forcing a selection on Roger. So, smiling and confident, he strode along to Roger's room - with his electronic card in his pocket. The door did not slide open for him and he knocked on it with his nose.

"Who is it?" shouted Roger.

"It's me. Jason," came the nasal reply.

"You don't sound like Jason Jackson to me. If it is you, just run along and get your new card like a good boy. This is the first of the month."

When Jason did get back to Roger's office he had dabbed his nose with a styptic pencil and put a small piece of toilet paper on the wound. His confidence was waning and his smile had waned. He pushed the list of names and appointments across the desk. Roger gave the paper a cursory glance and cursed.

"This looks like two days work and I am hellish busy just now."

"I'll do it if you like," offered Jason.

"Oh, no you won't. You couldn't pick the caterers for the office party without giving us all food poisoning. This needs a very special skill. It could be a dangerous operation. I will be doing this alone."

Jason thought it unfair of Roger to keep bringing up that unfortunate meal although that's exactly what they had all done on the night of the party. He winced as he thought of the receptacles that had been used to relieve the hard pressed toilet facilities - and the hard-pressed staff.

"But I thought - as it was my idea-"

"Forget it Jason. In the service, as you will learn, eventually, I hope, it is always best that as few people as possible know all about a project. You understand?"

Jason overcame an impulse to shake his head and nodded intelligently.

"So. Interviews tomorrow. 10 a.m. Any questions?" growled Roger.

"No arms, I assume?" Enquired Jason. Roger nodded, his plump jowls shaking. "Any special equipment, codes, instructions, anything like that?

"We'll wait to see what task we give to each individual. Then we'll decide."

"Will I then lay on a group briefing to make sure they all understand?" asked Jason.

"Jason, will you never learn? None of them must know what the others are up to or it will upset my plan completely."

Jason hid the hurt he felt at it being referred to by Roger as 'my plan'. "You mean they will all be working independently?"

"In a way yes, but I will give out some dummy tasks to create diversions and confuse them."

"That's a very clever idea," said Jason fearing that his unhappy expression might be interpreted, correctly, by Roger as a sign that he was not enamoured of the way the project was going. He feared he was going to be the first to be confused.

"Not one of them will know that their companions are other than ordinary tourists." explained Roger. "Each one will work on his own entirely oblivious to what the others are up to."

So what's different, thought Jason.

CHAPTER FOUR

Jason was not happy. It was now Roger's plan and he was making a real cock up of the selection. Several of his dummies had been issued with visas. His best man, the man he would have liked to have with him on such a mission, if going on missions had been part of his duties, had been sent off on a canoeing trip up the Ompopo. He had been an intelligent all rounder, fit and strong, with a record of daring sporting adventures behind him. Roger had said that he would have looked out of place and conspicuous on a bus trip. The lot he has picked so far, thought Jason, wouldn't look out of place in a fairground. He thanked his lucky stars that he would be hundreds of miles away when they all had to prove their worth - or worthlessness. He visualized himself taking the progress reports into Roger and making it abundantly clear that he was refraining from saying 'I told you so' only because he was above such trivial triumphs. Alternatively, he thought, I could say - 'I told you so.'

In a long line of failures by the Section, well covered up but still failures, this threatened to be outstanding. As it was his idea this worried Jason and he fell asleep trying to think of ways of improving its meagre chance of success.

At the end of the next day Jason was again less than chuffed. He would not have made the same selections. He was however favourably surprised that the blonde had been included. Jason hadn't really short-listed her, not in any positive way, it was just that he had this weakness in his character - he could not refuse anything that a good-looking woman asked of him. And this blonde was good looking all right. She was one of these rare, charmed human beings in whom all the parts are in perfect proportion - and then some. Everything was generous. Her legs were just a fraction longer than they need be, her breasts a little more ample than was strictly necessary and she would have got by quite nicely with lips less full and luscious. Her hair was blonde right up to the roots. Miss Hilary Pert was not perfect, she possessed just too much of everything to be perfect, and she dressed in a way which proved that there was an art in revealing art. She was indeed well blessed.

And even more so, thought Jason, would be any fortunate suitor. He expressed this to himself somewhat more specifically. It even crossed his mind, fleetingly; that he wished he were going on this crazy venture; but just fleetingly. He comforted himself with the knowledge that this aberration of Roger's would give him the pleasure of being involved in the kitting out of this beautiful creature before the party left and on their return - debriefing her. The ambiguity of this brought a smile to his face.

Roger replied to Jason's question, on this choice of someone even more conspicuous than the gentleman rejected yesterday, with the curt answer. "Even in real life a beautiful spy can be useful."

The next blow to Jason's idea of how things for the big trip should be ordered came when he was told that Bruce Dunlop was to be the professional - the decoy. Bruce was a James Bond lookalike. James Bond was fit, intelligent and brave. Bruce, thought Jason, had all but three of these qualities. He protested but Roger brushed his objections aside saying that this was just a fill in job. Jason had visualized the pro at least carrying the ball for a few yards before he was brought down: make a bit of ground for the others.

Roger produced the final list to go over the admin details with Jason. There were five women and six men on the list. The six men included the staff man Dunlop.

"Not a very strong looking team - in fact they look quite ordinary," ventured Jason grudgingly, still feeling sore that he had not had more influence on the make-up of the group.

"What has strong got to do with it? And, Jason, there is no such thing as an ordinary person. Everyone has a spark about them. This lot has resilience and spirit. I can promise you that - and they'll show it. To the superficial observer -," he looked hard at Jason. "They might look ordinary. I hope so. It's a bus trip, remember. But they're just right for what I have in mind - and I have given them a very good driver." Roger went on emphatically. "The best we have. They'll need him. The more I think about this the more I realize it could be a dicey venture. Pyke will be invaluable if it gets really dangerous. Nothing can divert him from his task. He's a man who does as he is told." Roger stressed this last remark as if it were to his mind the most important quality.

Jason grunted and Roger said testily. "The trouble with you, Jason is that you're not dedicated."

"Dedicated to what?" asked Jason.

Roger raised his eyes to heaven but Jason was pleased that he seemed to be taking the project more seriously now so he continued. "Yes, Pyke's a good man but I still think it's a pity there isn't a bit more backbone in the team. And why only eleven? Are you counting Pyke as one of the dozen?"

"No. We have another place to fill. I think we might be able to do that in a way that will meet all your objections. Someone who looks just like a tour guide. It will give the whole holiday theme an air of authenticity."

"That sounds good. When will you make this appointment? There isn't much time."

"Oh. I've made the appointment. I just have to tell the chosen man to get ready in double quick time."

"Good. Anything I can do?"

"Yes, there is. You can get ready in double quick time. You are the chosen man, Jason. You are going." Jason was speechless. "I knew you'd be delighted to be involved. After all, it was your idea."

CHAPTER FIVE

Jason did not sleep well that night. He struggled with the decision he had to make - what to do? He could resign. He thought long and hard about this option. He enjoyed his modest job and he was good at it. He had the vague feeling that on balance the Unit did some good. He loved the total complexity of the department which was such that no one knew exactly what the end product was so there was no need to feel responsible for or about anything. Jason didn't want to lead the mission and Emil Mocha standing in for him at the office would be a disaster. Emil was good.

Jason then thought about what else he could do if he did resign but he could think of nothing. I could work, he thought. He decided not to resign. He was unsure of his ability to get another job. He knew that he had been taken on in the service because he spoke well and came of a good family. He spoke well because his parents spoke well, they had never spoken to him but they had spoken well to each other. He did come of a good family - by the standards applied in the service - but the family had had its own life to live and he had been largely ignored - not neglected - but ignored. Jason often wondered if his appointment had been justified. He could appeal to higher authority. But he knew that after the office-catering debacle he did not appeal to higher authority.

As the day he had to face came nearer and nearer he reluctantly decided it would have to be a brave face. He would lead the group with élan, éclat and even le courage. He would return a hero. That would surprise them, thought Jason. He ignored that nasty little honest part in his mind which told him that he himself would also be surprised but he also thought how good it would be to have a group of people looking to him for leadership, looking up to him - including that blonde.

As Jason dressed in his brightest and most casual clothes he felt better. After carefully checking his security card he strode purposefully in to Roger's office as befits a project leader.

"Good morning," he said cheerfully, determined that the sinking feeling in his nether regions would not reflect in his face but Roger did not look up at his face, just bade him sit down and carried on writing.

"My brief I presume," suggested Jason chirpily.

"No. My expenses, actually."

What, Jason wondered, could Roger possibly do to incur such a sheet of expenses, then while he was kept waiting he started to speculate as to what his expense allowance would be for leading this important and dangerous mission.

Roger drew a double line, looked at the total, smiled and signed the paper. He looked up, the smile quickly fading.

"This damned paper work - so time consuming."

"Oh, I like it. I am a paper man," said Jason.

In more ways than one, thought Roger, glancing up the fair haired, mild looking young man.

He reached for the next file on his desk, opened it then appeared to notice that Jason was still waiting. "Ah yes, you wanted to see me."

"Yes. About the project."

"What project?"

Jason was too used to this putting down technique to let it worry him; anger him yes, but not worry him. "I thought you might wish to brief me personally."

"Not much briefing to be done actually. You are going as tour guide so you will have to mug up about the countries you pass through so that you are credible. Remember that at all times you must look and act the part so that even those who have a task to perform will think that all the others are on a normal adventure holiday. You should set off very soon to be in the right area when the balloon goes up. We haven't yet heard that contact has been made; overdue, but we should hear soon. So, go to the kitmaster and get your uniform and that's about it."

"But the assignment - the objective - the method - when do I get the details of that?"

"I am presently involved in the briefing of those members of the party who need to know what we are up to. That does not include you."

"What do you mean? How can I lead--?"

A disbelieving smile flickered across Roger's face as he interrupted. "You will guide, Jason my boy - not lead - guide. You will do just that. You will serve the best interests of the mission if you know nothing. Absolutely nothing."

Jason sank back in his seat. "I don't understand."

"Well, you should by now. I have selected members of the team each for one of a variety of tasks. I am using the scatter gun approach - not the sniper. No one will know all of the plan. Some will know nothing."

"And I will know nothing."

"1 knew you would catch on. It is vital that you know nothing. As tour guide you will have a high profile. They might have a go at you." He looked across at a wilting Jason with relish. "This means whatever they do to you, you will divulge nothing."

"Whatever they do to me?" Jason bit his lip to stem the quaver.

"Exactly. So you see the logic old boy."

"So, why not send a real guide?" asked Jason as a hope, which he instantly knew to be forlorn, struck him. "He would be really credible. I mean what is there for me to do?"

"You have an important task. You have to bring 'em back alive - as they used to say in the old talkies. Now that's a challenge. What have you to say to that?"

"Nothing - as they used to say in the silent pictures."

"Good. I like that. That spirit should stand you in good stead. I knew I had picked the right man. Keep that up and you might be still around for the last reel."

CHAPTER SIX

And so Jason set forth not knowing why, for what, or how but knowing where in great detail.

The squat little brown bus rolled off the ferry and was soon out on the dusty roads of France. The route took them on no motorways but along the narrower roads through villages of faded peeling pastel buildings and flat fields. The air smelt different, rich and fertile.

Only the hard faced Pyke was awake as they drove through some of the most beautiful scenery in France; and Jason, but only fitfully. Over the soft purr of the engine there could occasionally be heard the rustic sounds of the animals in the fields, the twittering of the birds in the dry still trees, some gentle snoring and the occasional belch. The thrill of foreign travel was being enjoyed by the zealous band.

But not by Jason. Pyke had been involved in long conferences with the kitmaster. The driver had insisted on four wheel drive, a souped up engine, a reserve petrol tank and special roll over bars. The spare wheels were deep tread rough country specials and almost every part had two or more purposes. The kitmaster had seen every spy movie and had a vivid imagination of his own. He had had his failures - the ejector seat with no opening in the roof and a grenade thrower, which, if the vehicle was travelling at sixty, returned the missile to sender. The oil slick which shot out of the front of the car was not his fault - that was the technical department's little boob. The kitmaster's real masterpiece was his placebo suicide pill. He issued some lethal pills and some harmless ones to find out whether, if a person thought a pill was going to do them harm, it would. This interesting experiment failed because it was so difficult to follow up as most of the guinea pigs did not return nor indeed did the control.

Jason therefore, knowing all this, which the regular field men did not, had less than full confidence in the equipment issued. Not that in this instance it involved him personally, he had been issued with a uniform, a whistle, maps and nothing else. He had complained to Roger that the purple blazer made him look like a refugee from Hi-De-Hi. To which Roger had replied with a belittling chuckle, "Good, I want you to look the part." Then he added. "And no mobile phones, covered or otherwise."

Jason looked puzzled. Roger continued emphatically, "Half of all serious crimes are solved nowadays because the idiot criminal has been traced through his mobile phone."

"Criminal," thought Jason.

An early stop had been planned for this first day - partly because it would give the inexperienced Jason a chance to sort out the accommodation without too much of a rush but mainly because Pyke on his visit to this area played boule for the Auberge team. It was rumoured within the department that he played without his boules after the game. The bus quickened pace as they approached the Auberge, reflecting Pyke's impatience to see how close he could get that night. He flexed and flicked expertly with his right wrist while the left hand, just as expertly, steered the bus over the potholes and pave of the rural road.

The sleepers awoke one by one as the speeding bus jostled and swung. Grumpy like children when first awakened, they were soon exchanging opinions on the beauty of the countryside they had not seen.

"I miss the green of England," moaned Monica, her heavy eyebrows coming together.

"Roads are not good. Wouldn't like to insure this bus," grumbled Chuck, an untidy looking friendly bundle of a man, knowingly. He was now clicking away with his camera.

Lucy, a bright little sparrow of a woman, shaking her greying head disapprovingly babbled. "The air doesn't seem so fresh,"

John, a dark subdued man with a worried air, rubbed his eyes "They seem to grow nothing but grapes - I wonder what they eat."

"I've had a lovely sleep." Hilary drowsily lifted her head from Jason's shoulder. "I hope I haven't been a nuisance leaning on you like this."

"Not at all, Miss Pert," replied Jason as well he might considering how carefully he had manoeuvred his shoulder under the slowly dropping blonde head. "I've been most comfortable."

"Thanks anyway, Jason - and it's Hilary, please."

Jason turned away and rubbed some blood into his cheeks then looked around as if he had been awake all afternoon. He nodded condescendingly to the sleepy faced passengers. The only person still slumped heavily in his seat was the ever alert Bruce Dunlop. Jason, noticing that one of the speakers was just above Dunlop's head, gave the microphone two sharp raps with his hand whereupon Dunlop flung himself on the floor and drew his arms over his head.

"Testing. Testing," shouted Jason cheerfully.

The size of the tables in the dining room that evening fragmented the party so Jason decided to dine with a small number and try to get to know them. He was determined to find out as much as he could about everyone so that he could still play the decisive part in this exercise that he knew he was cut out for - until Roger cut him out.

He knew only that the project had something to do with a gentleman called Torow who had evidently been sent instructions on an important project and had not acknowledged them. "Not like Torow." everyone said. "Torow's one of the best," everyone said. Everyone knows more than I do, thought Jason. Bloody Superman.

Jason had worked out from that one fact that this team, as Roger described it, must have to - find Torow - or do what Torow was to have done - or abort the project in view of Torow's disappearance. Of the three choices Jason preferred the third.

Hilary did not appear for dinner. She asked that a tray be sent to her room. This helped Jason to keep his mind on his self-imposed task. He arranged a table with the two younger ladies - both under thirty he guessed - and to avoid a party split by sex he invited Alan Mutch and Rory Brora to join them. Pyke and Bruce were not to be seen.

The evening was not a great success, socially or otherwise. Julia, the slimmer of the young ladies looked ill and was quiet and withdrawn. Grace looked thoughtful and was quiet and withdrawn. Alan and Rory were a bright pair and started off with merry leg pulling but the absence of an appreciative audience soon put a damper on that.

Jason tried to improve matters by asking questions and encouraging conversation. Julia was sitting opposite him, she was neatly dressed with a pleasant finely chiselled face and neat straight black hair. The face however had an unhealthy pallor and she had a timid dispirited look. She needs this holiday, he thought.

He was determined from the start that everyone should be on first name terms as he felt that the first defence was thus breached. "Rory isn't it?" Jason looked at the large man. Rory nodded. "I'm good at guessing what people do. Mind if I try?" Jason paused. Rory nodded again.

"You're a professional sportsman -," ventured Jason casting an eye over the other man's considerable physique. Rory looked pleased. "- who has played for Scotland." Rory looked even more pleased.

"A darts player perhaps?" said Jason. Rory raised his fist. "I'm just joking. You look like a rugby player who has -,

"Drunk too much beer," interrupted Alan.

"-retired," finished Jason.

"You're not far out. I played football - real football - not rugby." As Alan scoffed he went on. "I can tell you when I was playing these legs were insured for ten thousand pounds."

"So what did you do with the money?" chipped in Alan.

Rory smiled. He liked a man who fired back. "But I'm past it now. And never for a living. I'm a builder."

"That must be rewarding. Leaving something behind when you go," said Alan.

"What do you do then? Blow bubbles?" asked Rory.

"Very similar sometimes. I'm a teacher - a school teacher," said Alan.

"But that's the most wonderful job of all. Your influence could be felt for generations," Grace enthused briefly then relaxed back into her chair.

"Yes, madam. I used to think that. Now I reckon my entire mission in life is to cast arti-ficial pearls before real swine."

"Madam's name is Grace," said Grace very softly.

"You look tired, Julia. Far to come to pick up the bus?" asked Jason.

"No. Not far." Her dark dull eyes only met his for a moment.

"You seem to be in need of this holiday." Jason remarked, determined to draw her out.

Julia grimaced, "Look that bad do I?"

"No. Of course not - just a little tired. You look - good." Jason was not being untruthful. He could see that with a smile and a bit of sparkle in her eyes she could be an attractive woman. "You work hard, obviously?" he went on.

"Yes."

"Now what do you do - let me see?"

Jason looked from Julia to Grace, and asked, "Do you both do the same job?"

"I shouldn't think so," murmured Julia.

"I'm sure not," agreed Grace a tiny smile touching her lips.

"You're both very serious looking. One of you is a social worker," Jason surmised.

Julia and Grace both spoke together.

"In a way," said Julia.

"Something like that," came from Grace.

"Right, you can tell me all about National Insurance for the self employed. I am in one devil of a mess," said Rory.

"Oh, I'm not qualified to talk about that. Anyway I don't want to think about work. I'm recovering from - a sort of breakdown." Julia winced. "I'm on this trip for a rest. I just want to be left alone."

Jason turned to Grace who was sitting alongside him. She was not tall, about the same height as Julia, but she was more curvaceous with brown loosely curled hair, which shone with a reddish glow, when the light touched it. A very feminine looking girl Jason thought, but she also looked less than happy. She had a thoughtful, sad expression.

"And you Grace, what are you qualified to do?"

"Me? Nothing yet. Still studying." She looked at Jason steadily but without any show of interest in what he was saying.

"Post-graduate obviously." Grace gave a quiet laugh. "That obvious?"

"Sorry, I didn't mean that. It's just that you have an educated face."

"Well, it's only partly educated. And I don't like to be pigeon-holed." "Oh. No pigeon holing, we don't want any of that. I'm not being nosey, just breaking the ice. We're all holidaymakers now. What's more to the point is - what do we want to get out of this holiday."

"A change," said Grace quickly.

"Me too," added Julia.

"Meeting the people for me. If the language is not too great a barrier, I find it difficult enough with you Englishmen," Rory spoke the last sentence in an affected English accent.

"I'll translate for you," offered Alan.

"Just speak proper and I'll understand."

Julia excused herself to go to her room for a bath.

"You'll be here to learn something to pass on then, Alan." Jason looked after the departing Julia anxiously.

"No chance. I'm here to forget learning, to forget teaching and above all to forget children."

"I've not been there before but I hear the locals are very friendly," Jason persisted. "I've got a phrase book for everyone so that you can all polish up a few helpful remarks."

"Like where is the nearest hos-tel-iy?' said Alan.

"I'm no good at language. I just point. I usually get what I want." Rory gestured towards the carafe of wine.

"And speak loudly and dis-tinc-tly," suggested Alan. As the others were to find out in the days ahead, he had an irritating habit of enunciating long words very clearly as if he were talking to a class room of infant idiots.

"You've travelled a lot?" Jason topped up the empty wineglasses.

"Often but not a lot." Rory replied. "All my travelling up to now has been to the south of Spain. But never no more. It gets more like one big building site every year

- and that's exactly what I am trying to get away from. At Nerja they've even started building right on the golf course. The best line to a green is often through a villa - and I mean through, as sure as God made little tatties."

"You play golf then?" Alan played an imaginary chip shot.

"Badly. That's another thing I want to get away from. Now I look for a

country without a single golf course. That way I'm not tempted. It's getting more difficult though. Spreading like chicken pox."

"You don't like being tempted then?" asked Alan.

"Ah. That depends."

"I thought you Scots invented the game," said Grace.

"So, what's different? We invented everything," declared Rory.

CHAPTER SEVEN

At breakfast Jason gave the party a time of departure and permission to do what they wished till then. Chuck went around the quaint village photographing the distinctive wrought iron signs above the various tradesmen's premises. They were lightly drawn and imaginative in design. He particularly liked the dancing spinning wheel above the door of the knitwear shop and the great outlined bull swinging macho-like outside the butcher's and the sheep whose wool was unwinding and becoming a knitted garment - the whole effect as if the blacksmith were working in filigree. In silhouette against the blue sky they looked magical. He also photographed some of the local peasantry, for the costumes he declared, but most of the shots were of females - young females. They, he said with a chuckle, were wearing the most interesting garments.

The sprightly Lucy and Monica, the same moaning Monica Jason had assumed would not be selected, had a walk through the fields, Monica half running to keep up, grumbling away under her breath. While Julia preferred to soak in the bath Grace, noticing John's worried look, joined him in a visit to the old church whose thin spire seemed like the end of a shaft from which the whole village radiated. Rory and Alan walked round the streets arguing about the relative merits of Glasgow Rangers and Liverpool, reaching no agreed conclusion. Jason mooched about the yard covertly watching Hilary who sat on her verandah enjoying the sun. He varied this by strolling to where Hubert, the oldest of the party, sat in the village square. He was enthralled by the sketch Hubert was producing in a casual scribbling style.

Jason rallied them together in real tour guide fashion and they set off. As they approached the border with Hornia, Jason shouted "Passports ready. " It looked like the customary customs post. A red barrier blocked the road and a soldier with a rifle stood by it. Pyke drove right up to the barrier and stopped. The soldier leaned forward and pressed a button on the upright supporting the barrier. Immediately a civilian came out of the border post followed by a soldier in full battle rig with a pistol in his belt. They both boarded the bus, did not return Jason's smile and with grim faces started at the back of the bus looking at the papers.

"Not from the tourist board obviously," quipped Jason.

As the soldier glared in response, Jason hastily averted his eyes. They lingered a long time over Hilary's papers. Everyone lingers over Hilary, thought Jason.

Nevertheless he was nervous when they came to him. They took what seemed an interminable time before they handed his papers back with that fixed, direct enquiring look that you get when you go through the 'nothing to declare' channel. Rory, a large, cheerful Scotsman, asked the soldier who was coming along behind his colleague if it was going to be a warm day but he received no reply. "Thank you," said Rory undaunted. "I'll no have to wear ma thermal semmit then."

While all this was happening Bruce Dunlop was leaning back in his seat looking out of the window with a relaxed almost bored look on his face. He handed his papers to the soldier without looking up. The soldier took a quick glance at his passport, put his hand on his shoulder, and said quietly but with total authority, "Come with me, Sir."

Bruce rose slowly from his seat and as he turned to follow the soldier down the aisle of the bus he surreptitiously thrust a piece of paper into Jason's reluctant hand. He was not, however, surreptitious enough and the soldier reached out, quickly and roughly twisted the paper out of Jason's hand, looked at it, looked at Jason then hurried off the bus to help push Bruce into the building. The dazed passengers could now see that what had looked like a colourful rural chalet had bars on all windows and an armed sentry on each side of the door.

Before any of them had gathered their wits enough to speak a civilian in a dark suit boarded the bus. He looked round quietly for a moment then said in excellent English. "The gentleman whom we have just removed from the bus is an undesirable. We would not wish him to go any further. You will be safer without him in your company. I hope you all have a pleasant journey. Good day."

As the man left the bus and walked back towards the border post the still silent passengers heard a piercing scream from the building. A soldier walked to the front of the bus and gave Pyke a wave. It was not so much a signal of permission to depart as a peremptory order to get moving at the double. Pyke responded by putting his foot down so quickly that the travellers were thrust back into their seats in a way which reminded Hubert, the only grey haired man in the group, of the old Caravelle take off. As the bus drew off past the uplifted red barrier pole there was a loud report. They all hoped that this was the protesting bus backfiring but each one knew that the sound was far too sharp for that.

The small energetic lady known to Jason only as Lucy was the first to explode. "We must go back. We can't just leave him."

Monica, mouth turned down in distaste, turned angrily to Jason. "What are you going to do?"

The bemused Jason struggled for words but Pyke cut in, "We are on a motorway. We cannot turn for twenty miles."

"So, what are you going to do?" repeated Monica in a tone which implied, you're going to do nothing aren't you.

"I'll phone the British Embassy at the first opportunity. I have their number." Jason tried to sound as if he were in complete command of the situation as indeed he hoped he was. He pulled off the purple blazer to regain some dignity.

"That's ab-solute-ly the right thing to do," agreed Alan with relief in his voice. Rory sitting beside him nodded. "I must say I'm not too surprised. Bruce looked a rum sort of cove to me." he grunted.

"What was that paper he tried to give you?" John Storey twisted round in his seat towards the harassed Jason.

Of all the passengers, Jason knew least about this quiet man and promised himself he would find out more.

"I don't know. I hardly had time to see it. Looked just like last night's menu to me."

"Who screamed?" asked Hilary as everyone found their voice and started talking at once.

"And the shot?" chipped in Chuck. He was fishing under the seat for the camera he had been hiding from the hostile soldiers.

"We must do something," Lucy bounced up and down in agitation.

"If I had been a man," Monica glared round the bus.

CHAPTER EIGHT

Bruce Dunlop was pushed over the threshold of the border guard's office and stumbled into the small sparsely furnished room rubbing the wrist, which had been savagely twisted by the soldier. He peered around the room and saw, sitting behind a small desk in the corner, a plump man with hard eyes. He wore a dark suit with a white shirt open at the neck and a dark tie hanging loosely. As he approached the desk the plump man rose and his hand shot out towards Bruce's injured arm. Bruce winced as the other man took him by the hand and shook it.

"Bruce. So good to see you. It's been a long time."

Bruce smiled, "Good to see you, Stefan. You look well."

"Can't complain. You look well also - and how is Mabel?"

"Great, great. And Natasha - recovered from the shingles? That must have been nasty."

"Yes, she's all right now, thanks. Didn't meet in the middle. She has quite a middle. Glad to see you Bruce. Good to welcome you back to our country."

"Some welcome. Your gorilla nearly had my arm off."

The large soldier smiled, "Sorry, my friend but I have no confidence in the acting ability of the British Service."

"You must admit the scream did come across as most authentic. We must keep up appearances." So saying Stefan nodded to the soldier who moved over to the back of the room and fired a shot out of the window.

"Have a seat Bruce and a drink perhaps?"

"That is most civil of you. A beer would go down nicely. The air in that bus was like a North African bordello. And you perhaps can have a whisky from my duty free." Bruce nodded towards his valise which had been taken from the bus.

"Most kind of you. We might just do that. The people at number seven will surely nick it anyway."

Bruce fished out the bottle and handed it to the soldier who was pouring the beer. "So, it's to be number seven. Is your charming brother still there?"

"Yes, and always will be I'm sure. He knows when he has it easy. He finds it a bit claustrophobic but enjoys his work. Give him my regards when you see him."

"I'll do that. And how long will it be this time?"

"Perhaps not long. We want Sven back by the end of the year so we hope to arrange an exchange by then which is why we have seized you. Things are getting so confused these days I think we are going to need people like Sven."

"Good. But please make it nearer the New Year if you can. We have the in-laws coming for Christmas."

Stefan laughed, "I understand. We will do our best. By the way what was the paper you tried to pass in the bus?"

"It was last night's dinner menu. Just a little dramatic touch. Our acting's not that bad. However I must say I'm pleased that you've lifted me. I believe they're getting a bit rough over the border."

"That's an understatement. I don't know what is troubling them but they have gone quite mad. Just when the big nations are getting together and talking sense the little ones are going crazy. People with dark secrets to hide are trying to dispose of people who share these secrets. People who might emerge as leaders are being hunted by people threatened by change. We just do not know where we are with them. You are well out of it."

"I'm sure. Well, thanks - and cheers."

CHAPTER NINE

So as a chubby little brown bus started on its hesitant journey across Europe Larry Hassall was looking forward to a parachute drop of SAS types who would arrive in the nick of time to save him.

Over the last four days the doctor had become almost friendly and Larry looked forward to his daily visit. Today however he had a forlorn and troubled look as he approached and Larry braced himself for bad news.

"You are getting better," the doctor mumbled sorrowfully.

"You don't sound too happy about that, Doctor." Larry looked into the doctor's sad eyes. "I really am very grateful to you for all you have done for me."

"I have not cured you. Time has done that." The doctor puckered his face as if he were near to tears. "Now I must report that you no longer need the special diet."

"That was a special diet?"

"Yes. To feed you up for the ---. You have not yet tasted the Table D'hôte." He smiled at his little joke.

"That bad?"

"And the day of your interrogation comes nearer."

"It must be difficult for a doctor."

The other man shrugged. "Doctors throughout the ages have repaired broken men to go back to the battle field. They have an ambiguous role in the welfare of mankind. I wanted to be a teacher - but my mother-." He shrugged.

"I sympathize. I would like to have been a pilot."

"Well, as you cannot fly I suggest that you co-operate from the start. They get very - sophisticated after the first few days."

"After the first few days? Why don't they start right in with the sophisticated stuff?"

"The overheads. The number two interrogation room is very expensive to run. Complicated, pricey equipment - all got to be depreciated. You would be horrified how much the department is charged per hour when we use that room."

"I'm sure I would."

"This place is run by bloody accountants now. We have all got to stick to our budgets.

"Quite right too. And what do they start with?" Larry looked around as if someone might be listening.

"It is all right. There are no listening devices here. Perhaps later when you are being interrogated. But anyway I am encouraged to tell you what is in store. To travel fearfully, they think, is better. But I was not sure you were strong enough."

"You have not mentioned truth drugs. I believe the latest are pretty nasty?"

"We cannot afford these now. Perhaps when we have better relations with the west again we will have such refinements available."

"That's good news. You have looked after me well."

"I can only promise you another two or three days. Luckily they are quite busy.

"How nice for them."

"They will bring in what you call, I think, a heavy if you don't talk. If everyone would just talk it would be so simple. Pointless heroism for causes they do not understand, causes I certainly do not understand, is folly. I could weep at times. I could weep." He shuffled off banging a clenched fist on the door as he left.

Larry was relieved, almost elated by what he had just been told. The timing was working well. Help would be at band just when required. Roger's top team would even now be heading relentlessly towards him. Two weeks from the date of arrest, that was the plan, to be confirmed or adjusted by Torow. However that was the one niggling doubt in his mind. Why had he had no contact, no sign from Torow? Torow was the inside man - the man who had to liaise with those outside. Without him - Larry banished the thought from his mind. He mustn't travel fearfully. 'Torow is a good man,' everyone had said to him, 'Good old Torow. He won't let you down. Never has. Infallible.'

Larry started his routine of exercises. This was where the years of wrestling experience stood him in good stead - particularly the faking and the acting but also, more importantly the hardness and resilience that countless hours on the mat had built into him.

He had to avoid the skilled looking feint and stick to obvious, natural looking ducking and dodging. He must not look experienced. He concentrated on simulating the rolling with the punches to minimize the impact but always leaving the movement so much to the last moment that it looked like a natural part of the reaction to the blow. Most important of all he must remember not to hit back - no reflex counter punch.

He also practiced over and over again the tightening of various groups of muscles suddenly as if a blow bad been thrown at a relaxed part of his body. He happily patted the layer of fat, which disguised the hard muscles.

He checked once more the tough rubber spheres, which protected the most sensitive parts of his anatomy. This was one of the kitmaster's little contributions. The simulations were most authentic. Minimizers the kitmaster called them. Larry had joked that he didn't like the implication of the mini bit but the kitmaster, a serious man, explained that he had deliberately named the protectors thus so that the recipient (of what? Larry had wondered) would know that some discomfort could be expected.

Discomfort, thought Larry, that's a good word. I must put that in my report - I suffered some discomfort at the hands of my jailers.

Larry chuckled at the recollection of the tray of samples brought in by the kitmaster for his choice. They had looked like the answer to a Tory Women's Conference dream. He carefully adjusted the minimizers just as a warder peeped in through the spyhole.

"Ah well, wouldn't you?" said the doctor when this was reported to him.

CHAPTER TEN

Jason climbed back into the bus, all eyes on him, all ready to question him. He started to speak as soon as he was aboard. He wanted to make a statement not answer questions.

"I got through. The Embassy will take care of it. They seemed to know of Mister Dunlop and were not too surprised. However they promised to get to him and see that he's all right."

"If they're not too late." Lucy bounced up to make her point.

"They know him do they?" asked Monica implying disapproval.

Alan shook his head in distaste. "Drugs probably."

"If so he's in dead trouble," said John, worried as always, "Jail first, trial next here."

"There's no point in speculating. The Embassy has the matter in hand so I suggest we try to forget it. I know it's been distressing but there is nothing we can do so let's look forward to our stay at Glocken. It should be fun. That's what you're here for isn't it?" Jason looked round to see if any eyes contradicted that statement.

Monica scowled. "I don't like us talking of fun when we don't know what dreadful things might be happening to poor Mister Dunlop." Her disapproval transferring to the captors.

"If he was involved in drugs he deserves what's coming to him. That's what I say," disagreed Lucy her usual smile disappearing for a moment.

"Let's not condemn the man. We know nothing of him," said Julia quietly and sunk back into her chair even as she spoke.

"Hear, hear," agreed Grace. She and Julia were sitting together saying very little, except to each other.

"Please. I repeat, let's not speculate. We don't know what Mister Dunlop has done or what has happened to him. Let's have faith in our Embassy. They must be used to this sort of thing. We're coming to the mountains now and I'm told this is one of the most beautiful parts of all Europe. Let's enjoy the scenery. That's what we came for."

Jason sat down to show that the discussion was closed as far as he was concerned. However each small group continued debating the incident fiercely until, one by one, they fell under the spell of the beauty of the steep grassy hills, punctuated by small round fields inhabited by fat contented looking cows. It was a most peaceful scene.

Hilary leant over to Jason and whispered, "Do you really think he'll be all right?"

Jason shrugged. "If he hasn't done something daft he'll be home before we will."

"If that is the case - and he hasn't been shot - will he get his money back?" Monica leaned over the back of her seat to put her query.

"If he makes a claim that would be for head office to decide. I am only a courier." Out of the side of his mouth he whispered to Hilary, "For which I am truly thankful."

Jason was delighted that Hilary was sitting beside him although he had misgivings about how it had come about. To his delight Hilary had asked as they started their journey if she could sit with him.

"If you don't mind," she had suggested, "I want some peace on this holiday. I don't want anyone to make a pass, flirt with me or, and especially, I don't want anyone to get serious with me. I want a complete break from people getting serious. I always end up hurting someone. I can't seem to have a platonic friendship, or a flirtation without problems.

Everyone gets so heavy. I just want to enjoy myself. This holiday I want to look - not be looked at. This all sounds terribly conceited but I know you'll understand. You must be used to this sort of thing. You won't want to rush into a holiday romance every trip." She had laughed. "You must be sick of holiday-makers by now. So if you don't mind, I'll sit with you and be safe. Get a bit of peace."

Every time she emphasized a point her large, blue eyes had opened still further and the hypnotised Jason had nodded as if his head were on puppet strings. She then sat back and put on a large pair of sunglasses as if to hide herself from the world but only succeeded in making herself look even more alluring.

She looked alluring now as Jason slumped back in his seat to discourage further questioning. He had indeed reported the incident to the Embassy. They bad been totally enigmatic about the affair and, as usual, Jason learned nothing. He had also sent one of his cryptic messages to Roger to the amazement of the Embassy staff who wondered why he should concern himself with the state of his grandmother's roses at a time like this. He decided that there was no need to wait for a reply as obviously it all fitted into the plan to which he was not privy.

At the same time he had taken the opportunity to phone ahead to Glocken to request that they beef up the wine tasting. It was Jason's hope and expectation that they would all drink enough of the local beverage to dull the memory of today's, to Jason's taste, too theatrical and, even worse, too real happening. He had explained to the innkeeper that they had had a mishap and could do with something to alleviate the shock of it.

The inn keeper had promised - "Don't worry I will provide wine of the very first water." Jason hoped that it was the English, which was weak.

CHAPTER ELEVEN

Jason was taken aback to find that the inn keeper had taken his plea so much to heart that he had arranged that the wine tasting take place before lunch instead of the planned pre dinner function. He now feared for the success of the afternoon's activity. Jason's earlier fear proved groundless; the wine was local but was rich and strong. Only red was offered and although to the more sensitive palates, and there weren't many of these present, there was a variation in the contents of the differently labelled bottles they all had this in common - if you held your glass up to the light not a glimmer penetrated the dark ruby liquid. The innkeeper joined with the tasters and in fact set a merry pace.

"It is my duty," he explained, "to drink with my guests to show that this is the wine what we ourselves drink. It would not be courteous to do otherwise.

His own florid face testified to this courtesy faithfully extended over many years. He beamed as the guests discussed the merits of the different wines with great enthusiasm and little expertise.

Hilary asked if it travelled well.

The innkeeper shook his head "Je ne sais pas." We do not know. We drink it all here. Wir drinken ihn hier" His great belly shook with laughter. The itinerary for the afternoon involved an orienteering run over the beautiful hills, which surrounded the hotel. There had been little opportunity for exercise since leaving London and Jason had strict instructions to keep his charges fit and alert for what lay ahead. He did protest to Pyke that this was ludicrous after only three days and on top of the wine but he was taken aback by the ferocity of Pyke's insistence that they had to stick precisely to the plan. This is some sort of diversion, thought Jason.

They set off in twos and threes. Hubert and Julia went off first. Julia wasn't looking at all well and Jason expressed the hope that they would take it easy. Julia insisted this was just what she needed - fresh air and exercise. Hubert looked at Julia and murmured that it would be easy. He had a stout stick he had picked up and they set off at a leisurely pace saying nothing to each other. The next pair were about to start and saw them stop at the edge of a dark woods at the top of the first hill looking undecided which way to go.

The course completed Jason, and the partner he had chosen for himself, Hilary, collapsed onto the grass just ahead of Grace and John. The younger men, Rory and Alan, were already stretched out on the grass, having arrived back first, and their team-mate, Lucy, was swinging on the branches of a tree doing some limbering exercises.

"That woman will be hoist by her own leotard some day," quipped Rory, mopping the perspiration from his face and neck with a large coloured handkerchief. Lucy had taken off her tracksuit and now looked at first glance like a teenage Russian gymnast whose tough training had turned her hair prematurely grey.

They all relaxed, some dozing, some complaining quietly. Monica, who had been an unwilling participant, had just arrived back with Chuck, and was annoyed that she had not had a picnic; she had seen Grace and John tucking in on the way round.

"You've got to learn to live off the land, my girl," said John looking pleased with himself for a change.

"Yes, Jason, why didn't we stop at that field of croissants?" Hilary laughed.

John bad to admit that the ingredients of their picnic had fallen off the back of a lunch table. "First time I've had a Camembert bully," he joked.

Most of them were dozing when a shot rang out and echoed round the hills followed by a grunt then silence.

Grace sat up startled. "What was that?"

"Hunter. There's lots of game up there. We saw a beautiful deer didn't we, Grace?" John pointed up the valley.

"Game! That little bambi. Yuch!" Grace, who looked flushed and healthy after her run, stretched out on the grass again and spread her skirt carefully over her knees.

"Come on, Jason give Lucy her chocolates," shouted Rory.

"The presentation will be this evening. But I had in mind it would be a team prize," said Jason.

"Forget it. We couldn't have done it without her." Alan threw a genuine look of respect at Lucy.

"We wouldn't have anyway. She was wonderful. However Alan and I have reluctantly agreed to give her a free transfer. She doesn't fit in with our team plans."

"She cer-tain-ly does not," said Alan stretching himself out with a groan and closing his eyes.

Jason looked around. "Hubert and Julia not in yet?"

"No. No sign of them. Must be taking it easy. Sensible pair," replied Chuck rubbing his thighs.

They all relaxed, some dozing, some talking quietly, all, except Lucy, feeling the effect of the wine. The sun was still hot and the garden was more inviting than the deep shadows of the inn. They were strewn about the lawn thus for almost an hour.

Jason, who was fast asleep, awoke with a start to find an anxious looking Grace shaking him. It took him a moment or two to remember where he was. Then he saw Lucy sitting in the lotus position on the lawn. Grace shook him again.

"Shouldn't Julia and Hubert be back by now? It's almost an hour since we finished. They can't be that slow. Something has happened to them."

Jason sat up. "I sure they'll be OK." He looked round. "Let's check where we all saw them last. Chuck when did you pass them?"

"We never saw them. Did we Monica?" He was trying to take a photograph of the energetic Lucy who was now leaping about.

"No. Not even when we got to the top of that first hill. I was surprised. I expected to see them then. They must have started too fast." She shook her head disapprovingly.

"That's right. Gone off too quickly." suggested Lucy.

"You can talk.' grumbled Rory.

Jason gritted his teeth. "That's over three hours. They could have gone round on their hands and knees in that time."

"That shot," croaked Grace and everyone then chipped in with their own lurid description of the strange gasping sound that had followed it.

Jason declared he was going to find Pyke to see if he could throw any light on the matter. He went into the kitchen and around the public parts of the inn but could see no sign of the driver, then as he entered the darker, staff only, parts of the inn he heard the unmistakable sound of a rifle bolt being cleared followed by footsteps on the cobbles by the back door.

He peered cautiously into the high walled courtyard. Pyke, with no gun, was walking towards him and there were sounds of footsteps going off round the inn.

"Pyke! Where have you been? What have you been up to?" asked Jason fiercely. He told Pyke, quickly, of the missing pair and of the anxiety of the others, and how that concern had been made frantic by the sound of the shot.

"Forget about the shot. I fired it." Seeing Jason's deepening panic he explained that he had gone to pick up rifles from a secret cache but had been spotted and had had to shoot the pig.

"You shot Hubert?"

"Hubert! Don't be daft."

"Well, whoever you shot you're crazy. If you've shot someone we'll never get out of the country." Jason tried to wring his hands and beat Pyke about the head at the same time.

"Calm down, Jason. I shot that pig," he pointed to a large boar sprawled liked a beached porpoise in the corner of the yard, "To make it look as if we were hunters. Guns are not permitted to others now - on penalty of death."

"But we don't want guns. We mustn't have guns."

"Agreed. But the innkeeper needs guns. This is a safe house, and these are dangerous times. He must have the means to defend himself, till things settle down again. He is very valuable to us. Oh, and Jason tell the party not to panic if they hear a loud explosion." He paused. "Quarry blasting - explain that."

Jason looked up at the heavily wooded slopes. "A quarry up there?

"Yes, Jason. That's what you say." Pyke now spoke tersely. "I had also to call at a cottage on the hill to get a message from Torow. It was deserted. Fresh signs of a struggle. There's equipment hidden there - transmitter and things. Too heavy to take away. They'll come back when there are not so many idiots running around the hills so I've fixed an impromptu bomb from some of the ammo to destroy the evidence. Will go off in less than five minutes. So quarrying - remember." Jason nodded his head.

"Worrying not getting the message from Torow. We've only got a day or two in hand." Pyke went off with a deep frown on his face.

Jason was worried. If the phlegmatic Pyke was worrying there must be something to worry about. He also thought how close to the cottage they had run. They were being used.

He returned, completely bewildered, to the garden to find the group going frantic and Grace near to hysterics. When Jason could offer no explanation from Pyke it added to the dismay.

"They must have had an accident. I'm game to go up and look for them," volunteered Lucy.

"It'll get dark soon so we had better go to it. But where do we start?" Rory began to put his shoes on.

"Listen, if none of us saw them they must have fallen by the wayside very early on," suggested John. "You say they were out of sight by the time you got to the top of the first hill. That's not possible. You could see right up the next slope. They couldn't have covered that in four minutes. They must have turned into those woods. Mad."

"Funny I nearly -," Jason began and Hilary's eyebrows shot up. "I nearly suggested we go that way," he stumbled on, "It looked very -." He stopped in embarrassed confusion, as he recalled exactly why he would have liked to have gone into the woods with Hilary, aware that she was giving him strange questioning looks.

"Jason! Jason! Hi, maybe that's what Hubert was after too. Maybe he's a dirty old man," joked Rory.

Jason squirmed.

"Don't say that. Poor Julia. She's just had - she's not been well." Grace's voice trailed into a mumble.

"Sorry Grace. Just joking. She'll be all right.

John rose and started towards the gate. "Well, let's get going."

"And take sticks just in case. He had one." Rory also rose to go.

"I'll get them," said Jason and turned towards the inn, stopped, looked back, did a double take and looked towards the inn again.

Julia advanced slowly down the steps in a crisp white dress and with colour in her cheeks. She looked around at the bedraggled group. "I feel wonderful. You'll feel good too when you've bad a bath and a change."

Hubert came down the steps behind her fresh and immaculate in an old fashioned but elegant dark blue blazer. "Ah, you've made it. Waited for a bit but needed a shower. Sticky up there. Fancy a lemonade, Julia?"

"Love one thanks, Hubert." Jason noted that this was the first time Julia had addressed any of the men by name.

"Sensible pair, to cut it short," John nodded thinking he had been the smartest up till then.

"We didn't cut it short. We covered every inch, thanks to my genius guide." said Julia

"Hubert, you've been here before, you rascal," mocked Rory.

Hubert spoke now, very diffidently. "No, not that but perhaps just as unfair. But it wasn't a serious race was it? You see I am a cartographer."

"A what?" asked Rory.

"I make maps. So I can read them."

"So you found a shorter route?" asked Lucy.

"And a flatter one. We never went higher than that first hill," said Julia.

"I had some difficulty persuading Julia to come into the woods with me." Hubert chuckled mischievously.

Jason caught Hilary's eye and felt his cheeks glow. The group exchanged embarrassed glances.

Julia had a piece of paper in her hand. She held it up. "Look at the drawing Hubert made of the little bridge."

There was a chorus of "What bridge?" and Lucy looked scornfully at Rory and Alan's stained trouser legs.

"That's really good," said Alan. "You've done to that bridge what Topolsky did to people."

"Thank you, Alan. That is indeed a compliment. But I just scribble. I enjoy it. You may have it, Julia."

From up in the hills came the sound of an explosion and a deep rumble. "Must be the quarry," said Jason without even looking up.

As they rose to get changed for dinner Hilary put a hand on Jason's shoulder and said gently, "Had you a little cartography in mind too?" Jason reddened but Hilary smiled and walked on.

Before he slept that night Jason lay trembling and worrying about the guns, the explosion and the undelivered message but when he fell asleep he dreamt happily of Hilary and uncharted territory.

CHAPTER TWELVE

Jason was now beginning to miss Bruce who had seemed to know what to expect. They had another border post to pass today and he was not looking forward to it. He certainly didn't know what to expect. Hilary had been teasingly pleasant to him all morning and he didn't know what to expect from that direction either. His heart thumped whenever she came near. However, he thought, the party is gelling well. They had enjoyed yesterday even, after the initial trauma, the Bruce incident. That was real adventure. They had talked themselves into the view that he must indeed have been an undesirable. Jason did wonder if those aboard who did know what was going on had been alarmed by the incident? Perhaps nobody knew what was going on? Perhaps Roger, as always, had made sure that not one of them knew what was really happening? This made him feel better. He didn't like the idea of some amateur being in on the act while he was excluded, although that was the essence of the plan - - his plan.

Jason knew that the State of Tyrnia was in a state of unrest. The thought of this reduced him to a state of nervousness. The whole of Eastern Europe was as shifting sand. Roger had said that in these circumstances information was power - then told him nothing. The casual Bruce had shown no signs of worry when he heard that they were going to Tyrnia; a tiny country but strident, aggressive and internationally unpopular, but of course Bruce wasn't going was he? Jason thought with a thrill how the failure to return of field man Bruce Dunlop would add to the flavour of the account of his exploits when he returned. Then he felt guilty. Poor old Bruce.

The chubby bus meandered slowly through the hills as if it too were reluctant to reach the dreaded land. There were dark mountains up ahead and no sun shone on this side of them. This seemed a chilling portent to Jason of what lay ahead. They passed without hassle through the departure border post from Hornia and drove about fifty metres to a heavily guarded post with a double barrier, one of which opened while the other, ten metres on, stayed firmly down so when the first barrier closed behind them they were trapped. As in the Grand old Duke of York, thought Jason, but not for a kiss.

A soldier came aboard the bus and brusquely shouted for Mister Bruce Dunlop.

"He is not with us now," Jason told the soldier. "He was taken off the bus as we entered Hornia and we haven't seen him since."

The soldier turned and marched back into the border post.

"Don't let's put up with any nonsense this time." whispered Lucy shaking a fist in the air.

"No. It's up to you to tell them, Jason," hissed Monica.

As they waited for the soldier to return Lucy looked around at her companions. She had always travelled alone before. She wondered if she had been wise to join this group. Well, it will be an experience, she thought.

Back in the comfort of his London office Roger thought of the bus party occasionally, more so as no news had yet been received of Torow. He wondered about Lucy. She was older than he would have liked for such a mission. But the group had to look normal and he had taken to the lady.

Roger had never interviewed a volunteer before; they were always discouraged. Recruiting was by recommendation, which had made, he thought, the service what it was today. He thought again about this and had looked up at the lady entering his room with more interest. She was slim and lively looking, dressed in a pale blue tracksuit and was, Roger guessed, in her early fifties. Her neat brown hair looked as if it had been sprinkled with salt. She talked, with little need of prompting, about her enthusiasms -and she was an enthusiastic woman. "I am," she said, but her tracksuit had said it first, "a keep fit fanatic." She clasped her hands behind her head and stuck her elbows up and her chest out. Her small breasts leapt upwards every time she pressed back her elbows. On the odd occasions when she was listening Roger had to speak up to be heard over the deep breathing.

"Why a bus tour?" asked Roger. "You look too active for that."

"Oh, I'm active all right but there is so much to see of the world and each of us has only a limited life-span however fit one keeps oneself. I've hiked in all five Continents and seen small parts in great detail now I would like to paint with a broad brush for a few years - get the whole picture you know. Then I'll go back and fill in the highlights of the parts which have interested me most."

"Excuse my curiosity Miss Sprig--"

"Lucy Sprig. Lucy please. Fire away."

"You have obviously led an interesting life. I was curious to know how you make your living?"

"I write a little. Travel articles. Pieces for keep fit magazines. Advice on proper eating. I even write about holidays occasionally -adventure holidays. Don't make much but I don't need much. Most people eat too much and live too soft."

Roger frowned to himself as he pulled in the paunch that had been resting very comfortably on the edge of his desk. He had a soft and pampered body but inside was a hard man of action - struggling to stay where it was. He liked his way of life.

Miss Sprig misunderstood the fleeting expression on his face. "Oh, don't worry, I'm not going to ask for any concessions. Never do. Can't give unbiased report then. I don't like to be obliged to anyone."

"Never thought that for a moment, dear lady. I am a good judge of character. But would you be averse to undertaking a little duty for me while you're away? Nothing to do with the holiday really. The payment for that could be offset against the cost of the holiday. I've been looking for someone like you, someone I could trust, someone with a bit of go about them."

"I don't know what the opposite of averse is but that's me. Willing. But only if it's not just a back-hand way of gagging me."

Roger hid the alarm that the prospect of an adverse report on the holiday in the Yalding Herald raised in his breast and told her as much as he wanted to tell her about the project. He could see by the way her face lit up that she was going to throw herself into her task in the same way as she undoubtedly threw herself into and at all life's opportunities. She left with only the details to be filled in and came at Roger so briskly to say good-day that he thought for one dreadful moment that she was going to hurdle his desk as if it were game, set and match.

The soldier returned a few minutes later and ordered all the passengers out of the bus and into the reinforced concrete building. Jason was called forward and taken to a small bare room and asked over and over again what had happened to Bruce Dunlop. Then all the others were asked, separately, to give their version of the story. Being true all the stories fitted and the border guards eventually came round to believing them. They had obviously been alerted to Bruce's arrival and were angry at being denied the chance to capture him. Pyke spoke to one guard who nodded grimly. The other guards discussed the matter bad-temperedly then left the room.

After a long wait a large grim looking lady came into the room and ran her eyes over the ladies. As they filed past she stopped Hilary and took the magazine Hilary was carrying under her arm. She called over another official and they examined the paper. They looked up at her from time to time, nodded grimly and then beckoned her to follow them through a door.

As they entered a bleak inner room the large lady shouted that she should strip. Hilary hesitated and the woman looked threateningly. Hilary stepped gracefully out of her clothes and laid them neatly on the floor. Standing there completely naked and completely blonde in the dreary room she was beautiful enough for even these hardened women to look in amazement.

"Good afternoon, madam," she said pleasantly, "Let's get this over with. I am sure this must be very tiresome for you."

"Over here," the command came with a sneer and a push.

"Oh, your hands are cold. Poor dear. It must be very uncomfortable for you working in conditions like this."

The large lady's eyes narrowed and she dragged Hilary over to the X-ray machine very roughly.

Hilary continued to smile pleasantly. "There is no need to help me over. I am sure you must be tired enough standing all day. Do they not even provide you with chairs?"

The scan completed the woman now started a thorough and rough body search. "This must be a most unpleasant thing to have to do. I hope it is not distressing you too much," said Hilary comfortingly, "I think I would rather be a dustman. You'll want a good shower after this. I hope they pay you well. Not a nice job," Hilary looked at the woman with a sympathetic smile

The woman looked at her hands and her shoulders sank. She shook her head. She turned away from Hilary and said quietly, "Off you go."

As Hilary was thus detained Pyke entered into apparently casual conversation with an uniformed official. The official left and Pyke leant on the wall looking unconcerned. He looked up when the official returned, smiled at him and offered him a packet of cigarettes. The official looked around as if nervous about accepting the gift, took it, thrust it in his pocket and appeared to thank Pyke profusely.

As they left the building Pyke was looking grim. He shook his head to Jason. "There is no message from Torow."

Hilary strode out with a relaxed look on her face but when they were out of sight of the post she slumped in her seat with her head in her hands.

Jason looked at her. "Why did they keep you so long."

Hilary explained, her voice choking, what had been done to her. The group fell silent. After a few moments she turned to Jason and whispered, "What is an acid house party?"

"I'm not sure exactly," he replied. "A lot of people getting together to take drugs and enjoy themselves. The police try to stop them. Why do you ask?"

"The paper Pyke gave me to carry," she stopped. "Forget it," she added emphatically and turned away.

Jason thought for a few minutes then slid over to Pyke and hissed angrily. "Did Hilary's diversion give you enough time?"

"Enough." Pyke replied curtly.

"You rotten bastard." Jason lifted his fist.

Pyke looked at him without any change of expression. "Perhaps you should speak to Roger."

Jason tightened his fists desperately wanting to do something to relieve the tension and fury inside him. Pyke calmly switched on the engine and Jason, deflated, turned away.

"Jason," the driver said quietly. "This is not a game. A man's life-!"

CHAPTER THIRTEEN

The little brown bus raced off as if to get away from the distressing experience as soon as possible. An uncomfortable silence continued for some miles, then Lucy gave a start as if she had forgotten something. She rose from her seat and with a studied casualness walked up the bus to Pyke.

"Do you know Ramstad, Pyke? Is it an interesting place?"

"Yes, Ma'am. Very interesting. We may pass that way."

Lucy looked uncertain what to do next then turned and went back to her seat.

Pyke slowed down as if in deference to the prevailing mood and the bus swung gently on the many curves in the narrow winding road. He looked round at the despondent group and then drove off the road, took a sharp turn down a steep hill into the valley, turned again onto a rough track through a wooded area which led to a small river then drew off the track and stopped in a clearing by the river.

"A picnic spot?" asked Jason.

Pyke nodded his head and climbed out of the bus and walked down towards the river. Without a word he lay down with his back against the trunk of a large tree, pulled his cap over his tough brown face and settled himself for a nap.

Lucy was the first of the passengers to descend from the bus. She saw the pool of still water calm between the waterfalls up and down river, gave a squeal of delight and the next thing those on the bus saw was her white body arching in a neat dive into the water.

In a minute or two the others started straggling out of the bus. They heard Lucy gasping and shrieking with pleasure. "In you come. This is marvellous."

Rory and Alan stripped to their underpants and jumped in. They yelled as their warm bodies hit the cold water. Jason decided he would have to show willing. He hurriedly divested himself and looking down regretted the pink and white striped Y fronts. He sprinted over to the spot where Lucy had dived in and took a graceless header into the water to the cheers of the others. He came up to the surface with a gurgling scream and a bleeding nose.

Lucy looked at him, "I'm afraid you need more depth than little me."

Jason shook his head but his eyes would not focus but he had the not too distinct impression that Hilary was trotting to the water's edge with very little on. He cursed and decided to stick to character, his cautious character, in future.

All, except Monica, were soon in the water splashing and laughing like a party of school children. After a time Lucy swam over to the steep bank and tried to clamber out. The bank was just too high for her. Chuck seeing her difficulty scrambled out to offer help. He grasped Lucy's cold wet hands tightly and pulled her up. As her dripping body emerged from the water he saw that she was completely naked. He was so taken aback that he let go and Lucy fell helplessly back into the water. She surfaced again shaking the water vigorously from her head like a dog, and laughing.

"That wasn't very gallant."

"I'm sorry. I d-didn't--," he broke off embarrassed.

Lucy held up her hand again but Chuck held back.

Lucy laughed. "Come on Chuck." she giggled. "Don't be shy. I've got nothing to hide. My figure has been likened to two aspirins on an ironing board.

Chuck bent down and this time positively plucked Lucy from the water to the loud cheers of the others. Lucy skipped and danced over to her clothes her extremely slim yet still feminine body dripping shimmering droplets as she went. She chose a sunny spot and, lying on her stomach and making no effort to dress, raised herself on her elbows and watched the others. "My underwear would have been more embarrassing," she sang out.

Hilary smiled, understanding and appreciating Lucy's gesture.

"It's bloody cold in here," shouted Rory as he splashed about, "I'm going to have nothing to hide either when I come out."

After their swim they settled in two groups sunbathing as their clothes dried beside them, the naked bodies a sign of empathy with Hilary. They laughed and joked and shouted across to each other. This wakened Pyke who went to the bus and brought out a case of local white wine. He opened some bottles and passed them to the two groups. As he handed the bottles to the naked ladies Jason realized this should have been his duty. And Pyke does it calmly as if he were above or beyond lecherous thoughts - but I know better, he reflected.

He recalled with embarrassment the first night in France. On arrival at the Auberge Ballon Jason had found himself with the difficult task of allocating rooms, some single, some double, before the members of the group had got to know each other. He attended to all the 'tourists'. This left one single and one double room to be filled by Dunlop, Pyke and himself.

As Jason was helping himself to the single key Pyke sidled up to him with a smile. Jason had never seen him smile before and was taken aback.

The driver to Jason's alarm had put a rough hand on his. If Pyke suggests we share I'm off, he thought in a panic. This is beyond the call of duty. Roger can find someone else. No difficulty in that department in our department I would have thought - but not me.

Pyke had tightened his grip on Jason's hand, a hand that was starting to shake. "Do me a favour chum. Just for tonight - and I'll look after you for the rest of the trip-I promise."

"What have you in mind, Mister Pyke?" Jason had squeaked unable to release himself from the stronger man's grip.

"Just Pyke please, pal. No Mister. For reasons I will not go into just now I would like the single room tonight. Just tonight. You can put me in the barn for the rest of the trip - but tonight - please."

Pyke had been surprised at the alacrity with which the key to the single room was thrust into his hand.

"Certainly. Be my guest. I mean have a good night - night's rest. You deserve it."

Pyke had gone off clutching the key and smiling.

Jason retired to bed early. He wished to be asleep before Bruce appeared so he washed and undressed quickly, got into bed and shut his eyes. He wanted no cosy chat with Bruce especially none of his tales of past dangers bravely suffered. He had lain awake, poised ready to pretend to be asleep at the first turn of the key. He had been almost asleep when the key scraped in the lock and Bruce Dunlop tiptoed in. Jason had shut his eyes and breathed heavily. The steady rhythmic sound of his owns breathing had soon lulled him to sleep.

If his transition to sleep could be likened to drifting his awakening was like striking a rock - in a storm. In fact the first sound to crash into his consciousness had been like the ripping of a great sail; this followed by a fierce gust of cold wind. His first sight had indeed been of flailing torn sails which as his eyes adjusted to the dim light turned to curtains being blown about in front of an open French window - all this illuminated by a big round moon.

Jason had felt that the boat - he hadn't quite returned to the bedroom -would soon lurch and start to sink. In the way that half-waking dreams seem to anticipate actuality the bed did lurch as across the room shot blue flapping pyjama tops carried on an otherwise naked body. Jason realised at last where he was and from his low viewpoint on the bed the sight of the figure - a near naked male figure - had made him wish he was indeed on a sinking ship - he would have reached for a lifebelt. Right then he hadn't known what to reach for. He had hugged his arms protectively around himself.

However without pausing for a second the apparition - no, it was too too solid flesh for that - the spectacle had shot to the door and disappeared through it - only pausing to say 'Sssh' to the inhabitants.

"What on earth was that?" Jason had asked of Bruce Dunlop as he put on the light. There was no answer and he saw that the great agent had not been disturbed by this kerfuffle. He had slept on with a contented smile on his face. Jason took some time to get back to sleep and as he had dozed off he was conscious of a faint smell of Pernod.

"Can you describe him?" Bruce had asked as they dressed in the morning. "Would you recognise him if you saw him again?"

"Possibly - but it would make an interesting identification parade. I didn't see his face."

"Pity. So it could have been anyone."

"Well, it wasn't you."

Bruce had turned away pulling down at his shirttail.

"Because you were fast asleep at the time," laughed Jason.

"Was I? Oh, it was late on then?"

"Must have been about three. I can't think what anyone would have been doing at that time of the night."

"I can - and it sounds as if he was dressed for it."

"And equipped for it. However - no damage done so I suggest we forget it."

"Forgotten," Bruce sniffed. "You must have been giving the Pernod big licks last night."

Next morning just as the departure time struck in the church spire Pyke had appeared and made his routine inspection of the bus. He had moved slowly and his eyelids were drooping.

"I'll bet that's not all that's drooping this morning," Bruce had whispered.

As Jason had sat down, last to board, he was conscious of two perfumes. One he had guessed was Chanel No. 5 and the other he had known for certain was Pernod. The two persons nearest to him were Hilary and Pyke. He reckoned it wasn't Pyke who was wearing the Chanel. He had nodded conspiratorially towards the fragrant driver.

Bruce shrugged. "Everyone in France smells of Pernod and he hasn't got red hair."

"He's mostly grey. Its lost its colour. It was Pyke all right. Look at her." Bruce followed Jason's gaze out of the bus.

Standing by the side doorway of the Auberge beneath a wrought iron cutout of a well-laden table with two plump diners, was a fresh, round-faced lady dressed in a pretty red dirndl skirt and white blouse topped by a bright yellow apron; smiling and waving. It had been a discreet little wave but it was unmistakably directed at Pyke who had acknowledged it with a slight nod.

Jason had whispered into Bruce's ear, "That's the patron's wife. So all that capering about last night was to avoid the husband. No wonder he looks tired."

"There is no husband. Madame du Pre is a widow."

"Then why all the do4ging about? I don't understand." Jason had stared at the plump lady and shook his head.

"Well, I can tell you about it but you might still not understand," Bruce had nodded his head knowingly.

"Try me"

"We've used this route for many years now. Pyke came here first because it was the last place his best friend was seen before he disappeared. It seems he digressed from Roger's plan. Pyke searched for a long time but found nothing. He and Madame N Pie became friends, close friends, very close friends. Anyway, I believe when Monsieur du Pie was still alive Pyke had a passionate and tempestuous affair with Madame. The husband died three years ago.

"So it's plain sailing now."

"Unfortunately not. Pyke found that without the excitement of the subterfuge there was no excitement in the lovemaking."

"That's hard."

"On the contrary," Bruce had laughingly disagreed, "It wasn't. My theory is that the affair was - wilting so, in desperation, Madame let Pyke believe that she was being passionately pursued by a member of the hotel staff. A very large member. She went to great lengths to make her story authentic. A combination of jealousy and danger to revive the excitement."

Jason had stared at Pyke willing his eyes to stay open. Then he noticed a large solemn faced man in a white jacket and a chef's hat who was looking at the departing group with no sign of goodwill.

"He looks authentic enough," Jason had remarked.

"Well, it seems to be working. We're a strange lot in the service." Bruce shut his eyes and lay back.

As Pyke head dropped and jerked up again Jason couldn't disagree with either of these comments.

He came back to the present and winced as Pyke bent over the recumbent Hilary to pass her a glass. He felt jealous now - a new emotion for him.

Monica seeing that food was being served came out of the bus, took a sandwich, looked at the bodies with a scowl and went back into the bus.

"How about sketching that lot, Hubert," suggested Rory. "Very artistic."

Hubert patted his bare flank and smiled. "Sorry, I don't seem to have my sketch pad with me."

So they lay there sunning themselves, letting their clothes dry and joking, the incident of the border post far from their minds.

Some of them were starting to doze off, Lucy was fast asleep, and all were relaxed and content when Pyke shouted loudly, "Who's that?"

Everyone started. "What is it?" asked Jason reaching for his underpants. "A peeping Tom."

"Probably," whispered Pyke as he moved rapidly towards a figure stirring in the woods by the road. He set off up the hill to give chase. Jason pulled on his pants and was about to leap up the track, thinking his long legs might take him after the newcomer more quickly than Pyke, when the driver came tumbling back down the track towards him.

"Beat it. It's a cop.," shouted Pyke.

As he said this an uniformed figure stood up and blew loudly on a whistle and shouted to the unclothed group. He stumbled forward and shouted again.

"That loosely translated was - what's all this then?" said Rory.

"To the bus everybody quick. Come on, grab your clothes and move." Jason led the way in a clumsy scramble.

The bus engine was already purring and Pyke had swung it onto the track. Hubert, Lucy and Grace were partly dressed but the others were only covered by the clothes they were carrying as they rushed, screaming and laughing, to the bus. As soon as they were aboard, it set off up the hill at a great speed. Nearing the top they passed within a few yards of the red-faced policeman who was now frantically blowing his whistle and lumbering towards them. Everyone rushed over to that side of the bus and waved to the discomfited man and Hilary flapped a minuscule wisp of silk and lace at him as they swept past. Monica had a 'I told you so' look on her face.

"Watch it. Back to your own side. You'll have me over," yelled Pyke as the bus lurched dangerously on two wheels as it swung onto the road. As the cheering group disentangled themselves and resumed their seats Pyke put his foot down and they sped off.

Still on a high from the day's events, and elevated even further by the wine, they wrestled with their almost dry underclothes and were soon all dressed more or less correctly. They started singing as the little bus positively darted along the road.

Then Grace screamed out, "Where's Julia? Julia's not on the bus."

CHAPTER FOURTEEN

Pyke swung the bus off the road down a bank into the shelter of some trees. "Are you sure? I can't go back. They'll have you all for indecent exposure."

"Quite right too," squeaked Monica.

Pyke ignored the interruption. "We mustn't get involved with the police." He turned to Jason and hissed, "Any delay could be fatal."

"I'll go back for Julia." Grace stood up and started to move to the door.

"No, I'll go," said Alan and Rory in unison.

"Where was she?" Jason peered back up the road as if hoping to see Julia coming after them.

"She was in a little pool downstream by herself. Floating. She seemed shy." Chuck smiled at the recollection.

"If that policeman goes down there she'll die of embarrassment. We must get to her quickly." Grace turned as she got to the door of the bus.

"Blast," exploded Pyke grumpily. "Well, whoever goes for her, the bus can't go back and I don't think it should wait here. You sort out who's going back for her and I'll show you a spot where I can wait for you about four miles down the road." So saying he took out a map and started to study it.

Hubert stood up from the back of the bus and came forward. "That settles it. I must go back for her. If it means reading a map - and she was my partner."

"I'll come with you. Just in case she's ---' Grace hesitated.

"Of course." Hubert took a look at the map, which Pyke had marked, put it in his pocket then said quietly. "Right let's go." The two of them disappeared into the woods.

The bus moved easily up the steep slope and back onto the road and Jason, for the first time, appreciated the great power of the deceptively dainty-looking little bus. After about two miles, to his surprise, they turned off on to a minor road. He checked his maps then asked Pyke, "What are you doing? Evading the police."

"No," replied Pyke. "Change of plan. We have to go to Ramstad."

"Whatever for? That's miles out of our way."

"No option. Need a spare part." Pyke turned away as if he did not wish to discuss the matter any further.

Is this, wondered Jason, Roger using Lucy to pass instructions? If so it means that even Pyke doesn't know the whole story. Then Jason remembered Roger's remark, 'So whatever they do to you, you'll divulge nothing.' Jason shivered but found a modest comfort in knowing that Pyke was in the same position. I'll have to keep my eyes and ears open now. Things are starting to happen. So as they headed towards Ramstad Jason was not happy.

A further two miles on, Pyke drew the bus into the prearranged meeting place. He took the bus well into the woods so that it could not be seen from the road. Jason again marvelled at the rugged capabilities of the vehicle and wondered what tasks lay ahead for this mighty midget of a bus.

"Four miles over this sort of ground - I reckon we have two hours to wait. So I suggest we just take the opportunity to rest quietly. It's been quite a day." Jason climbed down from the bus.

Pyke, Alan and Rory joined him and lay by the side of the bus but the others made themselves comfortable on the seats and soon all but Jason were fast asleep. He felt responsible for the first time since the tour started and an almost proprietorial feeling towards the group was growing within him. This troubled him.

They had been dozing for less than an hour when Jason heard a rustle in the trees below them - then heavy breathing. He rolled over to Pyke and shook him. "Wake up, Pyke someone coming. We'll have to go." With a "Ssssh" he woke Alan and Rory and beckoned them towards the bus.

Chuck, now awake, leaned out of the bus and whispered surprisingly emphatically, "We can't go without them."

The three men turned to Jason. He thought of the man (what man?) whose life was at stake, then of Julia and Grace, then back to the man.

"Sorry, we must go on."

"No." shouted Lucy and Chuck in unison.

Jason hesitated then said, "OK. OK. We'll wait. If it's the policeman, Lucy and 1 will try to fob him off. We look respectable."

Chuck grunted, "Respectable! It was Lucy who--"

"Bloody hell! He's done it again!" Rory stared into the woods in disbelief.

Out of the trees walked Hubert with Julia and Grace, all three smiling and relaxed.

"How on earth did you manage four miles in this time," asked Jason.

Hubert laughed. "The Pyke pantechnicon flies but it doesn't fly as the crow does. It was less than two miles across country."

"Right, let's be off," Jason pushed them back into the bus. There was a round of applause as the embarrassed Hubert climbed aboard.

"Where did you find her?" asked Lucy.

"You've held us up you know," complained Monica.

"She was still in the pool just where we left her. She's not of this world - our Julia," said Grace affectionately.

Julia curled up beside a window and said nothing.

Pyke muttered "Ramstad," under his breath with a question in the tone. He looked around but noone spoke. With a shake of his head he started towards that town.

CHAPTER FIFTEEN

Ramstad is a colourful small walled town by a lake. It is a resort popular with those who can afford not to go to a popular resort. There are some modern houses and hotels outside the wall at the lakeside but inside the walls the buildings and the narrow streets have not changed in centuries. The roofs, set low and higgledy-piggledy around the one large church, are all pantiled in a deep russet which turns to bright orange in the setting sun.

And the sun was setting now as the bus swung through the main archway into the town. Jason could see the burning glow of the rooftops as they approached but as they passed through the gateway the great walls shaded the narrow streets and made them look cool and dim. His eyes gradually adapted to the lower level of light and he could see the irregular buildings, some leaning out over the roadway. Like a European York, he thought.

As they reduced speed Pyke opened the door to let in some fresh air. Jason inhaled the aroma of cooking from the open doorways; it certainly wasn't Yorkshire pudding. It brought sharply to his mind that he didn't know where they were eating this evening or for that matter where they were going to sleep. Even assuming that whatever Pyke had come here to get could be obtained quickly and at this time of night, it was now too late to retrace their steps and get to the scheduled destination. Pyke also looked uncertain and Jason glanced enquiringly at Lucy hoping she would produce another magic word but the greying head was slumped against the back of her seat. She was dozing quietly. He wondered whether to waken her.

Pyke turned into the town square and then said in a loud voice, "Isn't this a nice place?" This was the first time Jason had heard the taciturn Pyke praise the passing scene or anything else for that matter.

"Yes, I just love these red roofs," agreed Hilary. Lucy now awake said nothing.

Pyke drove around the town centre, stopped, mumbled something unintelligible, left the bus, and went a small tourist cubicle. It wasn't long before he returned looking red faced and perplexed. He sat down and thought for a few minutes then he started off with an uncharacteristically loud crashing of gears. He looked round at the group and said again this time very distinctly, "Isn't this a nice place?"

Everyone nodded bemused then Alan who had just been wakened by the jarring start said, "Yes, isn't it? Um - I mean - Aren't the grey walls lovely."

Pyke drove almost round the block then dismounted and shot round the corner back to the same tourist office. This time he returned looking less glum. He drove the bus a few blocks through the narrow streets and stopped at a small hostelry above the entrance to which swung a sign bearing the name Grievals against a background of a section of the castellated walls. Surprise, surprise, thought Jason. I wonder what would have happened if there had been a Red Roofs Hotel.

Jason found to his relief, but again not to his surprise, that there was accommodation available for them. After the alarming experiences of the day there was now a marked enthusiasm for the sharing of rooms. Jason let those who had already shared do so again and he ranged that Hubert occupy a room with an adjoining door to that occupied by Pyke. This left only Hilary on her own so Jason suggested a similar arrangement for her and himself. To his surprise she accepted with alacrity.

They all ate together at a huge oak refectory table, subdued but more together than previously. They did not talk of the day's events except to describe them as unbelievable.

"Not at all," disagreed Chuck with a smile. He seemed pleased to have a chance to speak. "No misfortune is impossible. I should know. I'm in insurance. You should see some of the claims we get."

"You're not implying that the British are dishonest?" queried Rory.

"'Of course not. But do you know that in ten per cent of accidents both cars are stationary at the time and moving lampposts also cause a lot."

"I've had just that experience myself Rory chuckled. "And it's not funny."

"And the explanations," continued Chuck. "Coming home I drove into the wrong house and collided with a tree I don't have."

"What is the most common claim nowadays?" asked Hubert.

"I can't think - but I know the one that's increasing most - since costs went up I suppose - false teeth. Holiday makers on boats being unwell. I'm sure there's a layer of artificial gnashers at the bottom of the English Channel."

"Maybe they'll break the surface some day like a coral reef," suggested Alan.

"And a thousand smiles of welcome as you approach the white cliffs of Dover," Rory intoned solemnly like a tour guide. He then turned to John who had been very quiet. "Does your line of business get you involved with these insurance sharks?"

"Not really," replied John. "I'm in - re-distribution but some of my clients may well need their services."

Chuck now carried away with the friendliness and the wine told them in great detail why he had absented himself to take time to think about the future.

He explained that he was not by nature an adventurous man, in fact he liked the security of routine. It enabled him to think of more important things, like swimming and his camera. But one day it had all been too much. First he had been reprimanded for hanging his coat on the wrong hook. Then he had been ticked off for stopping and speaking to the only attractive girl in the office. Actually she had stopped him to ask about a claim form that had gone astray but he would not demean himself by explaining.

The last cartload of straw was when all hell was let loose because he allowed the claim of an elderly widow for a burnt carpet to be paid without investigation. Any company who could not pay a poor dear old lady, it was thus he visualised her, forty-six pounds without a fuss was not for him. His indignation was aggravated by the knowledge that after two years with the company he could not have filled in one of the company claim forms himself so complicated were they. His department head, Mr. Dunn prided himself on the number of claims, which were not pursued.

Chuck told them he had had a couple of promotions and deeply resented being treated like a junior. Unfortunately, every time he moved up Mr. Dunn moved up too so their relative positions remained the same.

"If he knew how I ran the swimming club he wouldn't have spoken to me like that," Chuck explained that he did not, in fact, officially run the swimming club. He was the secretary but he wrote the minutes and he had learnt that the man who writes the minutes rules the world. If he didn't agree with a decision he wrote a vague account of the discussion and put the subject on the agenda again for the next meeting and fixed it for an evening when a different mixture of committee members would be present. But he shared no committee with Mister Dunn.

So, Chuck explained, when walking home that night boiling over with righteous indignation he was vulnerable. The poster was attractively and colourfully printed and was right at eye level for him. LAST MINUTE HOLIDAYS the poster was headed in lurid letters. Then it went on to proclaim the opportunity of a lifetime -vacant spaces on adventure holidays at reduced prices for those willing to leave in one weeks time. 'Are you bored with your humdrum life?' asked the poster.

"Yes," Chuck had hissed so loudly that a parcel laden man who had been peering at a life size picture of a Bengal tiger in the window jumped back, knocked over another man and his shopping and scurried off quickly down the road.

Chuck had decided he would not phone his office. He would just disappear for a few weeks. That would stick a spanner right up their routine. He had slept well that night, he said laughing, dreaming of visiting exotic lands where, when poor old ladies burnt their carpet, an insurance man swam across a sunlit bay and was on the doorstep, before the rug had stopped burning, with a cheque in his hand.

"You're a good man," said Julia to Chuck's embarrassment.

Rory disagreed scornfully. "You're a mug. If I were in insurance I wouldn't trust my own granny."

"Nor would I." agreed Alan.

"How come you know my granny?" asked Rory. "We try to keep quiet about her."

"Would you like something a little stronger, Rory?" Alan rose with his own empty tankard in his hand.

"Aye. I would," Rory answered with exaggerated Scottishness, "I'd be nane the war o' a wee dram."

"And what was that about?" asked Chuck.

"That was idio-ma-tic," explained Alan.

"Sounded idiotic to me," said Chuck.

"Would you like a knee in the spermaries, pal?" asked Rory.

"And what does a bonny lass like you do when you're at home?" Rory turned to Hilary with an appreciative smile. "A model or something?"

Hilary shook her head deprecatingly.

"An actress I'll bet," ventured Alan.

Hilary was silent for some moments then she said quietly, "I would quite like to act. I have done a bit of amateur dramatics but it's difficult to break into the profession."

"For a girl like you? Surely ~ What's so difficult?" said Rory.

"A lot of competition for a start but apart from that you've got to be in Equity. You can't get membership unless you have experience and you can't get an acting job unless you are a member. It's a chicken and egg situation."

"Does it help if you get laid?" Jason quipped. The others laughed but Jason looked closely at Hilary to see if his quick tongue had got him into trouble again; however after a sharp lift of the eyebrows she joined in the mirth.

"I didn't try that," she giggled, "I had other parts in mind."

"Well, you seem to need that sort of experience in more and more so called dramas nowadays," sniffed Monica.

"You're dead right." agreed Rory and went on, "But I do think there are too many films where the girl keeps her clothes on all through the film even when it's not absolutely necessary to the story. Don't you?" There was some scoffing laughter. Monica did not join in.

Julia abruptly excused herself to go and have a bath, John, mumbling something about an early rise, left and Pyke had already disappeared, but the others seemed in no hurry to end the day. It did cross Jason's mind several times that he was going to be very close to Hilary tonight so he made up his mind not to go upstairs until she made a move.

The wine kept flowing and the conversation grew in liveliness as it diminished in coherence. Eventually and reluctantly they started to break up and, in twos and threes, wend their way upstairs. The old floorboards creaked as they clumsily tiptoed past the sleeping guests with much ssshhing and tittering. They all felt merry and Jason particularly so. He was happy and tingling with nervous anticipation. It had almost been as if

Hilary had been signalling her interest. He would give her two or three minutes to get ready. All he had to do was to persuade her that he was not getting serious. He gloated to himself.

Hilary pushed open the door of her bedroom and looked at the huge four poster bed. Jason had been kind to allocate her such a good room. Jason, she decided, was a nice boy. She giggled as she tried to focus on the eight posts of the bed. She looked at the door to Jason's room, laughed and thought, he is witty too, I like that. She was in two befuddled minds as she started to undress. She reached for the zip at the back of her dress. It wouldn't budge. She pulled again - no movement.

As if this were the sign she was waiting for she went over to the adjoining door, knocked gently, and pushed the door open and slid quietly in. There lying on the bed was Jason. He was still partly dressed but spread-eagled across the patchwork quilt completely and noisily asleep. Hilary coughed but there was no response. She turned and went slowly back to her own room and pulled savagely at the zip. It came away easily.

CHAPTER SIXTEEN

Less than a hundred and fifty miles away from the revellers Larry Hassall was being visited in his grim cell by an even more doleful than usual Doctor.

"Cheer up, Doctor. It might never happen."

"It will happen and it is going to happen tomorrow. I hope you will pay heed to the advice I have given you - whatever you do - keep talking. Talk about anything but always be saying something. If they are listening to you they cannot be doing anything else. Always be saying something," pleaded the Doctor.

"I'll try to think of something appropriate to say. A merry quip perhaps," Larry forced a smile.

"Just keep talking."

"But do I want to prolong the agony? What am I saying? This place is getting to me."

The Doctor was going through the motions of examining Larry more for something to do than anything else. He knew that Larry was fit enough now. In fact he realised Larry was a very fit man. He also appreciated that he was a man of great strength of character. This worried him. This was just the sort of man who suffered most. Even to slip him a painkiller, a very risky business, would, to use Larry's own words, just prolong the agony. Oh, why did he identify with his patients! "This is just a job," he kept telling himself and it had not been easy to get any employment since he had been caught identifying too closely with his own patients.

Larry looked at the glum face. "So, you've come to cheer me up?"

"Sorry. I can't do that. Is there anything else I can do?"

"Yes. Tell me a bit about the big fella. The one who looked me over when I first accepted the kind invitation to visit your Health Farm as if I were a one-man dirty protest. What sort of man is he - anything underneath? Or is he just a mindless thug?"

"No. Unfortunately he is not that. He is worse. He is an idealist. He believes totally and passionately in the cause."

"What cause?"

"You know I am not sure - or I have forgotten. We have had many causes in this country."

"That's a big help."

"It might just be. He wants to believe in the rightness of the cause. It is good so it must be true. But even he must realise time is running out. He must be desperate. You might provoke him to argue a bit and prolong --." He stopped.

"The agony." They both laughed.

"You are a brave man." The Doctor turned to go. "But remember you cannot win against obsession and time may be on your side now. Do not throw away your life. It can be good - I seem to remember."

Larry spent the night remembering.

CHAPTER SEVENTEEN

Jason's door opened and a girl's face peeped round the door. Jason looked up startled, "Heavens above I must have dropped off. Oh, Hilary. So pleased to see--."

He broke off as he saw a tray come in followed by a young lady who was not Hilary. Jason looked at his digital watch but he could just make out that the blurred figures were still glowing. The girl laid the tray on the bedside table. She said something, which Jason could not understand. He nodded his head - gently - and the girl pulled open the curtains and the sunshine poured into the room. Jason groaned and blinked his eyes then closed them again.

He eased his head off the feather filled pillow, which seemed much too hard and looked at the breakfast tray. Something on it was making a thunderous noise. He shook his head then hastily desisted from shaking his head. He leant forward and peered at the tray. The noise was coming from a foaming glass of grey white liquid. He reached forward and grasped the glass and greedily gulped down the Alka Seltzer. 'Good girl,' he thought.

As he replaced the empty glass he noticed a piece of paper. He lifted it and with dint of much eye screwing he read the message. 'You are a good boy,' signed H. Jason groaned and fell back on the pillow. Then he noticed the adjoining door ajar. He swung himself out of bed, pulled on his dressing gown and lurched over to the door and went through. There, hanging over the end of the bed, was a dream of a wispy nightdress and the air held the merest hint of a most delicate fragrance but of Hilary there was no sign

Jason returned to his room threw off his garments and stood under the shower for a very long time. It was icy cold but he didn't care. He was punishing himself. He was mortified so he would mortify his flesh. The water streaming down his face might well have been hiding tears of frustration. He didn't care. He had difficulty shaving because he couldn't bear to look himself in the face and he had to stop frequently to kick himself

Meanwhile, down in the charming old dark-timbered dining room with the sun streaming in through chintz curtains, Hilary was finishing her breakfast. She had not slept well. This was the first time this had happened to her. She was not promiscuous but when she reached the stage of acquiescence that had always been that. She realised that she overawed most men so much that they sought Dutch courage, and she had come across brewer's droop before but not so that it affected the whole body - or was it that Jason had heeded her early request to be left alone and faked sleep? Of course that was it. Perhaps it was for the best. She sighed and turned her attention to identifying the strange preserve she was spreading on her toast.

She was surprised when John Storey came in and joined her. It was still very early. "Someone else couldn't sleep. It was an odd sort of day yesterday wasn't it?" said Hilary beckoning him to share her table.

"It was indeed. A bit of everything," agreed John.

'Well, not everything,' thought Hilary. "You've been out. There's rain on your shoulders."

"Yes. I had a look around the town. It wasn't raining when I first went out,"

"And?"

"It's delightful. Very old - everything. But I like old things." He thought of the locks that he had had to pick during the night. They had been interesting but not easy.

John Storey didn't know what he was doing nor why that night, but he had enjoyed the old thrill, particularly as he had been specifically instructed to use no violence whatever happened and that fitted in nicely to his own philosophy of work. He laughed when he thought of the nickname the police had given him - Fairy Storey - because the only thing that had made him apprehensive about being apprehended last night was that he didn't know the language so could not spin the fairy tale - no alibi. He had felt quite naked.

Mind you he had not managed to palm off a fairy story on Roger at the interview. Clever bastard that Roger Stafford. He had been so relaxed and friendly as if he had nothing more to do with his day than indulge in pleasant chatter. Then he had started probing.

"So you're free to go off next week? Not tied to a job then?"

"No. I'm me own man - for the present anyway."

John Storey had looked to Roger like a tough character - not big and strong but resilient and with quick intelligent eyes. But as the interview had progressed Roger had got the distinct impression that some of his answers were more intelligent than truthful. He also realised that on the present tack he was not going to get any information that this lively man did not want to part with. As the verbal sparring continued Roger found himself growing to like Mister Storey. This was a man who could look after himself. However as Roger's questions grew ever more searching John had started to show signs of irritation and when he began to ask about his employment and earnings John had exploded.

"You're a bit bloody nosey - aren't you? All I want is a holiday. Look, do I get my visa or not? There isn't much time to get ready."

Roger was pleased that the calm imperturbable front was breached. He decided to push through. "Would the police object to you leaving the country?"

John had started slightly but quickly recovered. 'Police. Why the hell would they be interested in me?"

"I don't know. You tell me. I'm asking the questions."

"Oh, no you're not. Not of me. Forget it, chum. I just want to go on a holiday."

"In a hurry?"

"Hi, what is this - some sort of interrogation? I'm off. Good day to you." John rose from the chair.

"No. Sit down - please. Sorry if I have upset you. I know the police have no interest in you - at present."

"So, why ask? What is all this? And how do you know?"

Roger decided to take the plunge while his man was confused.

"We need someone who will undertake a little task en route - in return for the cost of the holiday being waived."

John thought about this for a time. He sat down. "Is this straight? I've got enough--" he stopped himself.

"I know," Roger had ventured - a shot in the dark.

The man opposite him had seemed to shrink a little in his chair and it was a good few moments before he spoke.

"So what are you trying to do? Force me to do some dirty work for you? Blackmail?"

"Not at all old boy. Nothing could be further. This is for Queen and Country. Tricky job but perfectly straight. At least--"

"At least what?"

"At least from our point of view. You see - what is in our national interest may not be in everyone's national interest."

John had seen very clearly. Underneath a natural apprehension he was warming to the idea. Might not get him out of his troubles but it sounded as if it would take his mind off them - and get him away from them for a bit; vital that he get away till things quietened down.

Roger then set about explaining the full, or what John took to be the full, background to the project. He then explained, genuinely in full this time, exactly what would happen to him if he breathed a word of what he had been told to anyone - ever. John left Jason's office not sure whether he had landed on his feet or on some other part of his anatomy. He would be glad of the respite but couldn't help worrying and wondering just what he had got himself into. Was he stepping out of his league? He prided himself that one of the reasons for his modest success - and successful he had been - in his chosen profession was his care never to take on a job that was too big for his considerable but still finite talents. He was a specialist.

There was no doubt in his mind that Roger's proposition was genuine. He had never been more impressed than with the sheer cunning and deviousness of this man. He could only be that good and that rotten in that job. He realised with professional shame that he had been trapped. The man known by the police in three counties as Fairy Storey on account of his skill in creating alibis - alibis which stood up - had walked right into it. After having been given the impression that Roger Stafford knew everything anyway - then the hint of the influence that could be used to get him off the hook - he really did tell him all. He did of course want off the hook but most of all he just wanted to return to his chosen profession with no hassle. This was looking increasingly unlikely. One bit of bad luck and the hush puppies seemed to have skids fitted.

The phrase 'We'll check it out,' rang in his mind. Found in distinctly incriminating, but circumstantial, circumstances he had confidently detailed his alibi to the police. The sergeant had cast a frustrated look at the constable and said with a resigned voice, "Still following in his father's fingerprints." Then turned to John. "OK Fairy, off you go. We'll check it out."

'I didn't start worrying till the following day - as the girl said to the doctor,' he had joked to himself . Then told himself that this was no joking matter.

He had met his friend - the alibi - the following day and listened with mounting horror as happenings of the previous evening unfolded. The club in which he had spent - in his story to the police - that evening had itself been the target for an audacious robbery. The contents of the cellar had been removed and trucked away under cover of the noise - considerable - of the three piece - amplified - band. A goodly number of the local constabulary had spent the remainder of the evening on the premises and had taken very full particulars of the assembled revellers. They had been working on the hunch that someone inside had been signalling to the waiting robbers.

Bastards, thought Storey, thieving bastards.

John Storey was respected by the police in spite of the fact that their pride was constantly being hurt by his successful evasions. They had a high regard for him because of the special range of his activities and victims. They hoped that this inflexible pattern would one day be his undoing. He burgled only from the well to do. He never resorted to violence even when in grave danger of apprehension - and he was tidy. No needless vandalism for him. He left a house as he found it - give or take a possession or two. This of course had the great advantage that it was often a long time before the victim realised he had been deprived of some of his treasure. In some few instances they never noticed the loss at all - ever. It was these latter cases which helped John Storey to sleep soundly at night in the sure knowledge that he wasn't really doing any harm. He wasn't exactly robbing the rich to give to the poor but he was undoubtedly poorer than those upon whom he made his professional visitations.

Now here he was in Ramstad. His task had been reasonably simple. His instructions were that if and when they arrived at Ramstad he had to go round every hotel in the town and look at the register until he found out where a man called Torow was staying. He had some other names to look for also, aliases he understood. He had left his foray until well into the night so that the hotels would most likely be closed. His instructions were not to ask for the information but to look with his own eyes so the lack of the local language was no disadvantage in that respect.

The first hotel had been easy. A small modern lock which a credit card had opened easily. The only difficulty had been the shiny marble floor. His shoes made no noise but they were slippery. The glass frontage made his task difficult and he had to lie on the floor as he looked through the recent entries in the book from the reception desk with his torch shaded. There was no Torow listed, nor any of the alternatives. Two other hotels were equally easy to get into but were unproductive.

The next hotel, a larger one right on the town square, was not so easy. It had a massive old cast-iron lock, designed for decorative purposes but impossible to open quietly. There was a light shining dimly in the hall and John could just detect a slumbering porter. He circled the hotel away from the conspicuous front entrance round some dark lanes, and came to a large ventilator, which indicated to him that this was the kitchen. If anyone leaves a window open it will be the kitchen staff, he thought, and, sure enough, he found a window ajar right beside the ventilator.

He reached in and expertly levered over the safety catch, pushed the window up squeakily and slithered silently into the room. He shone his torch about, confident that no man or animal would spend the night in a kitchen. There was a large painted door past many smaller doors. He took the smaller ones to be for storage. He walked gingerly towards the larger one, avoiding the resonant tools of the chef's trade, which strewed the floor. The door was locked. He examined it with his light shining. It did not look difficult. He fumbled in his pocket for a small strong lever that he knew would be just right. As his light shone on the keyhole he heard a low growl from the other side.

A dog! A tremor shook his normally steady hand. He turned quietly and swept his torch round the kitchen. Meat, he thought, that should keep it quiet. He went over to the freezer and pulled out a large piece of meat covered with the black coarse hair of the wild boar and made his way to the door. As the meat swung by his side it hit his leg and he realised with a start how hard and solid it was. That's just the thing, he thought, it breaks its teeth and howls the whole town awake.

He looked around more carefully and after opening many of the side doors, came upon some smoked sausages and hams. He picked up a partly used ham, extracted the bone with a large knife, dropped it out of the window, and then returned to the door. He slid the lock quietly open and holding the ham between himself and the opening pulled the door gently inwards. The dog sunk his teeth into the joint without a murmur. It was a Rotweiller and it was a joke of his trade that their bite was worse than their bark. He had no wish to put the idea to the test.

John now moved quickly through unlocked doors and reached the lobby where a plump uniformed man lay asleep on a huge chaise longue. A small lamp shone on the reception desk and in the ring of light it shed John could see a large leather bound book. He crept stealthily forward, lifted the book and returned to the dark passageway. Here he shone his torch and searched the list of names, scribbled mostly and difficult to decipher, then after turning over the most recent two pages - there - the name Torow. The date opposite the name was more than two weeks ago. Would he still be here? thought John. That's none of my business he told himself. He had done what was asked of him.

He memorised the date and room number, returned to reception, saw the porter stir and rise, waited for a moment, heard a toilet flush then quickly replaced the book and headed quietly back to the kitchen. The dog did not even look up as it wolfed the remains of the meat. John noted with satisfaction that without the bone there would be no trace of the ham left to arouse suspicion and it might well not be missed; it was not a well ordered kitchen.

He thrust out of his mind any thoughts of who Torow was or what might now happen to him.

CHAPTER EIGHTEEN

"I thought we were going to be offered ham for breakfast." Hilary sniffed the air. "I can distinctly smell it. Delicious. I like ham, do you?"

"At times I appreciate it very much," John wiped his still greasy hands vigorously on his trousers.

John now waited impatiently until all the guests were down so that he could complete his assignment. He would rather have gone upstairs and had a good wash as Grace, who was next down, also mentioned the aroma of ham. The very basic continental breakfast seemed to heighten the guests' awareness of the elusive, unobtainable ham. It was becoming embarrassing.

Jason then came hesitantly down the stairs, hesitantly for two reasons: the uncertainty as to how he would be received by Hilary; and the uncertainty as to how to put one foot in front of the other.

John looked at him as he stumbled into a chair. "Quite an evening wasn't it?" Jason grunted. "You look bad," added John sympathetically.

Hilary, who was almost as pallid as Jason, looked up at him and asked. "Do I look as rough as I feel?"

"I don't know. I haven't felt --" Jason broke off and groaned.

Hilary's eyebrows shot up. "Quite!"

Alan shook his head. "You suffer from verbal pre-ma-ture ejac-u-lation, Jason my boy."

Hilary leaned over and whispered to Jason. "Listen Jason, I appreciate your not taking advantage of me last night." Jason looked quizzical or as near to it as he could in his present state but Hilary continued. "Oh, I know you were just feigning sleep. I had had too much to drink. I would have been very vulnerable. You remembered what I said. Thanks - you're a gentleman."

Jason groaned. I would fain not have feigned sleep, he thought. That sounds Shakespearean. To sleep perchance to - damn - perchance not to - perchance is a fine thing - taken at the tide too - ha bloody ha. Out loud he blurted "Stuff Shakespeare."

"I beg your pardon," said the startled Hilary.

"Sorry I'm befuddled this morning."

"What you need is a cup of hot black coffee. Allow me." So saying she poured the black pungent brew into his cup.

When all the party had gathered and was breakfasting John told them of his pleasant morning walk. "It is a lovely old town. Maybe if we put a wall round all our towns they could stay like this."

"Bit late for Cowdenbeath," said Rory.

"There is a quaint old hotel, an Inn really. The Vernia. Lovely. Even more old fashioned than this one. It's a nice little place. Well, I'm going up to change my jacket. It was raining earlier." John said all this unusually clearly then rose abruptly and left the breakfast room.

Jason looked round the room for a reaction. This sounded to him like another part of Roger's childish relay of coded instructions. Every member of the party was present but he could see no change of expression.

Things are going to happen soon and I'm in no state to cope, thought Jason. Ah well, must remember my motto - when all else fails - give up.

CHAPTER NINETEEN

Jason decided the best thing was to get the group on its way as soon as possible. He went after Pyke who had followed John out.

Pyke was under the bus. Jason bent down to speak. "Morning Pyke. Got what you came here for?"

"I cannot move off until everyone is here." Pyke continued his work without getting up and without answering the question.

"Right, I'll round them up." So saying Jason went back into the hotel and attempted to assemble the party. He shouted round the corridors but when he arrived back in the hall Rory, Chuck and Hilary were not present. He sent some of the others to look for them but they could not be found. He learned that Rory had gone off into town but that Chuck had turned the other way and headed towards the lakeside. No one had seen Hilary go.

"Roger's bloody scatter gun," he muttered to himself "No hope of finding them."

He told the remnants of his group that he was going upstairs to make some arrangements and asked that he be called as soon as the others appeared. He went to his room and was asleep in two minutes.

Meanwhile Chuck was enjoying his first project. He had to photograph the underside of the little pier on the lake. This was outside the walls of the town and a good mile away. The photography would take some time, as there were a number of different shots he had to take. He strode off whistling; thinking how nice it was to stretch his legs. He stopped to photograph two pure white egrets wading at the lakeside and watched a great pelican glide in to meet its own reflection on the still water.

Rory saw Chuck leave the hotel and was about to fall into step with him but, self conscious about not knowing really what he was doing or why, he thought better of it.

I don't want to sound a right wally, he thought. Feeling just that he saw Chuck turn and stride off in the opposite direction.

Hilary also left the hotel about the same time. She had instructions to look conspicuous but not recognisable, so she pretended to herself that she was playing a part - a French tart. French because she could speak that language quite well and a tart because that seemed fairly conspicuous. She had put on some of her most attractive clothes, but she had tried a mix and not match, and the result was striking. The blue blouse was décolleté enough to attract attention anyway but with the green silk skirt it was a cynosure. She had bound her usually loose hair into a tight bun held in place by an orange ribbon. Her bare legs were ornamented with a thin gold chain and a pair of vermilion shoes. She wore dark glasses. "Shades," she laughed. "To make me feel like a shady lady.

Hilary passed Rory who quickened pace to observe the fluctuations of the lovely silk-covered buttocks. He didn't recognise them as the same buttocks, which had disported themselves, without the silk, by the stream the previous day. He just hoped this lovely creature was going his way for a bit to take his mind off the mindless task he had in front of him. She was. She strode along taking each turning that Rory had to take and turned into the Vernia - the very hotel he was bound for.

Hilary strode into the lobby of the hotel and made straight for the reception desk. She dinged the little brass bell imperiously, looked around the lobby, lowered her glasses and winked at the small man sitting in the corner. His reflexes caused him to lower his own dark glasses and return the stare of this outrageous looking woman. Even more quickly he pushed the glasses back up again and hid his face in his paper. Hilary hit the bell again. Diversion they had asked for. Diversion they would get.

As the receptionist came out from the back office Hilary started to talk in loud slow French. To her relief he could speak the language and to her even greater relief his
French was not any better than hers. "Puis-je avoir une chambre s'il vous plait?" she asked.

"Certainement" he replied in hesitant French, "for how long?"

"For always if the price is right." She asserted firmly also in French.

"Always. You mean a permanent booking?"

"Exactly."

"You will pay weekly?" asked the receptionist. Hilary nodded. "You wish a single room?"

"If you like. But it must have a large double bed."

"I see."

"And I will have callers - business visitors. You will have to send them up for me."

"I see."

"That will be all right then?"

"No madam, it will not be all right. It will certainly not be all right. This is not a bordello. This is a respectable hotel. Please leave at once."

Hilary's voice rose an octave. "A bordello! How dare you. I am a respectable businesswoman. I will report you to - to the Chamber of Commerce."

"Get out of here or I will call the police." The receptionist turned and disappeared into the back office.

Hilary turned on the quiet man in the corner. "Did you hear what he said to me? Did you?"

The small man nodded sheepishly.

She strode towards him. "Well, why don't you do something about it? Why do you let him speak to a lady like that? A gentleman would have stopped him. I have never been so insulted in my life."

As the alarmed man wilted under this tirade Rory darted into the hotel and shot upstairs. He detected a faint smell of ham. Must eat it all the time here, he thought

Rory knocked gently at door thirty-eight. There was no reply but he could hear someone moving inside the room. He knocked again a little more loudly. Someone spoke curtly from inside the room. Rory guessed he must be saying 'Who's that?' so he put his lips to the door and whispered in German, "I have come to invite you to a picnic."

There was another prolonged silence and Rory, feeling even more of a fool than previously, was about to turn tail and rush back to the Greivals when the door quietly opened and a pale gnome like face looked out at him.

The man said, "Come in," in German. Rory stepped just inside the room and stopped. He wished to get the business over with and get back to his new friends and normality as soon as ever possible but the man pulled him further into the room.

"Over here. We can not talk by the door," whispered the small white-faced man, this time in English.

"Oh! Why were we speaking in German out there?" asked Rory.

"English would make you conspicuous. That you would not want, would you?"

"Wouldn't I?"

"Not if you want to live. Well?"

"Ah yes. Are you Torow?"

"I am."

"Right. The message. It is now D plus ten - whatever that means."

"Good God! Why was not I told this earlier?" Torow demanded fiercely reaching for Rory's lapels then changing his mind as he saw just how broad the chest was.

"Listen, I know nothing about this. I was asked to deliver that message. Full stop." I make that sound like the opposite of fools rush in, Rory thought, but never again. Not this fool. This fool will stop next time.

Torow explained, in understandable but convoluted English, to a Rory who didn't want to know, that he had been ill and had been convalescing so had been out of contact. He asked Rory if he could get a message back but Rory protested that he had done what he had undertaken to do and now just wanted to get back to the bus as soon as possible or it might go without him. On Torow's insistence he explained where the bus was and where they were heading. To Rory's bewilderment Torow congratulated him on getting past the guard downstairs. Rory edged towards the door.

"This is bad. I am late - perhaps too late - the life of a man is at stake." Torow looked worried. Rory looked unmoved. Torow added. "A fellow Englishman."

"Watch it. I'm a Scotsman."

"Ah, well then. A Scotsman. Then I can rely definitely on you."

"Forget the soft soap," said Rory while warming to the man. "I know nothing about this and I've done what I was asked to do."

"And you have done it very well. To get past Olaf in the hall was very brave."

"Brave?"

"To the teeth he is armed. To protect me. I think. He would shoot you in a second if he knew to what you were up."

"Shoot me. Look, I'm up to nothing. I'm getting out of this."

Rory looked around for his way out and now saw two handguns, one lying on a desk and the other on a coffee table.

"That's a bit daft - or do you belief in the cowboy's fair shootout."

"Not very fair. I pick up the one that's loaded."

Rory grimaced and moved towards the door. "Look, I'm off."

"Right, but go this way." Torow led him to the window and opened it. "Down there and like lightning go when you hit the ground - and thank you."

Rory swung his legs over the sill. There was no fire escape only a drainpipe but Rory didn't hesitate. In Glasgow it was a routine part of a street education to climb the rhone pipes and this one looked a good deal safer than the ones he had clambered up in his youth. He didn't think about his somewhat increased weight as he clambered down. Torow squeezed his arm as he disappeared out of the window and promised to keep in touch.

'Not if I can help it,' thought Rory.

The drainpipe swung away from the wall and Rory hung above the concrete backcourt. Remembering a long unused skill he expertly lowered himself speedily to a bracket and paused to let it stabilise. It held and Rory got back to the hotel in one third of the time it had taken to get there. He passed Hilary and nearly tripped when he saw the tart come into the Greivals behind him. He collapsed into a large chair in the hotel lobby and saw the fancy looking woman disappear into the ladies room. Thank Heavens for the fuss the cow made. He didn't see her again but Hilary came out looking tastefully beautiful as always and to his delight sat down beside him and started to chat. The tart was forgotten.

CHAPTER TWENTY

Lucy entered the lobby at the double having completed her fifth run round the square. "Ah you're here. I'll let Jason know that we are all present and correct."

Jason responded to Lucy's knock and shout with a forced cheerfulness. He now felt better - physically. He was completely bemused otherwise. What was everyone getting up to? He certainly wasn't getting up to anything. He hurried downstairs.

Rory noticed Chuck's sea stained shoes and wet trousers and Chuck looked at the rust marks on Rory's jerkin. They just forbore to wink at each other. Their instructions did not allow for even such hinting confidences.

Hilary relaxed into her seat in the bus with a smile on her face. Jason dropped into the seat beside her wondering what she was smiling at. 'She's laughing at me - and no wonder,' he thought miserably.

But Hilary was not thinking of Jason at all, which, if he had but known, would have hurt him even more. She was thinking of her debut as a professional actress. The concession she was to get for this morning's work made it a professional job - and she was pleased with it. She must have been convincing and the required diversion effective. She had been thrown out of the hotel bodily. The broken heel had made the journey back more difficult and she felt an ache in her calf. Gingerly she ran a hand up her leg.

'She's doing that to tantalise me,' thought Jason.

As they moved off from the hotel Rory thought the man sitting in a blue car parked opposite looked like Torow. He looked back as the bus gathered speed and the car turned and followed them. He shivered. "I'm not scared," he told himself.

Rory saw the blue car pass them and disappear at speed down the road and began to relax. Pyke was now assiduously looking at the road ahead and when he slowed down they all hoped he had spotted another picnic site. However he swung the bus in front of a broken down car - a blue car. Rory didn't have to look but he did. Sure enough it was Torow. He was waving them down with a blue handkerchief. The bonnet of the car was raised and a bag of tools lay on the ground.

Pyke lowered himself from the bus with a sign that the others should stay where they were. He spoke briefly with Torow then returned to the bus, took something out of his toolcase and gave it to Torow. He rejoined the bus and told Jason that the tool would be returned to him in Felsober, their next stop.

Shortly after that they drew to the side of the road by a wooded hillside for a picnic. As they started to unload Alan indicated the blue car flashing past.

"Can't have been much wrong with him."

"No," agreed Rory, "he must have got just what he wanted from Pyke." 'And Pyke is just the sort of man who would stop his bus to help a motorist,' he thought.

CHAPTER TWENTY ONE

As the bus sped towards Felsober, Larry Hassall sat on a hard chair in the interrogation room with a bright light shining in his face. He had been brought no breakfast this morning and the cell had been even colder than usual. He knew that these were signs that his ordeal was about to start, but he was ready. Fortunately it was summer so the room was warming up as the sun rose and shone obliquely through the small barred window. There were two other chairs and a small table - no apparatus Larry was relieved to notice.

The interrogator came in with a clipboard in his hand and a small sly looking man by his side. No thuggery yet so keep them talking, he thought, remembering the doctor's advice. But I'll have to watch my tongue, not provoke the man. I'll know all I need to know very soon. Then just wait for Torow. But where the hell is Torow?

The interrogator sat down, a small half smile played about his lips, then disappeared as if it had decided this was a dangerous place to play: he looked undecided whether to be threatening or conciliatory. The face rested somewhere half way between the two expressions. Larry decided to influence the opening shots by acknowledging the conciliatory side with a tentative, deferential smile.

"I hear you have been unwell" started the interrogator, shrugging his broad shoulders in the loose jacket as if to emphasise his own fitness. "I hope you are feeling better now?"

"Much better, thank you."

"And you have been well looked after?"

"Until to-day - yes. I have had no breakfast this morning. I'm hungry."

"There have been difficulties in the kitchen this morning." The interrogator did not try too hard to make it sound convincing, "Perhaps later we can arrange something"

"Thank you," said Larry sweetly.

"How did your accident happen? None of our people I hope. We do not use violence," he paused, "unless it is absolutely necessary."

"I don't know if it was your people but it was your countrymen. I was mugged- beaten up and all my money and papers taken"

The sly man leaned over, "That is why we cannot positively check his identity."

"How very convenient." The interrogator beckoned the smaller man to stand back and stepped nearer to Larry.

Larry looked accusingly at the interrogator. "In our country the police would have arrested the attackers not the victim."

"We arrest everyone involved in a fight. We do not here like fighting."

"Why have I not been permitted to speak to the Embassy? That is my right. I demand to see someone from the British Embassy," said Larry firmly.

"You can be back in your Embassy to-day if you answer one question - one simple question."

"If I did know the answer to your question, which I doubt, what chance is there of my being set free? You could just kill me and that would be that."

"I am a professional interrogator. I keep my word." He now spoke angrily. "Stupid amateurs spoil it for all of us. If all tortu - interrogated people were confident that they would be treated as promised we would have a much higher rate of success. And so much time saved. Our questions would be answered more readily if our bargains were trusted."

"Trust. And I would go to Sweeney Todd for a shave."

The interrogator ignored the remark. "We should have agreed standards. Fools."

"I would go along with that but anyway I cannot speak without someone from the Embassy with me." Larry stalled to hide his eagerness to hear the question

"You do not want your solicitor as well, do you?" The interrogator's lips curled.

"Listen, I am a member of the Consular staff. I have diplomatic immunity. There will be big trouble if I am harmed"

"You will not be harmed - if you just converse with us a little. And do not waste our time by contending you are an ordinary member of the Consular staff. We have records of your movements since you left Whitehall. We know exactly where you came from and the people you spoke to before you left. We know who you are - and what you are. We know it and you know it. Why delay your breakfast further by debating something we both know?

"Well, industrial espionage is not so bad is it? Everyone is at it. It doesn't justify this sort of treatment."

The interrogator's face hardened. "Do not you play with me. Your espionage is not industrial. We know of the part - small but important - you played in Ecuador in the former year. We know what you are."

"How flattering."

"So, let us forget the charading and get down to the business."

"Let's. But if you know so much about me you must know that I am new to this country. I have done nothing here so I cannot be of any help to you."

"I think you can. In fact I know you can."

"I think you flatter me again. I am a small man - a little cog. I know nothing of importance".

"What we want to know is not important. Except to us. And you know it. We know you know it."

"And I know that you know that I know that you know it."

"Pardon?"

"British music hall joke."

"This for jokes is no time."

"When we British feel a joke coming there is no stopping us. One of our failings - one of our few failings."

"Enough of this," snapped the interrogator, "I will ask of you a simple question

- you answer it and you will go. Understood?"

"Understood." Larry concentrated so that he would rememher the question.

"Where is Lenci Dolitin?" hissed the interrogator.

"Who?"

"Lenci Dolitin. I want to know precisely where he is at this moment and what name is he using."

"Never heard of him, " lied Larry. He had heard of Dolitin, a defector from Tyrnia but not a spy, but he genuinely didn't know of the gentleman's present whereabouts. A painful dilemma if Torow didn't appear.

"Of course you do. He was in your Whitehall office three months ago. You were there at that time also; we know that."

"Tell me more about him. Refresh my memory."

The interrogator bit his lip. Was this man playing with him? "Dolitin is a well known scientist from this country. We must contact him. He took away some documents, which to him did not belong. Industrial espionage you might call it. A more serious view we take. Anyway we need these documents. They are ours. We are not anything improper doing. We wish to have what is ours. I am sure you will co-operate with that."

"Dolitin. I have heard that name somewhere. He was a defector from Poland
was he not?"

"He was not," exploded the interrogator. "He was from Tyrnia - from here. And he was not a defector. He fled for personal reasons."

"I would have thought most people who defect do so for personal reasons."

"Nonsense. Most do so for financial reasons. Either greed or because they are in financial difficulties. It was for the latter in the case of Dolitin".

"I will take your word for it. I don't really know anything about him".

"I think that is not true. Look - if your conscience is worrying you I can assure you he will come to no harm, in fact we will clear his debts."

Larry shrugged his shoulders.

"If you do not trust us we will give you the money to clear him of his debts. We just want Dolitin and our documents. He will come willingly when we explain it to him."

"I am sure you can be very persuasive."

The interrogator nodded grimly. "So tell us where he is. Is he still in Britain or has he gone into hiding in one of your colonies - or where?"

"1 don't know but if he has gone to one of our Colonies you should have no difficulty in finding him; there aren't many left."

After two hours of verbal sparring the interrogator nodded to the other man who turned and left the room. The interrogator was quiet and grim as he awaited the oilier s return He was gone only for a few minutes. When he returned he had a package in his hand, which he passed to the interrogator.

"I think talk you now will," the interrogator smiled.

CHAPTER TWENTY TWO

While Larry Hassall was wondering anxiously where Torow was at least two persons on the little brown bus knew that he had just raced past.

Come early evening the bus stopped at a large house on a hillside. It had a small tower, which commanded a panoramic view of the valley below and the wooded hills opposite. There were several similar mansions dotted about the hillside each about half a mile from the other. There were a few smaller houses in clusters with the characteristic overhanging eaves, which cast deep shadows over the ochre stonework. It was a lush prosperous looking landscape. The white wooden fences in the valley were well kept and the livestock looked fit and healthy. A church tower peeped out from the village at Felsober in the woods some miles to the east.

Jason allocated the rooms in what had become the established pattern. The rooms were large and, like the corridors, were panelled in a dark wood. There were heavy pieces of antique furniture in the local style spread about the public rooms and on the walls of the main lounge were the heads of several wild boar. Their eyes surveyed the room like anti-shoplifting cameras in a department store. It looks like the right setting for the sort of weekend house party which traditionally ends with a murder, thought Jason gloomily.

Before he could settle himself in, the receptionist asked that he arrange to have all the guests in the sitting room before dinner to meet the organiser of the next day's activities.

When all were gathered together, Rory and Alan each with a pint of the local brew in front of them, the man they were waiting for came in.

"This beer is like wild boar's piss," complained Rory making his only reference ever to the magnificent wildlife of the region.

"Aye. One suffering from an-e-mia." Alan took a large noisy gulp.

"Like another?" asked Rory as he downed the last of his third pint.

"And why not," said Alan wiping the froth from his mouth.

Hilary raised her glass to Jason and mockingly pretended to throw it back. Jason smiled weakly and sipped infinitesimally from his glass of local cognac tasting only the damp sugar on the rim of the glass. He prepared to relax and let this talk flow over him. He would take a day off. He hardly heard the preliminary courtesies offered in a strong local accent by the elfin faced man standing in front of them then he heard, "My name is Torow," and his glass shot up out of his hand, spilling the contents all over his trousers.

"You're determined not to drink to-night, Jason - but remember temptation never knocks twice," whispered Hilary.

Jason wiped his trousers and wondered which of the two shocks he had just received to concentrate on. He saw that Torow looked strangely at him then looked at Pyke who nodded.

Torow continued, "During the daytime to-morrow, and after a rest, also at night we will indulge in a soft of adult treasure hunt. This one has a serious purpose, which may become clear to you as it proceeds. You will experience some of the thrills you came to seek on an adventure holiday, indeed some of the thrills very real will be. Although we will be often scattered it is to be a team effort. If we each do a small part we will achieve the end."

"And we will meet here later to hear who done it? "asked Rory.

"Not here."

"Can I be the corpse?" Hilary sighed "I'm tired."

"Don't say that," hissed Jason half audibly.

"I will give you all fuller instructions to-morrow morning immediately after breakfast. I hope the meal you all enjoy. In the meantime I will require three of you to take instructions now and then make a brief reconnaissance tonight after dinner. John, Hubert and Hilary."

Torow crumpled his impish face into a smile and left the room. Jason saw that although the slim dark haired man moved quickly he had a pronounced limp and dragged his left foot.

Rory was unusually quiet over dinner but the others were in a holiday mood so in an attempt to draw him in Jason asked, "Why are you not married Rory? You seem to have a healthy interest in the women."

"Och, I like women fine - but I'm no so sure about marriage."

"Don't you have a serious girl friend?" asked Lucy.

"1 had, I had. I wanted her to be my bidie- in."

"Your what?" asked Alan.

"My bidie-in."

"As in Abide With Me?"

"Something like that, Alan. A live-in as you Sassenachs call it. Or is it a partner nowadays? Anyway she said no. She would consider getting married, she said, but not a bidie-in. That didn't have the same ring to it she said - and she wanted a ring to it." Rory finished amid laughter.

"Do you still see her?" asked Lucy.

"No. She put it about that I put it about so I chucked her," replied Rory.

"Oh, what a tangled web we weave when first we practice to conceive," said Alan.

"And you, Chuck. You scared to take the plunge too." Lucy looked Chuck straight in the eyes.

"No, not really scared - more terrified. Things are changing too quickly for me. I think I'll wait till this sexual freedom business has settled down."

"You're joking, Chuck. You don't give me that impression. Not when you put that hand of yours on the girls' knees," said Lucy. "I wouldn't trust you."

"Ah, you'd be all right Lucy." Rory gave out a deep chortle. "Chuck is the soft of man who would walk confidently up to a brothel door then wait for the light to change to green."

"Give over," protested Chuck.

Jason turned to John for a contribution.

"Not me," John spoke emphatically. "Hours too irregular. Maybe some day."

Jason turned to Alan. Alan shook his head. "No. A bachelor me. That's a man who doesn't make the same mistake once."

"So, none of us have experienced the delights of matrimony," said Jason.

"I suppose the nature of the holiday makes that very likely," said Chuck. "Maybe we're all waiting for the perfect woman - sorry - spouse."

"I've been married," Hubert spoke softly and for the first time that evening. "Sadly she died - more than ten years ago now."

There was a short silence.

"And you still miss her?" asked Lucy.

"Oh, yes. Particularly when I'm enjoying myself I feel guilty. I've thought of her a lot this week." The older man smiled at his companions then sat back to indicate that his contribution to the conversation was over.

"Grace and Julia. Never been tempted?" asked Jason.

The two girls looked at each other both reluctant to speak, then Julia scowled 'My work has made that impossible for me I'm afraid," she said hesitantly.

"Me too. My vocation also precludes marriage," added Grace. Both girls blushed and Julia rose and excused herself to go upstairs to have a bath.

"Well, I'll be damned. Career girls. No wonder they're having to knock down schools. We'll be ex-tinct soon," scoffed Alan.

"Well, you're doing nothing about it, young man." Lucy jabbed a finger at him.

"Give me a chance Lucy, give me a chance. I'm just waiting for a beaut-iful woman like you."

"Flatterer."

"Well, faint praise never won fair lady. No, I'm too wicked for the likes of you,

"You'll reform in time, Alan. You all do."

"Oh I do - regularly. Like Dos-to-evsky 1 repent in haste so that I can sin again at leisure."

Jason would dearly have liked to ask Lucy why someone so bright and attractive had never been married as she was older than all the others except Hubert but instead he asked her to tell them of her travels.

She required little coaxing and happily started to talk of the time she walked high in the foothills of the Himalayas with a group of Sherpas.

"Were there no other women with you?" enquired Grace.

"No, there weren't many women walking in the mountains in those days."

"I'll bet they treated you like a lady. Foreigners do." Monica looked round at the assembled examples of British manhood with a disparaging eye.

"I don't think any of them realised I was a female. I wore about fifty layers of clothes and we even slept in them for warmth. All huddled together. I'm not sure it would have made any difference if they had. It was rough. Sex wasn't uppermost in our minds."

"It must have been rough," growled Rory.

"And cold I'm sure. Whatever is the opposite of aph-ro-disiac that's what cold is. How the Eskimos have survived as a race I can't imagine." Alan shuddered.

"You've got quite the wrong impression there. The Eskimos are a highly-sexed people." Lucy contradicted. "I remember when I was in Greenland," There was a groan of mock anguish, "I came across the custom whereby a visiting guest was extended the hospitality of the wife's bed during his stay. It was considered polite."

Rory nodded enthusiastically. "Very polite."

"Very civilised." Alan smiled lecherously.

"A good place to be a commercial traveller," added Rory.

"A sort of droit de salesman," suggested Alan.

"And a visiting lady," asked Hilary, "was she extended the same - or equivalent facility?"

"Not then she wasn't. I don't think they saw any lady travellers in those days. So no - not in my experience."

"But that's not fair. That's sex discrimination," protested Hilary.

"Maybe the new act applies there now," said Jason eager to enter the conversation now that Hilary had shown an interest.

"If it does and there have been changes you can be sure it's the men's perks which have been cut off," complained Alan.

"I know what I would cut off," said Monica tight mouthed.

"Yes, but only afterwards - like a Praying Mantis," suggested Hilary.

CHAPTER TWENTY THREE

As Larry braced himself the interrogator took some photographs out of the envelope and fanned them out on the table.

"Your holiday snaps. How interesting," quipped Larry.

"Do not have joke with me. These photographs could ruin you."

Larry reached forward and picked one up. It was a very clear black and white shot of himself embracing a lovely girl. Both of them were naked.

"Remember that?" gloated the interrogator.

"Indeed I do," replied Larry. "Yes, I remember it very well. It doesn't happen to me so often, I am sorry to say, that I would be likely to forget."

The interrogator stood back looking triumphant.

"I thought it was a safe house," said Larry.

"A semi-detached safe house? You British."

"You're right. Anyway I have admiration for nothing but your ingenuity." The interrogator smiled. "So you admit that that is you in these photographs?"

Larry peered at the photographs and almost bumped heads with the little man who was obviously finding some of the prints very interesting. "Yes, it's me all right although I think my other profile is better. Mind you I wouldn't vouch for all of them." He picked up one. "This one for instance, I don't think I've seen myself from this angle. That must be print number sixty-nine. No, I'm not sure about that one but I'll take your word for it. Here that's not a bad one; innovative lass she was," he said reaching for the print the small man was drooling over. "Is that really me? Not bad. Not bad for a man of my age."

"Stop this fooling about. This could be serious for you. These photographs will be destroyed if you talk."

"Oh, pity. Could I have a copy of that one and that one please before you destroy them?"

"Do not pretend that concerned you are not. These disgusting photographs will be sent to a few chosen people if co-operate you do not."

Larry laughed "To whom?"

"To your wife and family for a start."

"Your intelligence is not good," said Larry. The interrogator scowled. "I am not married and I have no family."

"You have friends."

"The sort of friends I have would envy me if they saw these. I'm sure they don't think I've got it in me. I'll tell you what you should do - sell them. Mind you I would want a royalty."

The interrogator took a photograph angrily from the little man and glared at Larry. "Right they will go to your employers, both to the Embassy here and your controller in London. You will be finished, a man in your position."

"What position?" Larry pointed, "1 liked that one best. Do me a favour. My employers asked me to do that. Don't you think I'm a lucky man," Larry reached forward and picked up a photograph of two naked bodies closely entwined. "Getting paid to do that?"

"I don't believe you.

"It's simple. I was sleeping - actually I didn't get a wink of sleep - with your lass because my employer thought I could get something from her."

"You would learn nothing from her."

"I wouldn't say that - but what I learnt wasn't relevant to my employer's enquiries. She must be a loyal girl to do all that for her country."

"She is well paid."

"I'm glad to hear that. I wondered whether I should have left her a tip."

The interrogator stood up abruptly, his fists clenched and a scar flamed red across his knuckles as he walked quickly out of the room barely able to contain his anger. He turned in the doorway, "I am sorry to be awkward you have decided. Think it over to-night. Tomorrow could be difficult for you."

The small man gathered up the photographs in his shaking hands and stood up.

"May I keep one as a souvenir?" Larry held out his hand.

The small man narrowed his eyes malevolently and left without replying.

"Remember me to Olga please." Larry shouted after him.

Larry thought of her warm, soft body that night as he curled up in his hard, cold bed.

CHAPTER TWENTY FOUR

Immediately after dinner the three whom Torow had named went off to another room to start their evening's activity. Torow himself had not appeared at dinner. Before they left Hilary came up to Jason.

"This is for real isn't it? I saw the man in the hotel. He had a gun."

"What man?" asked Jason.

Ignoring the question which questioned her assumption that he knew what was going on Hilary continued, "I thought I had done my bit, what I was asked to do. What's going on now? I'm scared,"

"I'm sure there is no need to be alarmed," comforted Jason but without conviction.

"Jason, wait up for me will you? Keep me a drink, I might need it. I'm not used to this sort of thing. It's something serious isn't it?

"I'll wait up. We'll discuss it to-night. If tomorrow's programme sounds unreasonable we'll scrub it." Jason put a reassuring hand on Hilary's arm.

"I don't think it's going to be as easy as that. We're into something. I hope it's worth all this. I hope its legal."

"It'll be all right - believe me, Hilary. I'll wait up - however late you are I'll be here - awake".

Hilary smiled. "Good." She rose and walked to join her team.

Jason joined Chuck, Grace, and Julia who had returned from her bath, for a quiet drink. He stuck mainly to a local lemon drink with no alcohol. He enjoyed the evening. Grace and Julia, who were very different persons, had however formed a strong bond of friendship. Both were given to bouts of depression and introversion but seemed to manage most of the time to suffer alternately, thus they were a comfort to each other.

Chuck, sensing that someone up above had torn up the claim forms of the two girls, tried to be as helpful as possible. He even flirted mildly with them both but received no encouragement. However, now that they knew him his lighthearted advances were not resented, but when he rested his hand lightly on Julia's knee she shrank back and shuddered but said nothing.

"Holy Mother of Jesus will you stop puffing your hand on her knee," protested Grace lightly. Julia looked aghast at the language.

"Sorry, Julia," said Chuck. "I'm one of the world touchers. You're either a toucher or you're not. All our family are touchers. I got a shock - and a slap or two when I first went out into the world. I thought everyone touched all the time. I'm sorry.

"I was just joking, Chuck. I think touching's nice. It's really a lovely way of communicating. Or it was. People put different connotations on it now. It's a pity -but there it is. We are all conditioned," said Grace. Her calm grey eyes trying to reassure the embarrassed Chuck.

"Don't fuss. I'm sorry. I can't help it," said Julia her shoulders tightening.

"The world has lost its innocence," mourned Chuck.

"You can say that again," agreed Julia.

When all but Jason had left the bar to go upstairs Rory and Alan, who had been drinking quietly in the other corner, rose also. As they entered their room Rory said, "If you don't mind I think I'll read for a while tonight. Help me get to sleep."

"You read!" scoffed Alan. "What have you got in there? The pop up edition of the Kama Sutra."

The lounge was empty apart from the now sagging Jason when Hilary returned, looking flushed and anxious. Jason pushed forward her Martini. She gulped it down.

"I feel like a duck," she said.

"You feel like a what?"

"A duck. This is the second time I am to be used as a decoy."

"Well, decoys don't get shot at as I understand it." Jason reassured her.

Hilary shuddered then explained in some detail her patrol around the Valhoose. "Creepy it was." She took the second drink that Jason brought from behind a curtain for her. She swallowed it quickly too while insisting on being told how much Jason knew of all this. He explained that he knew a little but not much.

"Well, don't tell me," Hilary said with devastating logic. "I don't want to know."

"I think you should go to bed."

Hilary nodded and downed the rest of her drink. They went up the dimly lit oak panelled corridor and parted at Hilary's door. Jason had decided it would be unfair to take advantage of her in her present fraught state. He kissed her gently on the cheek, gave her a comforting hug and went on to his bedroom.

He had just settled in his bed and was dozing off when his phone rang; it was Hilary, "I can't sleep, Jason. I'm having nightmares and I'm still wide awake"

"Oh! Anything I can do to help?" asked Jason.

"I don't know. I feel frightened - and lonely."

"Would it help if I came along?"

"Please" entreated Hilary.

He rushed to the door, got into the corridor, rushed back and put his dressing gown on, out into the corridor then back into the room for a dab of after shave, out into the corridor, then back again to put his pyjama trousers on. He stopped, breathed deeply and strode with dignity to Hilary's room. He knocked at the door and said, "It's me," in a squeaky voice he did not recognise.

In contrast the voice which bade him "Come in," was deep and husky.

The lighting in the bedroom was subdued. Jason could see Hilary looking tiny in the massive bed with her shoulders just peeping out of the sheets - bare shoulders. Her hair gleamed on the pillow. Her eyes were wide.

"I'm sorry, Jason. It's so late and I'm so tired but I can't sleep. I keep thinking about tomorrow. It's all racing round and round in my mind. I'm scared. Really scared."

"There's no need, Hilary. Everything will be alright," said Jason sitting on the edge of the bed.

"Will it? What have I let myself in for?"

"An adventure," said Jason.

She shuddered and he could see that she was trembling. He held her hand.

"You're tired," he murmured.

"Then why can't I sleep?" asked Hilary.

She shuddered again more violently this time. "Hold me." She reached a hand towards him.

When Jason had his arms around her, just to comfort her, he found that he was under the blanket. Without thinking about it, it had just happened - so naturally. She clung to him and gradually the shivering stopped. He held her close trying to be reassuring. After a few moments he realised that she was naked. Hilary was naked in his arms.

He started to pull gently away and to make a stumbling apology. "Don't," whispered Hilary. "Stay with me. I feel a lot better already." She snuggled in so that it soon became less of a cling and more of a cuddle. They were both silent for a moment. She moved again. This time it was a sensual writhe. She leaned her head back from Jason's and smiled - a slow sweet smile. "Maybe this is what I need," she said.

Jason was the one who was trembling now. His senses were in a whirl. He started to caress Hilary but as he gently stroked her he recalled with sharp pleasure the texture of the scrap of blanket he had taken to bed for years as an infant. This caused him a few moments of extremely disconcerting mental confusion. She purred as his hands sought her soft secrets and his own stimulation. She laughed softly as he kissed and fondled her, then shuddered - a different sort of shudder this time and she whispered, "Ah, Jason has found the Golden Fleece at last."

She rolled slowly on to her back. Jason allowed himself to roll with her. For the next few minutes Jason felt as if he were in heaven. He seemed to do nothing - but it happened - my how it happened. After the joyous explosion he lay back. The whole experience was so dream-like that in the days to come when he wished to relive in his mind the beautiful moments they were blurred and unreal. But for now the powerful sensation completely blotted out his fears for the days ahead. He now lay exhausted but exulted; drained but dauntless.

CHAPTER TWENTY FIVE

Torow called the party together just after breakfast to outline the plans for the day. He looked confident but Jason thought of Larry and shuddered. Hilary had not appeared for breakfast but she entered the lounge just in time for the briefing. She looked composed and beautiful as always. I hope she has forgotten her fear of last night, thought Jason. He wasn't sure whether he wanted her to forget last night altogether. I haven't - I won't ever, he promised himself. He looked at her to see if he could learn anything from her smile but her lovely face was serene and expressionless.

"It is going to be very hot to-day. This will suit us. Particularly our decoy." Torow cast an impish smile towards Hilary. She didn't smile back.

"Hubert will go out first. He will double-check for us a route to our target - the Valhoose -, which I will point out to you in a moment. A route to be used in darkness. He will also indicate the best way to the village for a group to get there in daytime -unnoticed. I think he will need an assistant to carry paper, compass, binoculars and others things. Could we have a volunteer?"

After a few moments of hesitation Julia put up her hand, then Chuck raised his.

"One should do Hubert. You want to be inconspicuous. Who do you want?"

Hubert looked embarrassed. "Well, I don't know. Julia was such a good partner at the orienteering - but I know she hasn't been well". He looked at Julia. "If you don't mind I'll take Chuck. He can take some photographs." Julia acknowledged this with a smile and Hubert went on, "And we'll have to go quite a bit faster this time."

"Come off it, Hubert. You couldn't move fast if your bus pass blew away," quipped Rory.

"Don't be rude, Rory. We all have our truss to bear," added Alan.

Torow looked bewildered. "Right - that is settled. Hubert, you know what to do so you and Chuck can go off as soon as you like." Hubert nodded to Chuck and they left the room.

"John, you will not be needed until four this afternoon but you can study these photographs and drawings in the meantime. When you do go you will need to take two strong men with you."

Jason sat up. John looked round. "I'll take Rory and Alan," he said. Jason slumped back in his chair, relieved but hurt.

"And you Hilary. You will not be needed until mid afternoon."

"Must I go by myself?" Hilary looked around at the others.

"Yes, I am afraid so. I have tasks for the other ladies," said Torow.

"Well, how about Jason? Can he come with me? Some of the guards might fancy him more than me." Hilary forced a smile. Jason frowned.

"I think not." Torow shook his head. "Before you disperse let me show you the Valhoose. Come upstairs to the tower."

They followed him up a stairway, which spiralled tightly up the small tower, which formed a corner of the building. The tiny room at the top could only contain four of them at a time so they took turns as Torow pointed out a large grim looking building far across on the other side of the valley. It looked very similar to the house they were in but was about twice as large. Through the binoculars they could see that there was barbed wire on the top of the high stone walls.

"And the treasure is in there?" asked Lucy.

"You could say that." Torow nodded.

"I don't want to get my clothes torn on this game." Monica smoothed her skirt in distaste.

"No-one need do what they don't want to do. You will not be near the barbs."

"Pity," whispered Rory.

"There's a lady who knows her lamentations," responded Alan

"And you can't tell us what we're looking for? It would help you know," queried Grace. "If it were something worthwhile I'm sure we would -" Her voice trailed away uncertainly.

"Not yet," replied Torow. "Not yet. We will see how the first part of the plan goes. It is better that you know only a little just now."

Sounds like Roger, thought Jason.

"Now the four remaining ladies, together with Jason and Pyke, will go into the village by bus and do some shopping. The purchases must be spread over as many shops as possible, and as much time as possible, and in as many different permutations of single and pairs of buyers as possible. You also should change your clothes from time to time. Be as unmemorable as you can.

Jason looked round the motley lot and reckoned that that was not going to be easy.

"They get a fair number of tourists," Torow went on, "Which should help. Those who can should speak French and German or a phrase or two of the local language. Do not create the impression of a great load of the English descending on the village.

"I could help there," chipped in Rory. "I speak effluent French."

"You will be busy. And the bus, Pyke. Keep it inconspicuous - and that does not mean hide it away so carefully that it will be conspicuous"

Pyke gave him an 'I know my job,' look.

Torow now took Pyke off to check the stock of tools and gadgets, which were stowed about the bus. Roger had avoided loading anything which would look out of place or which could reasonably be obtained locally. Torow looked appreciatively at the plentiful supply of ropes and climbing material - the sturdy shoes and the axes. They checked the inflatable boat and the outboard motor.

"Right," said Torow to the assembled shoppers. "To start with get chocolate, biscuits, anything like that to carry with you to-night. Enough for everyone. Then I want, and don't write this down, remember it, each of you to get one or two of the following articles. I want wire cutters, another two torches, some glue - super glue, silk stockings if you can get them if not tights will do".

"Oh no," said Rory. "I've heard the one about the bank robbers who had to work closely together because they had a pair of tights over their heads."

Torow did not acknowledge the interruption. "Some large handkerchiefs, a pair of insulated pliers, two whistles, two large penknives, string, cellotape. He went on at length. "Do not use British money, either use local currency or better still use Francs or Deutschmarks if that suits the language you are going to use. 1 have some of those currencies available. Do not in the village use the restaurants, tea rooms or bars."

Jason had a quick word with Hilary before he departed on his shopping trip. He didn't feel as if he was being given the chance to shine in this enterprise. "Am I allowed to know what you have to do this afternoon Hilary?"

Hilary shrugged her shoulders. "Can't see why not. Simple really. Don't know why I'm worried. I've just got to sunbathe in the meadow by the Valhoose building."

"Sunbathe?" shrieked Jason.

"Topless"

"That's disgusting."

"Thank you very much."

"I didn't mean that Hilary. You~w..."

"Forget it. I am supposed to distract any guards or watchman so that John can do his reconnaissance unobserved."

"Well, I hope you just distract them - not attract them. You have a pretty powerful appeal, Hilary"

"I get a pretty powerful response sometimes."

Jason flushed - and smiled.

By three o'clock they had all returned. Hubert looked exhausted and was despatched to bed after Torow had looked at his drawings and expressed approval. "Exactly what we want. This should make things a lot easier. We will call you about midnight to guide the raiding party to the Valhoose. We should manage the village without you from these drawings. Thank you, Hubert."

Chuck went off to develop some black and white shots be had taken.

Torow called Jason aside. "I didn't know you were one of us."

Jason looked non-committal. Torow went on, "Pyke told me. We are one day behind so we have the niceties to cut out. I did not get the message. I was unwell -convalescing when you contacted me. So I have the task of getting someone inside the Valhoose when I am not on duty at head office to fix it; not easy." Torow face was puckered but he talked with a relaxed authority.

"What can I do to help?" asked Jason.

"Come with me this evening. John is leading a party to pick up the interrogator. He is the only person who lives outside the Valhoose who is permitted to have keys. Some back up they might need. Can you run?"

"Like lightning when I'm frightened", said Jason.

"You should just right be then."

Jason didn't like the sound of that. He then felt he had to admit his ignorance to Torow, "I don't really know what's going on."

"Of course not - if Roger briefed you," said Torow. "I know his technique of old. I just hope between us we know enough or in trouble is poor Hassall."

"Hassall?" queried Jason.

"Larry Hassall. He is captive in the Valhoose. Interrogation started yesterday I think. He is probably having a- tough time right now. And if they stick to the usual routine it will get really unpleasant tomorrow." He shuddered, "We must tonight get him out".

"I think I've met Hassall once. Nice chap. Boxer isn't be?. I don't like this bit of the business - the thought of him in there being --. Back in the office we don't realise ---."

"I am sure you do not."

"What are we going to do tonight?" asked Jason.

"Get the keys of the Valhoose from the interrogator to start with," replied Torow.

The small party set off for the village on the route plotted by Hubert. On the way they stopped above the meadow where Hilary was disporting herself while John and Rory made a detour to inspect the target house at close quarters. At the pre-arranged signal Hilary, lying resplendent on a red tartan rug and with a yellow parasol, sat up and started combing her hair - behind her head. She felt nervous but to those in the grim building she showed a bold - and beautiful - front.

When John and Rory left some of the ropes and hooks hidden near the house, so that they could travel light and fast in the dark that night, not a guard was looking in their direction.

CHAPTER TWENTY SIX

In the interrogation room Larry Hassall was indeed having a tough time. For the first hour the interrogator with his small friend threatened, cajoled and even tried to bribe their prisoner.

Larry listened to what they said and answered and debated at length. He was not at his best. Last night he had been served a small bowl of the gruel of some unrecognisable grain. This morning he again had no breakfast.

"Still having trouble in the kitchen?" he had started by saying, as his tormentors came in. "I could help if you like. I was a good cook."

"We know that," leapt in the interrogator happy with the chance to display the intelligence at his disposal. "In the Royal Navy. At least we know you were a cook. Our records however say you were not so good. In fact you were transferred to submarines after a petition from your crew."

"That's not kind. It's true but it's not kind. I cooked badly deliberately because I--" Larry hesitated.

"Because you what?"

"Because I was bored."

"Nonsense," snapped the Interrogator. "It was because you wanted to be in the action. You wanted to fight someone. Not for a cause - but for a country - anyone - you would fight anyone." His voice stayed cold and unemotional.

He followed up these comments by reiterating his, and his country's objections to the Western powers. "I suppose you enjoyed your time in the Navy - fighting. The Americans, the British and the French make so many arms. They keep the whole world fighting."

"And the Russians," said Larry.

"And the Russians. We have no time for any of the big powers. We want to stand on our own feet. Defend ourselves. Live in peace. No interference from anyone."

"Not even from your own people? I don't disagree with your criticism of the arms trade but I would think better of your Government if your own people decided what sort of country they wanted."

"We govern for the good of the people. We cannot counter the propaganda from the West - or from Russia. Therefore we cannot hold truly free elections. You will not allow us," protested the interrogator.

"I respect your opinions. I don't share them because I trust your rulers even less than I trust ours. There are some checks on ours - a democracy is not perfect - but it has these checks."

"Nonsense - all evil comes from the big powers and we will not put up with it much longer. We will start by procuring the return of Lenci Dolitin. It is a matter of principle with us."

"I'm sorry I can't help."

"I am sorry that you will not. I will just say this for the last time. We know that you know the whereabouts of Lenci Dolitin. We can this interrogation keep up for weeks if necessary. After some weeks your release would be academic. You would not be fit, physically or mentally to return to the outside. Go now and you will be well."

"You are mistaken about my knowledge - so you will be wasting your time and incidentally a quite useful life."

The Interrogator nodded to the small man who left the room. He then sat down at the table and scowled. He did not look at Larry as he composed himself and set his resolve for the task ahead.

A large man entered the room. He looked like the sort of man Larry might have faced across the ring in days past. He was bigger than Larry but had the same kind of face - a face which evoked the question, 'If a man built like that has got like this what does the other guy look like?' Larry hoped that his own much-molested countenance was discounted as being due to his recent mugging. He didn't want the thug to take into account his skills.

"He is being difficult. Show him what you can do. Gently to begin with." The interrogator nodded to the big man.

Larry braced himself. The heavy blow to the side of his head came at him obviously deliberately signalled for maximum psychological effect. Larry moved with it and felt little pain. He grumbled in simulated distress.

"Right", said the interrogator. "That was just a sighting shot. Now let us save time and trouble. Tell me where Lenci Dolitin is?"

"In the circumstances I would obviously be pleased if I could. You would save us both time and trouble just by believing me."

"Right. Mark him this time."

The big man shot a short blow to the head, which would have taken most people by surprise. Larry rode it easily but felt a sting and a warm trickle of blood on his forehead. The big man had turned his hand sharply as he made contact. This boy knows his job, thought Larry. He saw a large ring on his tormentor's finger.

"Stop protesting your innocence or it will go bad for you."

"I'm not protesting my innocence. I'm admitting my ignorance."

"We know you know."

"Don't let's start that again. You have been misinformed. I am a little man. You want someone bigger."

"Who?"

"I don't know. It's not my department."

"What is your department?"

"I'm a courier - a messenger - that's all."

"For that job you are a bit bright."

"Don't knock it. It requires great ingenuity to get through sometimes."

"I am sure." The interrogator nodded to the big man who raised his knee sharply into Larry's groin.

Paradoxically, it flashed through Larry's mind; this is not a blow you can ride.

Larry was protected but the howl he let out was spontaneous and genuine as the two reinforced rubber spheres, on impact, tried to go in diametrically opposite directions.

Discomfort the man said, thought Larry as he bent double to gain a little time. "I hope those people for whose cause you do this know about it. Most people are quite nice you know - even in Tyrnia," he said, but this merely provoked another blow to his head.

After three hours of this, the assaults spread out by Larry's desperate attempts to engage the interrogator in conversation, Larry was in a much worse state than he would have been after a full bout on the mat - having lost badly! He made a point of repeating the question to himself after each blow - 'Where is Lenci Dolitin'.

"Pity," said the interrogator - not expressing his feelings for Larry. "We will have to go into the theatre tomorrow."

"Something good on?" said Larry spitting blood from his broken lips but still trying desperately to establish some rapport with this man.

"A tragedy perhaps. And the men with the black hats will win. Think about it. Think about it all night." He turned and left the room.

Larry realised the significance of this last remark when he got back to his cell and found that a loud noise, like music concrete, was coming from next door and the machine was obviously on auto-reverse: and from further away he could hear the howling of a man in torment.

"Torow can come as soon as he likes now," Larry muttered to himself.

CHAPTER TWENTY SEVEN

They took dinner early at the hotel. It was a subdued affair. Torow and Pyke did not dine with the others but Torow had given Jason instructions to keep a rein on the drink consumed. They discussed the afternoon's activities and swapped experiences. Hilary complained about some tenderness where she had been exposed to the sun but only received some jocular offers to rub soothing unguents into the affected parts.

"Did you find the route to the Valhoose easy to follow?" asked Hubert of John.

"Excellent," John offered the salt to Hilary. "No problems".

"I wouldn't say that," disagreed Rory.

"Oh, what was the difficulty? "asked Hubert looking disappointed.

"There were two features we had great difficulty in passing - and they weren't marked on your map."

"What features?" asked Hubert.

Rory looked at Hilary who threw a roll at him as the others laughed.

Monica complained of the surliness of the shopkeepers in the village and looked surprised when the others laughed.

Grace told them of going into a big ironmonger's shop in Felsober and using her best French to make a purchase when she was embraced by a big fat friendly Frenchman who spoke at her at such a speed she hadn't the foggiest notion what he was saying. She only extricated herself with difficulty by simulating a faint, when Julia, speaking in poor but loud German, pushed in and led her away. They left the Frenchman shrugging his shoulders and smiling deprecatingly around as if he were accustomed to young ladies fainting at his feet.

"First hug I've had for a long time," joked Grace.

Darkness was intensifying the shadows in the valley as John and Torow crept out of the hotel and headed for the village. Jason, Rory and Alan followed five minutes later. After half an hour of fast walking they were in a disused barn, a short way from the cluster of houses. The clouds were high and scurrying across the sky but for the present the moon was hidden.

Torow led them to a small stone-built house slightly apart from the others. He posted Rory and Alan at the front and left Jason at the back gate. John and Torow slunk up to the rear door; ducking under the ray of light emanating from one of the windows.

John shone a narrow beamed torch on the lock and nodded then took a small bunch of levers and prods and worked away without a sound for several minutes, during which period Jason had to duck behind a wall as a courting couple sauntered and simpered past. John shook his head from time to time as he struggled with the lock, then came the gentlest of clicks and he eased the door open. Torow stood back against the wall and signalled Rory to precede John into the house.

Rory paced forward, his broad shoulders hunched in anticipation of a fray, his training shoes making little noise on the path. They disappeared into the house. They reappeared in two minutes.

"There is no one in there," hissed John.

"There must be," insisted Torow. "He goes out never."

"That's what you think. He'll have gone to the pub for a bevy," suggested Rory.

"He does not drink." Torow thought for a moment then added. "However it is possible that he has gone to the bar to meet someone. We will look. I cannot go in. He would recognise me. I have described him to you, so to see if he is there you go in, Rory."

They collected Jason and slipped along the shadows of the lane and turned into a slightly broader street which was not well lit but there were slivers of light peeking out from between curtains and about fifty yards on there shone the warmer glow of the stained glass windows of the public house. Rory walked up the street and pushed through the swing door releasing a short burst of noise into the silent street. The four men hid in a narrow arched passageway awaiting his return.

About ten minutes later Rory strolled down the road to-wards them and was pulled into the passageway. "Well. Was he there?" asked Torow.

"No. No sign of him."

"What the hell took you so long?" asked Alan.

"I had to have a drink, didn't I? Would have looked conspicuous otherwise. Beer's not bad."

"What now?" Jason looked anxiously around the dark village streets.

Torow was quiet for a while, then, "The butcher's shop," he exclaimed

"And what would he be doing in a butcher's shop at this time of night?" asked Jason in exasperation.

"The shop-window. All the village notices are displayed in the butcher's window."

"So?" queried Jason.

"If there is anything on in the village to-night there will be a notice in the window. I will go. Wait for me here." Torow disappeared up the road.

He returned with news of two events; one a choir practice and the other a children's party. They headed off for the church hall. Torow looked at his little band.

"Not me this time. Not my scene," whispered Rory.

Torow beckoned to Jason. Jason looked nervously around and saw a light in a leaded window high above the ground. He noticed that there was a raised stone step just beneath it so he went over and climbed on to it. By standing on tip- toes he could just see over the sill. He hung there for some time then turned shaking his head.

"Handy that gravestone was just there," whispered Alan.

"That what?" Jason jumped down, stumbled on a raised mound of earth and knocked over some vases of flowers sending a metallic noise through the still churchyard. This, happily, coincided with an almost equally metallic crescendo from the tenors inside the hall.

As he scrambled to his feet and made towards the gate Torow limped over to him, swung him round by the shoulders and directed him towards the entrance door to the hall. "Make sure."

John pointed to a white coat and a brush just inside the door. Jason donned the coat, which was a few sizes too big for him, picked up the brush and walked slowly into the hall. He came back in a very short time carrying a bucket. He was tempted to do a Charlie Chaplin walk.

"No. Only six of them in there. No one like the man you want," He told Torow.

"Where did you get the bucket?" asked Alan.

"I picked it up in there - added veri-si-mil-itude," he hissed at Alan.

He dropped the bucket with a clatter.

"Right - the children's party. School hall this time." Torow turned shaking his head and hurried off with the others scampering in his wake.

The school hall was a low wooden building so looking through the windows was easier this time. The only problem was to do this unseen by the persons inside, particularly the sharp-eyed children. However they were at this moment, although indeed bright eyed, looking in another direction as they sat in a circle playing a game which Jason recognised as similar to pass the parcel of his childhood. They were concentrating. There were two men in the middle of the circle and three ladies, two spreading out lemonade and biscuits on a table and one playing the piano. The children were in full fancy dress and the adults had all donned some odd garment to enter into the spirit of the thing.

Torow darkened his face with some earth and peered intently at the two men in the room. "Not here I think," he whispered after a time. "I did not think we would find a man like him here. We will have to wait at his house for his return; a waste of valuable time." He thought of Hassall and sadly shook his head. "I hope he is not somewhere away." The others joined him and surveyed the happy scene inside. The adults were as absorbed in the simple game as were the boys and girls.

As they were just about to abandon the search the game ended, the children shot towards the spread table and the pianist, like the others in fancy dress, turned round, her Shirley Temple mask grinning towards the children.

"Good pianist," hissed Alan.

"The Shirley Temple films have got here already, have they?" quipped Rory.

They turned to go; Torow looked worried and shook his head as if uncertain what to do next. His limp was more pronounced and his shoulders slumped.

"Don't go. Look," hissed Jason, "aren't Shirley's hands a bit big?"

Torow turned back and peered through the window again.

"So they are," gasped Torow. "And look at that scar. It's him all right. I would know that scar anywhere. He burnt himself cooking someone."

Jason heard this and thought of Larry Hassall and his resolve, which had been ebbing rapidly away, returned, still shaky but returned.

"Does he have a car?" asked Rory.

"No. He will walk," whispered Torow. "Jason run to Pyke and get him to bring the bus to that gateway. We will seize him here and do not want to carry him far."

Jason sped off, glad not to be involved in the actual snatch.

"He is coming away. Not waiting for his lemonade," gloated Torow. "Rory you take that side of the porch. John with me. Quick."

The interrogator came out of the hall backwards waving to the laughing children, nodding his head to them in his ludicrous mask. As he raised his hand to take it off a rolled up sleeping bag was pulled over his head and he was swept off his feet. His cries were muffled by the thick bag and the children's laughter helped drown the stifled shouts. A strap, pulled tight where his legs were, ended the kicking. It was now easy for the three of them to carry him to the bus and bundle him inside.

The bus shot off down the street and out of the village just as soon as they all clambered on. Pyke stopped out in the countryside where any noise would go unnoticed. Torow kept out of sight while the others took two bunches of keys from the interrogator's pockets. They were about to thrust the violently protesting man back into the bag when Torow whispered to Jason to get the Shirley Temple mask. When the interrogator was almost secure again Torow pressed a bottle into the struggling man's hand and then took it away again and wrapped it carefully in a cloth.

CHAPTER TWENTY EIGHT

Back at the hotel Jason was sent to alert Hubert that he was now on duty. Torow examined the keys closely and discussed them with John. They sifted out the personal looking ones, looked closely at the others and picked out those, which looked likely. Torow explained that no one; not even the interrogator had a key to the gate. However it had been agreed that an approach through the gate would have been undesirable anyway. John confirmed that he had already decided at what point to go over the wall.

"Good." Torow nodded approvingly. "John, you take Rory up to heave you, Chuck as a look out and Jason to run back to the bus if need be."

Torow leant over, cupped his mouth, and whispered to Jason. "Must have some professional input.

That's exactly what the genius who thought out this plan planned wouldn't happen, thought Jason.

"Do we have grappling irons?" asked John.

"No." answered Torow. "Roger probably thought that they would be too conspicuous in the baggage. There are climbing axes and pitons but I do not think we will need them."

Hubert led them into the darkness and Jason found himself once again full of admiration for this man who could read the countryside as easily as most people could read a picture book, and interpret contour lines as if the features were set out on page three. They arrived within fifty yards of the darkened Valhoose and posted Chuck by a junction of dense beech hedges. Jason had feared they would have to cross a ring of light but all was in darkness. Torow had explained that the authorities kept a low profile here:

They did not want to draw attention to the building and its use so they had tried to keep as domestic looking as possible. It looked just like a typical large private house to which strangers are not welcome and where security is good, but it was not a fortress they were tackling. They conducted, he was informed, this activity out here because they didn't even trust their regular prison staff.

Hubert now left them and went back to the hotel, his next task being to ensure that the bus got to the rendezvous. The three remaining now slipped balaclavas over their heads and crept forward towards the high walls. Jason carried a roll of heavy insulated material.

"Just in case the wire is live," Pyke had warned.

'Live!' thought the now quivering Jason recalling Pyke's words. 'I hope I'm still live tomorrow.'

The three men stopped where their reconnaissance had indicated the optimum place to be; as far from a sentry as possible; the wall as low as possible and the barbed wire at its flattest. The dim grey light changed to black as they came alongside the stone wall. All was quiet except for a strange, grating sound from the house. Rory put his back to the wall and joined his hands in a strong grip. Jason put one foot in Rory's hands and braced himself upwards helped by a push from John. As Jason reached his highest stretch with his feet on Rory's shoulders he slung the heavy bundle upwards so that it unrolled and lay across the wire. As soon as this was done Rory moved a step away from the wall forcing Jason to be the top of a half arch. John scrambled up, his training shoes leaving an impression on Jason's head, slung himself carefully onto the protective sheet and dropped down silently to the other side.

"Thank heavens there's not a cold frame there," whispered Jason.

"You don't have a cold frame on a north wall," scoffed Rory.

Just then there was a loud trumpeting noise from the corner of the wall - just thirty yards away. They froze and shrunk into the shadows. There was complete silence for some moments as they stood there petrified. Then the sentry blew his nose again noisily, snorted a few more times then resumed his silent, secret vigil.

Rory now gripped Jason's ankles and raised him as high as he could. Jason, surprised how easily the big man thrust him upwards, almost fell backwards. He regained his balance and stretched. It was still an awkward reach. His fingertips scratched for a fold in the sheet and found a shallow indentation and with all the strength he could muster he pulled himself upwards and clambered over the sheet. It was not now lying as smoothly as when John had just bounced on and over it so he had to scramble awkwardly to avoid the millions of volts he feared were surging through the wires. He dropped heavily down inside the wall. The strange sound coming from the house was now louder; like a pop record from the bottom twenty - in poor condition.

John tiptoed forward. The moon was just peeping out from the clouds which obviated the dangerous necessity of using a torch although John did not seem at all disadvantaged by the darkness. Jason followed closely. He enjoyed the proximity of this confident man; but the confidence did not rub off. Jason was puzzled that there was no light to be seen yet there was, coming from inside the house, the blare of discordant music and the sound of voices. It was not pleasant to the ear, but it covered the noise of Jason's nervous stumbles.

John beckoned Jason to support him so that he could reach a small box high on the wall. Jason leant against the house as Rory had done for him outside. John took some cutters and something that looked like an electric socket from his overall pocket climbed onto Jason's shoulders and worked quietly for two minutes then scrambled down. He nodded. They now slunk along the wall to the front door. John went to the lock, took out his little bag of levers and three minutes later they were stepping inside the house. Jason knew the layout of the large house as well as he knew the shape of Hilary's blouse. He had studied Torow's drawing almost as intently.

There was a faint light upstairs and Jason could just see a door ajar right by the upper landing. He could not hear if anyone was stirring as the ghastly music from downstairs drowned all lesser sounds. John tied a string at knee level across the stairway and they headed towards the noise. It was now pitch black but John only shone his torch briefly when they came to a door. They found the stairs leading to the basement and moved slowly down them.

John put his mouth close to Jason's ear, "Torow said not to look in any cell other than the one our man is in. We might get distracted." Jason shuddered.

They passed the room from which the 'music' was emanating holding their hands over their ears. Jason crept along, resolutely ignoring the peepholes of the cells they passed, and then they came to the door Torow had marked on the plan. John selected the key, flashed the torch briefly at the keyhole, and turned the lock.

The small room was brightly lit. To keep the poor sod from sleeping, thought Jason.

Larry Hassall was huddled in a corner of the cell with his hands over his ears. His eyes were puffed with lack of sleep and he stared ahead as if in a trance. His face was swollen and bruised and his lips were bleeding. His right forearm was black. He did not see and certainly could not have heard them enter. Jason just recognised the man he had once met. He walked over to him and passed his hand before the dazed man's eyes like a hypnotist waking someone who had gone under.

Hassall blinked, then started. He swung his head away from the expected blow.

"It's me. Jason. Jason Jackson."

Hassall looked bewildered.

"Torow sent us".

At the name Torow, Larry's eyes lit up. His cracked lips almost smiled. "You're bloody late," he grumbled.

CHAPTER TWENTY NINE

Jason and John helped the limp Larry to his feet and into overalls and rubber shoes. Jason noted they fitted perfectly. John led the way out of the dark cell, dropping a torn scrap of a Shirley Temple mask as he went.

As John was locking the door of the cell behind them they heard an agonised scream from further down the passage.

"What's that?" croaked Jason.

Larry shook his head. "The poor wretch has been at that all night. We must get him out."

"No chance," John turned to go. "We can't take anyone with us. This is difficult enough. Let's get out - quick."

"No, wait please," pleaded Larry. "We can't just leave him. I feel as if I know him."

"Don't be daft." John pulled at Larry. "One more passenger and we sink."

Larry gripped at the bars and resisted. "At least let's go and see if we can do something for him." He paused blinking as his tired eyes tried to cope with the change of light. "Even if only to put him out of his pain."

Jason shuddered. He had once broken the neck of a wounded rabbit and hadn't slept for a week afterwards. He pulled at Larry but he could not be budged.

John shook his head in dismay. "Right, let's take a look."

The three men tiptoed down towards the scream. There was silence broken only by the music. They stopped and listened, not knowing which door to go to. After a long interval the scream again reverberated along the passage, echoing and multiplying. Jason stiffened in honor and John stepped back, bumping into him. Larry rushed forward. "This is the door."

There was a small peephole, which gave a fish-eye view of the cell. John peered in. " I can't see anyone in there. Come on, let's go."

"No." said Larry firmly. "Let's get in. See if one of the keys fit. The scream didn't come from nowhere and I don't believe in ghosts."

Jason tried hard to believe in ghosts as preferable to what he feared they might find behind the rusting iron door. John shuffled the keys in his hand and picked the one he thought most likely. It would not turn. He tried another with no success then a third, this time the lock clicked and as he pushed the door creaked open. Jason stood back as Larry then John looked round the door then slipped into the cell. Jason finding himself alone in the dark corridor hastily followed them. He heard Larry laugh and grunt, "Bastards."

As Jason's eyes adjusted he saw that the torch beam lit up a tape deck.

They stood silent then Larry cursed. "How I've suffered for that man - and he doesn't even exist." Again there was a long silence.

Jason shuddered. "He did once." He strode across and switched off the player.

"No. Don't do that," John commanded. "That can't help him now. We don't want to attract attention." Jason switched it back on.

He swung the torch around the room and had to support himself on a bench to keep his knees from going from under him. There were pliers and pokers and whips in one corner but even more sinister, on another wall there were electric panels with switches and dials and long leads. There were racks and rings and chains the purpose of which Jason energetically avoided thinking about.

Larry looked round, shaking he head. "Come on, let's go."

This time it was John who deferred their departure. "No, hold on a minute. Shine the torch over here."

Jason took the torch and cast a shaking light towards the dials.

"Hold it steady, man."

Jason braced himself against the bench and looking down saw a vice like piece of apparatus. He dropped the torch - hastily picked it up and steadied it against the bench. John took some small tools out of his bag. He worked away for two minutes stripping the insulation off a large electrical switch then took a cable and stripped a short section at the end of that. He now wrapped the end of the cable round the switch. He then put back the insulation but with some bare wires wound outside it and rubbed it all with some dirt from the floor.

"Looks like new," he whispered. He then adjusted the power control - upwards but so that it did not show on the dial. He touched the bare wire with a small tool and there was a shower of sparks. He nodded grimly.

"That's shocking," quipped Jason.

"I hope so," Larry nodded and smiled grimly.

"O.K. Let's go." So saying John led the way out wiping off fingerprints as he went. He locked the door and moved quickly upstairs.

He checked the string on the stairway and then made for the front door. They crossed the lawn and over to the place where they had surmounted the wall. Once there John threw a stone over. There was no response. He threw another stone and this time a stone came back over. It crashed with a loud shattering noise into a cold frame just three feet away from them. Jason hissed over the wall at Rory. "A north wall." John clapped his hand over Jason's mouth.

The sentry deafened by the dreadful music and the screaming heard nothing. A knotted rope came hurtling across the wall then, after an interval, another stone indicating that Rory had secured his end. John took a bottle out of his pocket, unwrapped it carefully and without touching it dropped it at his feet. He then climbed effortlessly over the wall, followed by a faltering but determined Larry who needed all the pulling power the mighty Rory could muster.

Jason shook uncontrollably while he waited alone in the dark for the signal to follow. If the sentry had blown his nose again Jason would surely have stopped shaking for a long time. After what seemed an eternity the signal came. On his way up and over greatly helped by another powerful pull from the other end of the rope, he wrenched off the insulation, threw it to the ground outside the wall then carefully stuck a small piece of white cloth on one of the barbs and dropped clumsily to the ground.

Larry ran quickly away from his grim prison but collapsed after fifty yards. Rory hoisted him up and with Jason taking his other arm they half dragged him as fast as they could, afraid that the alarm would be sounded at any moment. They had not gone more than four hundred yards when the siren wailed. Rory took the injured man, slung him across his shoulders and set off in a lurching unsteady run.

But the first planned meeting place was dark, quiet and empty.

CHAPTER THIRTY

Rory was strong but not fit and the noise of his great snorts as he desperately drew in breath unnerved the others. Torow had not told them where they had to rendezvous with Pyke only that they had to meet, half a mile away, with Grace and Julia who would lead them to the arranged meeting place. Trained by Roger, thought Jason.

They waited in the quiet, laying Larry down to rest. Lost, thought Jason, without the foggiest idea what to do next. But after what seemed many minutes Grace and Julia materialised from the gloom.

"We thought the whole Tyrnian army had arrived," complained Grace.

"We had gone fifty yards before we recognised Rory's gentle breathing," added Julia.

The girls had instructions for the next three possible legs of the journey. Julia knew the first and third. Grace knew the second. The idea was to go to these places in sequence as Pyke would have abandoned any which proved dangerous and moved on. Both girls seemed remarkably calm and business like; pleased to have something absorbing to occupy their minds.

As they approached the first meeting place the sound of the siren was replaced by an even more intimidating silence. There was no bus at the first of the appointed places.

"Right, Grace, where to next?" Jason peered at the paper Grace held.

"We go there." Grace whispered and pointed to the sketch map. "It's about two miles so we had better get moving. You all right, Julia?"

"Fit as a fiddle".

"And you, Larry?" asked Jason.

"A bit banjoed - but I'll manage. Lead on. I won't grunt as much as the big fella." Larry gasped as he rose.

They headed across a field and over a wooded hill away from the road. They moved slowly, realising that if they once strayed from the path set by Hubert they would never find it again and they would be lost in a strange and very hostile land. Julia led the way hoping after her brief experience with Hubert, that she knew how his mind worked. Several times as they neared the road they heard the roar of vehicles and once, when they looked down from a hilltop, they saw that from some of them searchlights were sweeping the countryside. It was hard going; between the smoother fields of cultivated land were stretches of rough scrubland punctuated with frequent boggy patches.

"Thank heavens we don't still have the interrogator with us. We could never have carried him over this lot," said Jason.

"The interrogator!" Larry looked at him in surprise. "Where is he?"

"We have him." Jason put out a hand to steady the injured man.

"Good. I'd like to meet him again. We were having a conversation, which had not quite completed.'t Larry punched a fist into his hand and winced.

The second route finished in a quarry cut into a hillside at the end of a rough track. Again there was no sign of the bus. They sat and waited partly in the hope that the friendly little vehicle would bob into sight but also for a rest. Larry had kept up without complaint but as soon as they stopped he slumped into the grass and fell asleep.

After an hour Jason decided that they should be on their way; he was trying to assert himself as the leader if only to avoid anyone being brave and foolhardy. They gently wakened Larry and Grace and fed him with some chocolate while Julia produced a small flask of something which appeared to sting his broken lips. He declared himself ready. The way ahead was up into the higher parts of a gently sloping valley. It was easier now, as there were no bogs, and they made good progress. Soon they could see a fast flowing river, ahead and below them, shining in the soft moonlight and they stayed parallel to it for about a mile.

"Making for a bridge," whispered Julia tapping the map.

They did indeed come to such a crossing. It was a narrow wooden bridge just broad enough for one vehicle.

"Right, rest for a bit. We'll have to take the bridge at a sprint. We'll be exposed." Jason sat down and signalled for the others to do the same.

The group collapsed in the grass and surveyed the bridge. They could get right up to it through bushy undergrowth and there were tall ferns by the water's edge but they had no cover once on the bridge.

After ten minutes Jason said, "We'll wait till that dark cloud comes across then go hell for leather."

As he spoke the sky was darkening and the group braced themselves for the dash. They crept quickly through the undergrowth and were within twenty yards of the bridge when they heard a vehicle approaching at great speed. They threw themselves on the ground. It hurtled past them and to their relief shot over the bridge. It seemed even darker now. They rose and as they started forward again they saw the lights of the vehicle swing round, illuminate the ferns and reeds on the other bank then back on to the bridge, stop, and with a blinding flash a searchlight played along the length of the bridge in both directions. They dropped back into the bushes. The whole area was now lit up and uniformed men leapt from the lorry and stationed themselves at each end of the bridge and spaced out along the banks of the river.

"Well Hubert, you never thought of this," murmured Julia.

They crouched just outside the circle of light, cowering and watching. Then a small deer broke cover and bounded along the riverbank. There was a burst of automatic gunfire from three different directions and the fawn's body rose, danced obscenely in the air, then fell broken to the ground.

Jason shuddered, rose quickly and led them, at least he ran and the others followed, back up the wooded slope away from the bridge. They kept well up from the river until they came to a broad straight road. It barred the way for as far as they could see in both directions. He decided it would be too dangerous to attempt to cross so they turned back and retraced their original route for half a mile. After fifteen minutes of silent scrambling they seemed to be well clear of the soldiers so they crept carefully back down to the river's edge. They were half a mile from the bridge.

"If we could get across the river could we get ourselves back on to Hubert's route?" asked Jason.

"I think so." Julia peered at the map with John's torch cupped over it. "Yes, I'm sure we could."

They looked at the river. It was about thirty yards broad at this point, in full flood and flowing fast.

"Well, could we make it?" asked Jason.

"No bother," said Chuck.

John and Rory muttered their less enthusiastic assent. Grace said she could do it. Jason himself was reasonably happy about the prospect but Julia and Larry were silent.

Then Julia dipped her head and frowned. "If I were fit I could just about make it. I'm not sure now."

"We could help," said Grace.

"In that race I think I would be too much of a drag. But I'll have a go if we have to."

Larry looked at the river for a long time his shoulders slumped. "Two days rest and I could manage it. Right now I would have quite a struggle walking across the bridge."

He beckoned to Jason to come to his side and whispered. "Look, I'm pretty far gone. Go on without me. I'll give you the message."

"Rubbish," proclaimed Jason not wanting to leave the sick man but equally not wanting to have anything to do with the message. Didn't Roger say he should know nothing? "We stick together."

Jason thought for a moment. "Rory, and you John, go up and down the bank a bit and look for a boat."

Without a word the two men disappeared into the darkness. Ten minutes later John came back and reported that he had gone back along the bank until he could see soldiers. There was no boat. Rory came back a little later saying that he had come to a full stop where a high, rough-hewn stone wall came right down to the river's edge. He suggested they all go along there either for shelter and to be together if they were going to attempt to get round it.

They soon reached the wall and huddled down in its lee to give Larry a rest. Rory and John went off again to see if they could detect any signs, which would show what sort of building lay behind the wall and who occupied it. They came back in ten minutes with the news that there was a large wrought-iron gate with a Madonna worked into the pattern, two sets of words one of which was Latin, and a collection box.

Grace and Julia went into a huddle and whispered then they stood up and Julia said, "Grace and I will go and find out who uses the building.

"We'll all come with you." Jason started to rise.

"No. I think we might do better by ourselves. We won't frighten anyone," insisted Grace puffing a hand on his shoulder and gently pushing him down, "And it will give Larry more time to recover."

The girls moved off silently. The others huddled together besides the wall but not as closely together as when Grace and Julia had been with them. Twice they had to cower down, scarcely daring to breath, when they heard soldiers come along the bank. After half an hour Jason was starting to get worried about the girls and he couldn't make up his mind whether it would be best to go after them or stay where they were. The irritating repeated call of an owl distracted his efforts to think clearly. He kept thinking of Red Indian films.

Just then, to his great relief, Julia and Grace reappeared. "Come with us," said Julia. "They will give us shelter."

"And who are they?" asked Jason.

"Nuns." Grace bent over Larry. "We've asked for sanctuary. We've told them about Larry so we'll go in front with him."

"Try to look as if you're not well, Larry," quipped Rory.

CHAPTER THIRTY ONE

Larry forced a smile and struggled to his feet to be helped along the path by the two girls. Soon their way was blocked and they had to turn away from the river. They came, by following the old wall of mellowing yellow stonework, to a large ornamental gate with massive locks. It looked forbiddingly shut and all beyond was dark. As they approached it swung open and a small woman in a dark olive green habit turned, beckoned them to follow, and walked staidly up the gravel path towards a complex of low stone buildings, dimly lit. The gate closed behind them with a solid clank, bolts were slid into place and a huge key was turned.

They were led in through a small arched door to a large hall lit only by candles. They could see the wooden beams but not the ceiling - only a dark cavern above them. On the stone floor was one long table solid and rough-hewn. At one end of the table seven places were set - or more precisely - seven spoons had been laid out. The nun pointed to the chairs and they sat down. Presently two similarly dressed nuns came in and put down seven bowls and a tureen of steaming soup. A large spherical loaf was placed on the table. The fugitives ladled soup into the bowls and supped hungrily. They looked at the loaf and saw no knife.

Rory leaned over and tore off a large piece. "Ma mither would hae belted me for this," he muttered with a grin then handed the bread to Larry who tore himself piece. The others followed suit.

When they had eaten a nun came with some hot water and bandages and tended to Larry's wounds. They were then each shown to a small cell-like bedroom with only a large crucifix to decorate the white walls. They slept on very hard beds with only one thin blanket; but they slept.

In the morning Jason heard pleasant soft bells ringing and later some gentle musical chanting but he heard them as from a great distance and was not awakened.

He was roused, much later, by a sharp rap on the door and saw through the high narrow window that it was daylight. The all-white room looked bright and cold. He dressed quickly and went out into the corridor. There was no one about nor a sound to be heard. He saw that the rooms next to him had already been vacated so turned in the direction that he thought he recollected having come from the previous evening. Halfway along the corridor a door opened and Rory joined him with a quiet, 'Good-morning'.

This place must be getting to us already, thought Jason. He couldn't remember Rory talking softly before.

Jason's guess had been right and they came to the big hall in which they had dined. John and Chuck were already at the table.

"You should be all right," Chuck said to Rory. "It's porridge this morning."

"Kippers to follow I hope?" Rory sat down and started to tuck in hungrily.

"Where are the girls and Larry?" asked Jason.

"The girls breakfasted with the nuns I gather and they've left Larry to sleep it off." John watched Rory pour milk over his porridge, did the same then took a tentative spoonful.

The four men emptied their bowls in silence and drank the mugs of milk left for them. Of the nuns they saw nothing.

Rory looked about curiously. "They obviously hadn't heard of timber frame construction when they put up this lot."

"Thank goodness for that," said Chuck.

"It wouldn't have been so ruddy cold." Rory rose and tapped the three-foot thick stone wall. "No cavity - and I'll bet there isn't even a damp-proof course." He shook his head.

After a time they saw two olive green clad figures come along the long corridor towards them. They stopped by the table and the leading one spoke.

"Morning boys. Enjoying breakfast?"

Jason blinked. "It's you Grace. Yes, very welcome. Morning Julia. When did you get up?"

"Early," said Julia. "Very early. We were asked to breakfast with the nuns."

"They're very hospitable," commented a smiling Grace.

"But not very chatty," added Julia.

"What have you learnt from them? How welcome are we and can we stay and can the soldiers come in after us?"

"Jason. Jason. One question at a time." Grace replied. "They seem very friendly. They are concerned about Larry and were distressed when I told them how he came by his injuries. I don't know how long we can stay. I would imagine until Larry has recovered."

"And the soldiers?" asked John.

"I don't know," said Julia. "We can ask when the time seems ripe."

"We are to see the Mother Superior after morning prayers." Grace informed them. "We might learn more then."

"Are we free to walk about?" Rory rose and looked out of the window towards the high stone walls.

"I don't know about that. I suggest you don't go out until we know the score," said Julia. "They didn't seem to want you at breakfast with the girls."

"They must have heard about Chuck," quipped Rory.

"Grace, you come with me and see what we can do for Larry. I'll bring his porridge." Jason rose from the table.

Larry was quite perky, enjoyed his porridge and expressed himself ready for the road as soon as necessary but he still looked dazed and tired.

"I'm sure you're ready," Jason looked anxiously at the pale faced man, "but you just lie doggo till we see what's what. If needs be we keep our heads down until we know that the soldiers have stopped guarding the bridge or that we can get a boat?"

"Suits me. I could do with a bit more rest".

Meantime Grace was gently washing the abrasions on Larry's face and body. As they left him he turned over and was instantly asleep.

When they returned from their audience with the Mother Superior, Grace and Julia looked remarkably happy in the circumstances. They found Jason, Rory and John in the latter's room; chosen because it was the nearest to Larry's. The men were worried because Larry was screaming out from time to time but on each occasion when they rushed to his side he was sleeping but restless and perspiring profusely.

"How is he now?" Grace asked.

"Delirious," replied Jason, "He certainly needs more rest. What did the head nun have to say?"

"The Mother Superior," corrected Julia. "She's keen we leave as soon as possible. She's obviously worried about the military. I gather the relationship is rather brittle."

"Let's plead for as long as possible. I'd hate to have to move Larry in his present state".

"I agree but we've got to be fair to them too. The Mother Superior sounded nervous," said Grace.

"If I don't sound nervous as well, I'm creating a false impression." Rory simulated a tremble in his voice.

"I like it here," said Jason. "Peace and quiet for a change."

"Yes, isn't --," Grace was beginning, when there was a great roar which grew louder and louder then swept away.

"You were saying, Jason?" Rory rushed to the window. He looked out. "A helicopter. It's coming this way. Just as well they kept us inside."

"Come away from the window," Jason urged. "They must have stepped up the search."

"Is Larry that important? I thought we were just helping a Brit who was being ill treated," said John.

"He is a Brit and he has been ill-treated. Who told you that anyway?" asked Jason.

"Torow," explained John. "Said it would be a piece of cake. A good turn - and a bit of a lark. But that Roger bloke back at the travel agency seemed to know something funny was going to happen. Have we been set up? I wouldn't buy a second-hand car from that man. Jason what do you know about all this?"

"Less than you do," answered Jason with some truth. "And Roger - I wouldn't buy a new car from him. But don't let's worry about that just now. Let's keep hidden and get to hell out of this as soon as Larry is fit."

"How?" asked Julia.

"I haven't the foggiest." Jason shook his head. "Do the nuns have any ideas? Do they have a boat?"

"I don't know - but we couldn't use a boat with a helicopter about - not in daylight anyway."

As if to underline the point the helicopter roared past again, this time more slowly and lower. As they cowered away from the window a nun appeared and beckoned to the girls who went off down the passage with her.

They returned a few minutes later. "The Mother Superior thinks they might land and search. She thinks they must have seen signs that you came in this direction to be hovering around like this. She wants you to come down to the crypt. If she is alarmed it must be serious." Grace's face reflected the Mother Superior's concern.

"We have to bring Larry with us," added Julia firmly.

They rounded up Chuck trying to take some photographs of the old stonework. Larry was still in a coma. They made a makeshift stretcher with broomsticks through the arms of overlapping anoraks and carried him along the dim corridor, through a large chapel and down some stone stairs then into another narrower corridor with no windows. By the light of flickering candles they stumbled along until they were led through a dour into a small vaulted room. They rested Larry on a convenient surface and looked around. Again there were no windows and only one spluttering candle so it took some time for their eyes to adjust. There were three narrow dark arched doorways, which looked as if they might be recesses or passages leading off from the crypt.

They stood there for some time before the Mother Superior hurried in with another older nun who lit some more candles. In spite of the haste she looked calm and Jason thought how fortunate she was to be able to put such little local difficulties as possible imminent death in their proper perspective.

The Mother Superior spoke in beautiful English with only the slightest hint of an accent. "We have a way by which you might escape but I must have your sworn assurance that you will never divulge anything of it to anyone."

Jason started to speak but she was looking at the girls. They both nodded vigorously and said in unison, "We swear."

"We are preparing a little food for you. Only a little because we think you should travel light." The Mother Superior spoke in a calm matter-of-fact way, only her eyes revealed how worried she was.

"Most kind of you," said Jason. He looked at Larry who was moving a little. "Be careful," he said to Chuck and John, "Don't let him fall off. That looks a bit narrow."

They all turned and looked at Larry whose facial injuries looked dreadful in the flickering light. One of the nuns lit another candle.

Larry's eyes opened and he became conscious that they were all gazing at him. "What are you all staring at? - Seen a ghost?" he asked.

They were silent. They had not seen a ghost but they had seen, with the improved lighting and adjusted eyes, that the convenient surface on which Larry was resting was a coffin.

The Mother Superior smiled, "I don't think Sister Bernadette will mind. I hope she will not be needing it for some time.

Larry looked baffled then relaxed and closed his eyes. There was a ripple of nervous laughter. A nun then appeared with some small parcels of food, which they stuffed into their anorak pockets.

"You will go that way." The Mother Superior pointed towards one of the black holes framed in an archway. "Do you have a light?" John held up a torch. "Good. It may be draughty for a candle. But take these in reserve. You will go through that door. We will lock it on this side. There is a bolt on the other side, slide it firmly shut and make sure the cord attached to it still comes through that hole."

"I don't understand. Why -," queried Jason.

"You do not need to understand. You will then find yourselves in a narrow passage. It will slope downwards with occasional steps. After a time it will start to slope up again and you will come to a heavy wooden door. You will then use this key to open it. It will be stiff. It has not been opened for years," John's eyes lit up and he reached for the key. The Mother Superior went on. "Throw the key in the river. We have another. You will emerge on the other side of the river. You will then be in a ruined building. You will have to find your way out of it and no doubt you will then make your way to your friends."

"How wonderful. And how propitious. What is this ruined building you were linked to? Another convent?" asked Jason.

"It was a monastery."

"Oy, Oy," chuckled Rory.

The others silenced him with a glare. The Mother Superior eyes flared.

"This river was, long ago, a national boundary. These were days of religious repression."

They all nodded vigorously while Rory squirmed.

Grace realising they were still in the borrowed habits suggested, "We should change."

"No time," said the Mother Superior. "Keep them," The other nun handed the girls each a bundle containing their own clothes.

John asked for a candle and with the wax gave the rusty old key he had been given a thorough rubbing.

"You may wish to lie up in the ruins until dark. That is for you to decide but go now. The soldiers may appear at any moment. Go now. It will be damp at the lower levels so go carefully. God bless you." The Mother Superior raised her hand.

The two girls crossed over to her and kissed her. They both gave her a tearful hug and whispered a heartfelt, "Thank you, Mother."

They passed through the narrow door into a dark passage Rory and John carrying Larry. Jason waited till they were all through, slid the bolt home and checked the cord. Chuck bent down beside him to tie his shoelace. In the silence as the others crept off down the passage they heard the two nuns talking in French.

"Who are they, Mother?"

"Travellers," replied the Mother Superior. "Travellers in trouble."

"We have many travellers; often in trouble - but of course the injured man. You risked using the old passage for him?"

"No. As you say, we have many such in these difficult times. It was for the girls. A remarkable pair. One was a novice nun, a tormented novice and the other a woman of the street. But both gracious ladies. I would happily have taken both of them. Happily."

As they tiptoed away Jason could tell by Chuck's expression in the faint light that, like himself, he had understood the French. But Jason did not understand the pang he felt.

CHAPTER THIRTY TWO

When Jason and Chuck had fumbled their way along the narrow passage and climbed down some steps they caught up with the five ahead.

"What's the hold up?" asked Jason.

"Water," said John. "We're going to have to paddle. Take off your shoes and tie them round your neck. It looks as if it might get deep. Someone with long legs should go first. Check how slippy it is. We might have to hoist the stretcher on our shoulders."

Being the tallest Jason felt obliged to volunteer, so he took off his shoes and socks and rolled up his trousers. He took a candle as he didn't want the torch to get wet, then half leaning on the wall, he eased himself along the now slimy floor. He almost immediately came to a step. He was now up past his knees and the ground was sloping steeply away from him then another step and the rolling up of the trousers was made pointless. After two more steps he was up to his waist in the chill water and there was still no sign of the upward slope so he leaned forward and held the candle out in front of him. A few feet further on the plunging roof met the surface of the water.

"It's flooded. We can't get through. We'll have to go back," he said as he squelched towards the others. "See what the Mother Superior can suggest. She'll think of something."

"If I could swim the river and get to Pyke," offered Chuck, "I could see if he could come with that rubber boat he has when it gets dark."

"Yes. Thanks, Chuck. That might be our best chance. I can't think of anything else." Jason tried not to sound dispirited.

They turned and struggled back up the steps to the door, Larry sleeping soundly through it all. As they approached the end of the passage they could hear voices. The nearer they got the clearer it was that some of the voices were male.

They froze and listened. The voices now sounded angry but were occasionally punctuated by the calm voice of the Mother Superior. They could not understand what was being said.

There followed the sound of heavy footsteps receding then the voice of the Mother Superior speaking artificially loudly and in English. "After hundreds of years they will break down the door in our crypt. It is a sacrilege."

"They're coming in after us. John how long will it take them to get through that door?" asked Jason.

"Depends what they use. If it's a big axe it might take them ten minutes. It's a good strong door. I don't think they would blast. It would bring the whole place down. I think we've got ten minutes."

"Chuck, I gather from your offer to swim across that you're a strong swimmer?" asked Jason.

"Not bad. Life saving and that," Chuck replied.

"That's a coincidence, we have some lives badly want saving," said Jason. "Do you think you could swim underground and see how much of the passage is blocked?"

"You want a pot-holer not a swimmer." Chuck shook his head in distaste.

"Any pot-holers." Jason looked around in simulated hope. There was silence.

"Rory's a pot holder - if it's a pint pot." quipped John in an attempt both to relieve the tension and disguise his own growing fears.

"Right, I'll have a go," said Chuck. There was a sound of approaching footsteps on the other side of the door. "Not much choice."

"Good for you, Chuck." Julia patted his shoulder then withdrew her hand quickly.

"Is that torch waterproof?" asked Chuck.

"I doubt it," said John.

"Never mind." Chuck, with a shudder, turned and made off down the passage.

The others followed. Without a word John handed Chuck the end of a rope. Hesitating only momentarily Chuck waded into the still, stagnant water. A putrid smell rose as he disturbed the scum on the surface. Just as he disappeared out of sight the sound of the first blow on the door came reverberating down to them.

"Someone is chapping at the door." Rory held his hands over his ears.

"I hope the hinges aren't rusted through," whispered John.

The blows now followed quickly on each other in a rhythm.

"There's two of them." John peered at his watch. "Make it six minutes."

"Thanks a lot," said Jason.

After about three minutes the noise made by the blows on the door was changing, there was now the distinct sound of splintering, but there was no sign of Chuck. The thuds stopped for a bit to be replaced by heavy breathing as the men paused then, with a gurgle, Chuck reappeared.

"About ten metres. That's all," gasped Chuck, choking and spitting furiously. "Now listen. Don't try to walk any of you - and it doesn't matter if you can swim well or not. Turn on your back and scramble with hands, knees and feet along the ceiling as fast as you can. Just hold your breath and do that. Don't swallow any, it's disgusting. Off you go quickly. John you go first."

"And Larry?" asked John.

"I'll bring him last. You take the rope end and give us a good pull when I tug. We'll come after Jason. Off you go now." Chuck spoke urgently and pushed John forward into the water.

"Should we leave everything heavy?" asked Grace.

"No. Leave absolutely nothing not even the broomsticks or they'll know we've come this way," said Jason.

"Of course. Stupid me."

"Don't panic any of you," instructed Chuck. "Just keep going. It's not far. Whatever you do keep going. Pull on the rope if you can't get a grip on the ceiling but don't stop. Not for a second - don't stop.

Grace quickly took off the nun's robe and stuffed it with her other clothes. Chuck grasped her firmly by the hand led her through the water then bent her down, turned her over and putting his hand on her bottom pushed her vigorously into the water. He kept on pushing even after she had disappeared below the surface. Then Chuck went back and gripped Julia firmly, almost roughly, and in the same way propelled her into the noxious fluid. Rory hesitated for a moment and found himself getting the same treatment from the slighter man and off he went.

Jason was the last to go before Chuck and Larry. The sound of splintering was becoming louder now as if the axes were coming right through. Chuck put his hand on Jason's shoulder and pushed firmly to indicate that he should follow Rory and quipped, "I've never believed these films with just in the nick of time escapes."

"I do now," said Jason as he peered at the disgusting slimy water ahead. "No-one would go into this muck until the last possible moment." So saying he took a deep breath turned over and disappeared.

The water pressed him against the ceiling as Chuck had said but he wobbled, bobbed and spun uncertainly as he tried to keep contact with the uneven stonework. He clawed desperately at the slimy surface, felt the rope and pulled frantically on that. He could not tell how much progress he was making. Panic surged within him as he willed himself not to breathe. The tunnel seemed endless. The stone ceiling felt crumbly and unsafe. His lungs seemed ready to burst and he was near to breaking point when he felt a slight upturn so, with a frantic scramble with fingernails and feet, he pushed on along the tunnel. Eventually his head bobbed out of the water and he gulped in air. He swam a few feet then lurched through the now shallowing water. He stood retching the foul taste out of his mouth. Rory came down past him and then turned and stood waist deep in the water.

"I'll just give Julia a hand." The big man was still spitting as he spoke.

Jason scrambled on up the slope then turned. "Julia! But Julia set off before me."

"Good God," exclaimed Rory and with a shudder but no hesitation he turned back and plunged into the water.

John by now had received the signal from Chuck and was pulling on the rope. "Give me a hand, Jason I can hardly budge it."

Jason turned and gripped the rope. There was still practically no movement. Grace leapt up and added her weight to the grim tug of war. Slowly the rope started to move with them.

"They'll drown at this rate. Pull for God's sake - pull." John was leaning right back straining every muscle.

The three found ridges on the floor to brace themselves and pulled for dear life -their friend's dear life. Gradually the rate of movement increased, bubbles disturbed the scum then came a sudden release of the tension which set the three of them on their backs and Rory emerged from the dark water dragging Julia like a limp rag. He rushed forward and laid Julia's still body down beyond the waterline.

CHAPTER THIRTY THREE

Rory now turned and pulled so feverishly on the rope that Chuck and Larry shot out of the water like a pair of dolphins. Grace crawled over to where Julia lay motionless and started to press rhythmically on her chest. There was no response. Chuck bent over them his face twisted in anguish. Grace soon cramped up and Chuck pushed her aside and started vigorously pumping away. Jason looked at the blue face, gave up hope and turned his tearful face away. But Chuck kept pushing, relaxing, pushing, relaxing. Rory offered to take over as Chuck seemed to tire but Chuck pushed him off. Years of tedious life saving drill went into the powerful controlled movement. Years of muscle racking early morning training at the local pool give him the stamina to continue. He brushed aside all offers to take over. Every part of him ached as he kept the rhythm without the slightest falter. His inner anguish made him realise how much this slip of a girl meant to him. Tears now ran down his cheeks. The others took this to be a sign of his painful efforts. After what seemed like eternity he suddenly stopped and collapsed beside the still body. A sigh rose from the group.

Grace kneeled down and cradled the body in her arms. The tunnel was still and silent. Grace broke into a sob and hugged the limp body tightly to her rocking her like a doll. The doll shuddered and there was a tiny movement of Julia's lips and she started to splutter. Jason choked then beckoned and everyone stood up.

Chuck sprang to his feet and gently picked Julia up and carried her out through the door at the end of the passage, which John had already opened. The others followed. Rory came last helping Larry who was also distressed and gasping; all of them felt absolutely nauseated after the ordeal in the foul water. He now carried Larry as easily as Chuck carried the tiny Julia. The passage opened into rough undergrowth with irregular piles of shaped stones at intervals. The air was cold and fresh and Chuck could feel Julia gasp feebly. They pushed through the shrubbery and came to the remnant of a tall wall at a corner of which a small part of roof still clung precariously. They huddled into the shelter. Chuck laid Julia down on a patch of smooth turf and she rolled over and vomited into the long grass, then as if set off by the sound Larry threw up violently. Chuck indicated to Grace to look after Julia, took one step and collapsed.

They lay for a long time all of them panting and spitting. Grace was holding Julia and thumping her back to help her to eject the foul liquid. Jason could not help noticing that the wet blouse and pants clinging to Julia's thin body make her look frail and vulnerable whereas the effect on Grace was quite different. She looked strong and healthy and oh so feminine. He tried not to look at the sharply outlined nipples.

Julia then lay back still choking from time to time. Then she raised herself on one elbow, looked over and gasped, "Is Larry all right?" Grace smiled, nodded, and hugged the slim girl.

After a further long silence Julia looked over at Chuck and said softly, "You went into that without knowing how far the end was or if there was an end." She leaned over and kissed him on the cheek.

"I second that," said Grace as she did the same.

"Hear! Hear!" agreed Rory. "I'd kiss you too but that sludge has played hell with my lipstick."

"Well, we were warned." Jason shook his soaking locks.

"How that?" asked Rory.

"The Mother Superior. She said it would be a bit wet."

Rory threw a small stone at Jason. "And I told you. No damp course."

Rory started peeling off his soaking clothes. "How about a swim to get all this muck off. The girls won't see us."

"No, but the helicopter will." Jason pointed upwards and as if to underline his point they heard the roar of the helicopter taking off. "Forget it. Although I don't think I'll ever feel clean again. Let's just have a rest. We've far to go before we sleep."

"That means they've left the Convent. That's good. I would have been most unhappy if the Mother Superior had suffered because of us," said Grace. Her voice grew quiet. "She told us of some dissidents who gained asylum in a church. During the night earth was bulldozed against the doors and the church was set alight."

The group fell silent.

"What a wonderful woman." Julia spoke perkily as if to break the spell, and smiled at her recollection of their saviour.

"Yes, she was but how on earth did you girls convince her we were worth saving? Chuck got all the kisses, I think you two deserve some as well," said Jason warmly.

"Well, don't come and give us them right now please," Grace held up a bare arm. "We've just got rid of our dirty habits."

They all laughed. The tension was broken.

"So now we're not decent," giggled Julia to further laughter.

"I think they're trying to tempt us," said Rory.

The helicopter was sweeping up and down the river and low over the far bank but it did not cross to the side where they lay. Jason warned everyone to keep their drying clothes out of sight from above.

"They seem sure we haven't crossed so they can't have thought we'd go through that water." Chuck lay back and closed his eyes.

"They didn't know we had a hero to lead us," said Julia softly.

"An idiot," corrected Chuck.

As they lay out in the sunshine, concealed by the remains of roofs and ceilings and the occasional small tree, the mud caked on their bodies so that they could brush and pick off the worst of it. With the sun streaming onto his naked body Jason thought of the two equally naked girls just through the bushes but he also thought of Hilary and wondered where she was. Not lying naked in the sun with the others, he hoped. He felt the pang of jealousy again. His thoughts turned back to the tunnel.

"Strange that tunnel. From a nunnery to a monastery. Makes you think of Decameron," he remarked.

"Yep" said John. "These Scots are a lecherous lot."

"Watch it you ignorant sassenach," muttered Rory.

Jason asked Julia if the maps had survived the ducking. She looked in her sandwich pack and found the maps fairly dry but the sandwiches soggy and uneatable. Only two of the other packages had kept the water from the food so they shared and had a spartan snack. Now, exhausted and lulled by the warm air, all but Jason fell asleep. He was disturbed by thoughts he did not understand. He was passionately in love with Hilary and yet disturbed, pleasantly disturbed, by the proximity of the two naked girls, hidden, but so close to him. His mind was a jumble of confused thoughts about Grace. She had seemed such a nice girl; but he wasn't just thinking of her niceness. This adventure was rousing - too rousing or was it just propinquity? That, they say, is the greatest aphrodisiac of all - propinquity - and, he thought - danger.

As the sun sunk lower in the sky Jason pulled on his clothes now stiff with caked mud but not smelling quite so badly. He called quietly for the others to wake and dress. Soon be saw Grace's plump bare shoulders above the bushes as she pulled her clothes over her head. He turned away sharply. The men grumbled about the discomfort of the brittle garments.

"How do you feel now?" Jason asked as they helped Larry to get dressed.

"A lot better. I'll walk for miles now." Larry stretched his legs and muffled a groan.

"You're lucky," said Rory strutting about like Frankenstein. "The man in the iron Y-fronts. If I swing my legs in this lot I'll lose my manhood. Julia I hope your bra is not as brittle as my breeks."

"That's alliteration," said Julia laughing.

"Ah what?" asked Rory.

"She says you're illiterate," Jason informed him.

"Awe you didn't mean that, Julia. After all I've done for you," complained Rory.

"You'll always have a place near my heart, Rory," Julia pale face creased in laughter as if her recent ordeal had released a sense of frivolity in her.

"Good, "

"I'll think of you if my bra hurts," she added.

Jason stood up. "To get back to the point--" He was interrupted by a gale of laughter, Julia's interrupted by a fit of coughing. "I am delighted everyone is in such high spirits," Jason went on. "But to get back to business - we'll leave as soon as it gets dark. I think it would be best if we got as far away from the river as we can as soon as possible. Does Hubert's map help with that, Julia?"

Julia studied the map for a few moments. "Not really. Our intended route goes parallel to the river for about a mile then swings north. The river is within a hundred yards of it most of that time."

"Could we cut across and join Hubert's route?" asked Jason.

"No doubt we could but Hubert has made no marking other than on or near the route. We wouldn't have the foggiest idea what was in our way."

"Hubert has done us well so far. I suggest we stick to his plan," said Chuck.

"Hear, hear," murmured the others.

"Right," agreed Jason. "There's sense in that. We'll try to rejoin Hubert's route as near to the bridge as possible. I think this is too big a party to travel unnoticed so I suggest we split into two and meet, say two miles along the way, when we're clear of the river." The others nodded. "Grace and Chuck come with me. John you lead the other party. You and Rory can give Larry a hand." Larry started to protest his ability to manage. "If need be." Jason added. "Julia can guide you. Julia could you do us a copy of the map. Has anyone got a paper and a pencil?"

A copy of the map was drawn on a sandwich wrapper and Jason studied it and pointed. "I suggest we meet here. If one party gets there and there's no sign of the others in one hour go on to the planned rendezvous with the main party."

"I thought we were the main party," protested Rory.

A roar disturbed the night and over by the river a light flashed. They saw the dim outline of the helicopter and the not so dim beam cast by a searchlight shining from it.

"They'll pick us up nae bother with that if we move." Rory's eyes followed the circle of light rising and falling with the land as it moved slowly towards them.

"Our only hope is that they stay well over to that side of the river," said Jason.

"No, it's not." Larry who was shaking himself awake painfully raised himself on one elbow. "It's been hot today. It's getting cold quickly. With this river here we'll have a mist settling soon. The helicopter can't work in that."

"That sounds reasonable. I hope you're right," said Jason.

"I've doubted it up to now Larry but I'm glad we brought you along." Rory helped Larry into a comfortable position, and they huddled together as it grew colder and damp, and waited

"This is the bit I like best," said Rory. "This cuddling in. No don't move - nothing personal, Chuck."

CHAPTER THIRTY FOUR

Gradually, almost imperceptibly, the mist closed in and sure enough the roar of the helicopter faded into the distance and died away.

"Mist is when the sky is tired of flight," murmured Grace softly.

A clever quip jumped to Jason's lips but he bit it back and the silent moment was enjoyed.

"And rests its soft machine upon the ground," continued Grace. "I read that somewhere." The others nodded appreciatively.

They stirred and Julia led off the first group and they were out of sight by the time they had gone thirty yards. The remaining three felt the raw wind blow along the river and they huddled up again. Jason found Grace soft and yielding against his body.

Then Chuck remarked, "You and Julia seemed to have cheered up enormously. What did the Mother Superior say to you to achieve that miracle?"

Grace smiled but replied simply, "She is a wonderful woman."

"She must be." Chuck shivered in the cold air.

The last three set off ten minutes after the others. Skirting a large field of grain, they crossed over a stile and took a path diagonally across a meadow. They were making steady progress when they heard footsteps and rustling ahead of them in the hazy darkness. They stopped, trembling, and peered into the mist. Grace slipped her shaking hand into Jason's. They stood petrified as a dark shape moved slowly towards them.

"Listen Jason," hissed Chuck. "Think what happened to Larry. Don't let's get captured. Shoot us. Don't let them get us."

"Shoot you. I don't even have a peashooter. Shoot you!" His hand tightened on Grace's.

They stood still, shaking. After what seemed a long time, long enough for one of Roger's coffee breaks, they heard a grunt close by, then something rubbed against Jason's leg. He stood perfectly still, feet sinking in churned up mud, resisting the strong urge to pull his leg violently away. There was another snort then two huge black pigs shuffled on unconcerned.

"What a boar," quipped Chuck. The three of them laughed quietly but it was a forced light-heartedness.

They were travelling slowly checking constantly to see if they had come to Hubert's route. They were pretty sure they had; marks on Julia's map seemed to match what they were passing though several times they had to circle round and round to make contact with a landmark marked on the sketch. Then suddenly it became easier. The mist was lifting.

"Good." Chuck strode a little faster. "Now I can see where I am putting my feet. Anybody chasing me will have a powerful scent to follow."

Then they heard the subdued roar of the helicopter far off but starting up.

'Damn them," exploded Jason. "Let's move." So saying he pulled at Grace and they set off more quickly up a hill. They could hear the roar getting nearer and saw the searchlight flash on the surface of the river and great beams bounce off into the sky. The moon was struggling through the last wisps of mist. The searchers swept far down the river then turned back towards them.

"They're on this side now. Hide. Quick." Jason found himself again pulling on Grace and together they dived onto a haystack then burrowed right into it. Jason could hear Grace's heartbeats and he very tentatively held her soft body tightly but her ready acquiescence made him feel uncomfortable.

The roar swept past and Jason pulled Grace out of the hay and abandoning caution they ran as fast as the dim light and the rough ground permitted. The sound of their puffing became so loud that they had to slow down but they were still breathing heavily as they passed over a small bridge. A head popped over the parapet.

"What a noise," hissed John. "We thought they'd put bloodhounds on us."

Julia stood up, came forward and took Grace's hand protectively. "Right let's go." She looked quickly at the map. "This way."

It was slightly uphill all the way now so they knew that they were climbing away from the river. Certainly the next time the helicopter passed it was back where they had come from and below them. They relaxed and walked slowly enough to give some respite to Larry who was limping heavily.

"We must be nearly there," whispered Julia as they rounded a corner by a dense pinewood. They crept nervously along the fringe of the unrelieved blackness of the trees. It crossed Jason's mind that if the others weren't here he didn't know what they would do next. Even when their eyes adjusted to the darkness only an occasional glimpse of sombre grey gave a third dimension to the flat blackness. It was a nerve-chilling scene.

The air was very cold now. It was as if the sun never reached this bleak spot. Jason shivered and shook. He was glad he was not holding Grace's hand. His heart sank as they crept on in silence.

Then a hissed "Jason?"

"Yes. It's me. Jason."

"Right, come this way." It was Alan's voice.

He led them deep into the woods. They had to link hands to follow him in the gloom. They came to a clearing where it was just possible to see a patch of sky away above them. Alan said he would report their arrival and sped off into the blackness.

They slumped down by a huge tree and leant against it, thankful for the support. As their eyes adjusted they could see that there were other shapes by the trees.

"Did you find the maps helpful?" The voice of Hubert broke the silence.

"We did. We did indeed," said Julia. "How has it been with you, Hubert?"

"Tedious I'm afraid," he replied. "Tedious and cold."

"Where has Alan gone? Who has he gone to report to - if you're here?"

"We have a council of war now. We don't know what is going on," groaned Monica from the gloom.

"What council of war? Who?" asked Jason.

"Torow, Pyke and Hilary," chirped in Lucy.

Jason could understand the two professionals getting together but why Hilary. "Why Hilary?" he asked.

"To represent our point of view," said Monica forcefully.

Rory growled, "Obligatory now,"

"What is?" asked Monica.

"On all committees. The statuesque woman," quipped Rory. Exasperated with this turn of events he added. "A committee. I prefer to get my bullshit straight from the horses mouth."

"That sounds a bit messy." retorted Chuck then asked if there was any food as he was famished. He was informed that Pyke now rationed their supply as t0hey were running short. Monica scoffed at this and expressed her opinion forcefully that Pyke just enjoyed exercising authority.

"That woman was weaned on a pickle." Rory hissed to Chuck.

A crunching noise heralded the approach of Alan with the others. As if he had heard the conversation Pyke announced that they would eat before instructions were issued.

Whose instructions? wondered Jason. However he said nothing until they had eaten some cold meat and chocolate washed down with a most welcome mug of hot tea. Jason noticed that Grace and Julia were cheerfully helping Larry to eat before having anything themselves.

'They are both gracious ladies.' The phrase came back into his mind. He hastily banished the recollection.

He could just make out Hilary in the dark. She was engaged in earnest conversation with Torow. Jason felt upset by this too. He gulped down the hot liquid and wondered when he should assert himself? Then he wondered if he should assert himself

"Where is the interrogator?" asked Larry quietly as they were finishing their modest meal.

Torow replied. "He is in the bus. We have him secured."

"What will you do with him?" Larry enquired as Grace took his cup from him.

"We have not made up our mind yet. I don't think it matters much. We might even let him escape."

"Let him escape! I don't understand." Larry sounded outraged. "No chance!"

"Listen, Mister Hassall. They find you're gone. The only keys, which could have been used, were his. He has carelessly dropped a scrap of his fancy dress mask at the Valhoose. A patch of torn blanket from his bed is hanging from the barbed wire and a bottle smelling strongly of chloroform left at the scene of your disappearance has his fingerprints on it. Need I go on?"

"Not at all, Mister Torow. Excellent. There is just one further thing I would like to know," said Larry.

"Oh. What's that?"

"How can I get a ticket to his interrogation?"

CHAPTER THIRTY FIVE

Pyke decreed that they should move off as soon as possible to get as far from the Valhoose and the river as they could. He also announced that the Council had decided that the interrogator should be taken with them some distance further before release - perhaps just before the border. He implied that he had received instructions - from whom he did not say - and was forced reluctantly to take command. They all sank with relief into the now familiar comfortable seats and swung easily with the soft suspension of the little bus. They felt cocooned from the hostile world. Each person automatically went to their own seat and Jason was pleased that this included Hilary.

Before they set off Pyke asked Larry to feed the interrogator so that no one else became known to him. Larry accepted this instruction with relish and when the prisoner would not open his mouth for the offered food decided this was just the excuse he needed for his first little retribution but Pyke stopped him in mid blow and angrily forbade any vengeance. He insisted that the prisoner be kept blindfolded except when being fed and kept in a compartment under the rear seat when they were travelling.

"If we are to arrange that he escape later the less he knows the better," said Pyke. "If he learns too much we must kill him. I would prefer not to have to do that."

"He doesn't deserve such leniency." Larry glowered at the man being bundled under the hinged seat.

"It is not leniency. It is tidiness - and he will suffer more this way I think," said Pyke.

"I agree," agreed Torow. "We should have no killing. Revenge is never an end - it is a continuation. All we are trying to do is directed to improving things."

Larry shook his head. "Whatever you say, boss."

"In the meantime," Torow went on, "You will be the only person who to him will speak. It will be obvious to him that you in this group will be but he must not know that I am here or that it is an English speaking party. So you will be the only contact, Larry. You will exercise restraint."

Larry grunted.

With that settled no one spoke for the entire journey. Most of the party dozed. The bus sped along narrow roads, which became progressively more convoluted and steep as they came to the foothills of the mountains which marked the border. After an hour of this they swung into a re-entrant cutting steeply into the hillside and slowed down over a rough track. The bus turned into a walled courtyard by some buildings and stopped.

Torow rose, roused everyone, and announced that they had arrived at a safe house so they should be all right for the night. He explained that the house did not have accommodation for so many guests so they would have to sleep in the barn.

"We have sleeping bags," interrupted Pyke.

"Good. The rats to keep out," said Torow at which there were squeals from the ladies. "We will be brought some soup shortly then I suggest you get some sleep. Things might start getting tough from now on."

"From now on!" protested Julia. "You should have been with us."

"Yes. I appreciate that. Others can take their turn the next stage to spearhead."

"Good," said Rory. "My spear's decidedly blunt."

"Mine got wet," added Chuck.

A huge witch's cauldron of soup arrived and a large tray of wooden bowls. They supped hungrily and noisily.

"This will put them off the scent," said Grace. "Anyone passing will think there are pigs in here."

Before he himself ate Larry went into the bus to feed the interrogator. He was not under the rear seat. Larry rushed back to the barn in alarm.

"He's escaped!" he hissed to Torow feeling sick with anger.

Torow turned in fury to Pyke. "How can this be?"

"Come with me," said Pyke calmly.

He led them out to the bus, opened the rear seat to show an empty recess just as Larry had found. He then pulled a small lever and a box like compartment slid forward into view.

"The kitmaster. If you open the seat the box slides back to the boot and if you open the boot it slides forward under the seat. Clever." He turned and hurried back to his soup.

Larry now approached the cowering interrogator. He proffered a spoonful to the mouth of the trussed prisoner who spat at it and glared.

"Suit yourself," said Larry. The interrogator spat again as Larry replaced the blindfold. Larry drew back his fist, hesitated, then punched the sleeping bag gently.

Pyke, Torow and Hilary conferred in a corner. This time it was Hilary who spoke for the trio. "There is evidently a building about three miles up the road. Whatever is the opposite of a safe house - that's it. It is important that we know whether it is occupied or not. We cannot go this way - which is by far the best unless we can get past this house. They think - we think that this would best be checked by some innocent looking passer-by passing by. Do we have any suggestions and or volunteers?"

"Do you wish me to check out a route to it?" asked Hubert anxious as always to be helpful.

"No, thank you." Torow shook his head. "To get to it we know exactly."

"You mean you want a couple of us to put on haversacks and just stroll past it like hikers?" asked Alan.

"Something like that. But it's bandit country up there. It had better be someone who can run. They'll cut off your dangly bits if they catch you." Pyke made a slashing gesture with his hand.

"Jason can run," said Hilary. "I've seen him. He's really fast."

"But Jason is tired," snapped Grace angrily.

And Jason wants to keep his dangly bits, thought Jason.

"It is perfectly simple," chipped in Lucy. "I have none of these appendages, to which you men are so attached, attached to me. I will dress up in my brightest track suit."

"Oh no!" squealed Rory.

"Quiet, young man. And I will jog past them. Have a good look and report back. Easy. I will go first thing in the morning."

"Not too early," said Torow. "We want to be sure up and about they are."

"Don't worry, that track suit is so loud it will waken them," joked Rory.

"I don't like the idea of a lady doing this," protested Hubert.

"Nor I," agreed Chuck.

"Listen I intend to have a run tomorrow morning so I might as well kill -," Lucy hesitated, "- accomplish two ends."

Torow leaned over and spoke to Hilary then indicated that Lucy's offer was accepted. He then suggested everyone get some sleep.

"Right, anyone afraid of rats, there is room in my sleeping bag." offered Rory. "What, no takers?"

"I think we would rather risks the rats," said Monica. However she placed her sleeping bag right beside Rory's and beckoned to Alan to come on her other side. This established a pattern and each lady was shielded by two men or two women by three men.

Jason found himself between Hilary and Grace but he did not hear Grace whisper to Julia, "Someone once said women pretend to be afraid so that men can pretend to be brave." He fell asleep and dreamt of glorious battles in which he repelled giant rats and was suitably rewarded. As always in such dreams the battles were more vivid than the rewards.

CHAPTER THIRTY SIX

As if wakened by an internal alarm clock Lucy rose early and slipped out of her sleeping bag, pulled on a purple and yellow tracksuit, and crept quietly out of the barn. The snores and grunts from the huddled sleepers covered the sound of her departure.

It was a still soft summer morn. The sun was low in the sky and the air was fresh and cool. The birds twittered as if startled by the colourful runner trotting past them. Lucy ran slowly up the hill. She was enjoying the easy jog; she was also, she thought, to her surprise, enjoying the holiday. She was a loner, normally shunning company, especially male company. In her youth she had been repelled by and had, therefore, repelled any young man who had the disgusting habit of eating meat. Time had passed and there were fewer opportunities either to attract or repel. She was now resigned to this and was content with her full and active life. She had, however, found her fellow travellers most congenial - even the steak eating and sometimes vulgar Rory. She smiled affectionately as she ran.

In little over half an hour she was at the house of potential danger. She circled it at some distance then seeing no sign of life she ran more closely past it. Still nothing moved. She now turned and ran through the yard making an elaborate pretence of curiosity for the benefit of possible watchers. She stopped to peep into a window. Eyes glinted back at her.

She jumped, fell backwards and scrambled round the corner of the building. She stood still for several minutes, trying to breathe quietly, and waited but there was no sound of movement within the house. She peeped round but could see nothing. A high wall joined the house to a large cattle shed; she had no alternative but to return the way she had come. She started creeping, then remembering her previous pretence of casualness, she straightened up and sauntered past the offending window. She glanced at it as she passed then giggled nervously as she saw a cat's unblinking eyes staring at her. She made a face back at it and it was the cat's turn to jump backwards. She turned and ran easily off down the hill.

She had barely gone half a mile when a rustling sound by the side of the road made her heartbeat falter and her legs quicken. Two men stood up from a hedge as she passed and came after her. She accelerated again and her heart quickened with her steps. She didn't look back.

"Hi, hold on Lucy not too fast," came a shout.

She slowed and turned and there were Rory and Alan striding after her.

"Your team remember, Lucy," said Alan.

"We couldn't sleep after we heard your track suit going out," said Rory.

"Thanks, boys," Lucy panted as she padded on.

"Just one thing, Lucy," puffed Rory.

"What's that?"

"Slow down a bit will you?"

Back at the barn the others were in various states of fairly modest undress trying to wash and clean themselves up. They looked up and gave a quiet cheer as Lucy strode in. She looked back for her companions to share the acclamation but they were nowhere to be seen. They crept in unnoticed by the back door soon afterwards. They joined in the praise for Lucy then slipped out again. Lucy reported that the house was deserted but that the presence of the cat indicated that this was only a temporary absence. The Council huddled together again to discuss the significance of this intelligence.

Rory and Alan returned in two minutes and Rory shouted. "Lucy. We have some hot water for you in the yard. If you don't mind washing in a bucket."

"That's wonderful. Thank you boys." She walked over to the door. "Don't go. If you promise to keep your eyes shut you can pour it over me."

CHAPTER THIRTY SEVEN

It was decided that an immediate departure was imperative while the bandit's early warning house was unmanned so the bus set off up the hill again. It was a stiff climb for a little, well loaded vehicle but Jason was again surprised by the ease with which it cruised upwards and the smooth effortless gear changes at the hairpin bends.

The view over the valley was now spectacular. Although the route was tortuous and the ascent steep the roadside was not too precipitous which meant that Jason who was not good at heights could enjoy the vista with the others. The banks of earth between the various levels of road were profusely covered with small trees and brightly coloured bushes. All this gave Jason a visual barrier between himself and the floor of the valley far below. He was enjoying himself.

He recounted the tale of the friendly nuns and of the fearsome tunnel to Hilary. He gave Chuck full credit for his part but made sure that his own contribution sounded reasonably worthy as indeed, he thought to himself, it was. Hilary sounded impressed and in turn told Jason of the other party's fairly dreary wait after being frightened off from the first two meeting places. The approach of the searching soldiers had caused them to skip the first and at the second the approach of an even more frightening band of the local peasantry on a summer hayride. They were waving great flagons obviously nearly empty and they had whooped and rushed towards them when they saw that there were women in the party. Evidently Monica had just made the bus in a leap as the men closed in on her but one swing with her ever handy handbag had felled the nearest reveller and thus discouraged the others.

"They must have been drunk," said Jason.

"Now don't be unkind. A woman is not an ornament. In any case I don't think they were in any state to be fussy," laughed Hilary.

The sun was shining, Hilary seemed relaxed and friendly and she looked at him with interest in her eyes. All was well in Jason's little world.

"You are a surprising person. I can't make you out," said Hilary.

"In what way? I think I am a fairly simple man," asked Jason, intrigued that she was intrigued.

"I thought that when I first met you but not now. I thought you were a very gentle man but what you've just told me shows you can be tough."

"That makes it sound as if I have been boasting. My part was really a small one. Everyone was great," protested Jason.

"You - boast! I don't think so. I listened between the lines. And I know that you can be pretty savage," she said this with just the slightest widening of her eyes but it was enough to bring the colour to Jason's cheeks.

"And of course I realise that you are a boxer," she went on.

"A boxer!" Jason exclaimed disbelievingly.

"You can tell by that nose. And don't sound so embarrassed. In England it's still regarded as the noble art of self-defence. It will do you no harm. In fact that nose will open doors for you."

Jason groaned and was searching for a way to change the subject when the bus accelerated rapidly.

"Hold on," shouted Pyke. "Someone is coming after us."

Everyone turned and sure enough a large black car was closing in on them at a frightening rate. Someone was leaning out signalling to them.

"Perhaps it's someone wanting to ask us the way," suggested Rory. Nobody laughed. They saw that the man doing the signalling was doing so with a pistol.

Torow shouted now. "If it's bandits they will have something up front so hold tight."

As soon as he said this Pyke pressed a button and the front bumper of the little bus lifted and thrust forward. The bus changed down a gear and surged forward as if it were looking forward to the fray. The passengers didn't know whether to look forward or backward. The bus slowed to take a sharp bend and there, immediately around the corner, was a small tree lying across the road. Pyke applied the brakes and at the same time lowered the bumper. He then changed down again to a gear far below anything he had used so far and growled towards the tree like a small bulldozer. The bus shuddered as it contacted the tree but it did not stop. Pyke steered towards the uphill end of the obstacle, the bus hesitated briefly but did not stop, the tree swung slowly round, poised for a moment then crashed over and down the slope. There was a subdued cheer.

The bus crept forward again as Pyke started to work up the gears but before they could gather speed marksmen hidden by the roadside bushes opened fire. The passengers threw themselves on the floor as the bullets zapped against the windows. Jason covered his head and threw himself on top of Hilary to save her from the shower of broken glass. There was no shower of broken glass. Jason looked up in disbelief

"Bullet proof," grunted Pyke.

Jason extricated himself from Hilary slowly, very slowly, and climbed back into his seat. She hadn't snuggled up like Grace. He looked round and saw that the black car had resumed the chase and was again gaining on them. He looked enquiringly at Pyke. The driver nodded grimly. He slowed down and the car was soon right behind and manoeuvering to overtake them. No one spoke although all were wondering why Pyke wasn't keeping his foot down. The driver then leaned forward and pulled a lever at his side and peered into his rear view mirror. Jason turned and saw that one of the bus's spare wheels had parted company with the vehicle and was rolling and bouncing straight towards the chasing car. The black car swerved violently and swung up a steep bank and came to an abrupt screeching halt. One up for the kitmaster, thought Jason.

"That should do it." Pyke smiled again and swung the bus around a hairpin and along the next stretch of road. They wound back and forth thus, looking up from time to time to see if they could catch sight of the thwarted pursuers. They were going along the third stretch down from the incident when there was a treeless patch with an unimpaired view upwards. They craned their necks and peered upwards to gloat over the plight of the hapless car when they saw, not the car, but a large black object bouncing and hurtling its way down the hill straight towards them. At least they all saw it but Pyke. He had his eyes firmly on the road.

As they let out a concerted scream of warning the missile dropped from right above them and smote the little bus smack on the radiator. There was a great burst of steam. The bus slewed as Pyke desperately tried to stay on the road. It squealed to a halt. The tyre, their own dual purpose spare tyre, bounced on down the hill.

When the bus came to a standstill and the steam ceased to billow over the entire vehicle, they were able to see where they were. Jason did not like it. Pyke had just managed to stay on the road but they were pointing out towards the valley away below them. If this is front wheel drive we've had it, he thought. He hesitated whether to get out or go to the back of the bus to add his weight to the precarious balance, which kept it on the roadside. He took one glance over the edge, dismissed the first option from his mind and crawled back up the bus with his eyes tightly shut.

Pyke rose to get out to assess the damage and as the others were all gazing spellbound over the precipice or gingerly leaning backwards Lucy, who had been looking upwards, gave a shout.

"Look, they've got the car back on the road. They're after us again."

All heads swung round simultaneously then back to see what Pyke was going to do. He jumped back onto the bus, engaged a reverse gear but the rear tyres just spun in the air.

"Back here, quick," shouted Jason impatiently, implying that it was intelligent anticipation, which was causing him to crouch thus in the back corner of the bus. The others cautiously climbed up the sloping floor and almost immediately the back tyres bit into the earth and the little bus was dragged along on its bottom until the front wheels gained contact again. They backed slowly onto the road. As soon however as they started going forward the steam enveloped them again so Pyke had to switch off the engine to reduce the steam output a little so that he could see. He let the bus freewheel down the road.

Lucy, who was now kneeling on the back seat, was the commentator. "We're pulling away. We're making ground." She bounced up and down.

"They must be damaged. If it's bad we might be all right." Jason turned back to see the danger recede behind them then turned in time to see another precipitous bend ahead. He closed his eyes.

Sure enough at each hairpin bend they seemed to have gained a hundred yards or so. They started to sing a mixture of 'We shall overcome.' and 'We shall not be moved.' By the time the bus reached the bottom of the hill they were a clear mile ahead. The impetus of the descent shot them along a level stretch of road and the bus was barely slowing down when the road started to climb again. Pyke switched on but only an angry growl came from the engine. The bus sped onwards and upwards but now slowing down rapidly. It just managed to the first bend when Pyke spied a little quarry and pulled sharply into it throwing the passengers into heaps on the floor. They could now hear the uncertain throb of the other car coming nearer and nearer down the hill. Pyke kept trying but the engine would not respond. They were trapped.

CHAPTER THIRTY EIGHT

"We must split up," shouted Pyke rising from his seat. "They won't know how many of us there are. Rory you take a party with Larry and leave now."

"I will go with the others. I know the bandit leader. I might be able to do a deal," said Torow. "Take the interrogator with you too, Rory. Blindfold him but make him walk. Our overriding priority is to get Larry back. Off you go, Rory. We will lead them away from you. Ditch the interrogator if you have to."

Larry smiled and thought of deep, deep ditches.

The impassive Pyke stood by the door and hurried the confused party off. "I will hide by the bus and try to get it going again later. If I do I will try to go back along the valley bottom to the village of Spandek. It is not in bandit country. I will wait for two days. If we don't meet up by then we all make, somehow, our way back to Britain. Remember - Spandek. Torow knows it. Others must find it as best you can."

"And report anyone missing to the British Embassy," added Jason.

"Missing presumed well, please," pleaded Rory.

Monica and Lucy were already out of the bus and strode off with Rory. Larry and Alan bundled the interrogator out onto the road, released his legs covered his eyes and pushed him on his way. Larry had a large spanner in his hand.

"You go with them, Hubert," said Torow. "I know the way to Spandek. Take this map. You lot hide close by and we will lead them away."

Rory led his group past the quarry and up the hill into dense scrub. They ducked down and were soon lost from sight. Pyke sunk behind some large boulders right by the bus. Torow took Jason's group at a run along the road for quarter of a mile and only turned into the rough country as the black car came within sight and they were sure they had led the bandits away from the others. Torow's limp did not slow him.

The car disgorged its occupants as soon as it drew level with where the bandits had seen the fleeing group disappear. They looked around, shielding their eyes with their hands, searching the hillside, then three of them returned to the car and drove on up the hill to outflank the fugitives. The other man waited for his companions from the roadblock then they too came into the scrub spread out like grouse beaters. The bushes, which were packed tight and tall promised to be good cover but after a hundred yards they thinned out and offered less protection. The bandits shot each time they caught a glimpse of the hunted party. Their bullets ricocheted about among the white flint-like boulders, which seemed to Jason to increase greatly the chance of a hit.

"We've taken them far enough from the others," said Torow. "Let's see what they want."

So saying he stood up with his hands above his head and beckoned to the little band to do likewise. There was silence for a long time but Jason, who was trying hard to look as small and insignificant as possible, could see glimpses of the bandits crawling towards them. He was hurt when Torow hissed to him to stand up and show them we were harmless. The bandits circled the area then, when apparently satisfied that there was no trap, one by one they stood up and approached Torow who shouted to them in the local language. There was no immediate reply.

"I am asking to speak to their leader. He owes me a favour," said Torow. One of the bandits shouted to him.

"What did he say?" Jason tried not even to move his lips.

"Mantos - their leader is on holiday," replied Torow.

"On holiday. A bandit. You're joking," scoffed Jason.

"I wish I were. Mantos, they say, goes off for a fortnight by the sea each year at this time. They have a rota but the others only get a week."

"Bandits who go on holiday. This is crazy," protested Julia.

"Maybe so but it is also serious. His son has a bad reputation. Be very careful and do just as they say," ordered Torow.

One of the bandits came towards them and indicated with his gun the direction he wanted them to go. They did just that. They saw the black car head off up the hill then, as they trudged upwards for three miles. Jason noticed that Torow was carefully trying to pick up landmarks as they went. They came to a ramshackle cluster of huts and tents and were bundled into one of the smaller huts. A sentry was posted at the door and the bandits went off to report their capture.

After a time which they spent assessing their improvised prison Torow engaged the sentry in conversation. The sentry obviously recognised him. He talked volubly, violently emphasising the points he made by thrusting a knife savagely into the doorpost.

When Torow rejoined them Jason did not like the expression on his face. "You look worried." He said, running his hand nervously through his hair.

"They're worried ," said Torow. "Zuko, Mantos's son is on the drink. Discipline is strict when the old man is here but Zuko always has a wild time in his father's absence."

"That could be good surely?" asked John.

"If his own men are worried about what he gets up to I think we should worry too. But I agree we for lapses in their security should watch. All the time." Torow ran his eyes over the hut.

"What are his weaknesses - or vices?" asked Grace.

"Bullying. That worries the gang. He shot one of them last holiday. None of the others dared tell the old man. Drink. He gets drunk most nights while his father is away - and women." Torow glanced towards the girls. The men all turned to look at them. They shuddered.

As John started to survey the hut for weaknesses and pointed them out to the others one of the bandits came with some bread and cheese. After they had eaten two bandits returned and Torow was taken from the hut. He was brought back an hour later. He looked unhappy.

"Zuko has been drinking. He has plundered the bus but could not make it start. Doesn't want it anyway. Says too many people get caught because they have someone else's vehicle. He was angry about the damaged car but confident he could get it repaired. One of them gets day release to learn motor-car maintenance."

"I don't believe this." Chuck shook his head.

"He will take what money we have and all the food and liquor from the bus. He wanted guns but I have persuaded him that we have none. He was delighted to get the rubber boat. Already planning when they can use it to advantage. Bad news is that he has taken all the petrol from the bus."

"Have you any good news?" asked Julia.

"I have pleaded that we be allowed to go. I have explained that you are all part of a cover for a rescue that I am doing," replied Torow.

"Well, that's true isn't it? Whether we like it or not," said Chuck.

"I have explained to Zuko that there is no point in him letting us go unless he our papers leaves us with. I think he understands this," said Torow.

"So we are in no danger?" asked Grace.

"I wouldn't say that. If his father were here we would be safe. They know that the police only come into these hills if they have to, and that is only when a killing has taken place, so they try to avoid killing people."

"How nice of them." Julia grimaced angrily.

"That is his father's philosophy. The son -," he shrugged his shoulders.

"So what happens now?" asked John.

"We wait and see. And rest." Torow settled down and laid his head on the table. He looked tired. For a time the silence seemed ominous and threatening. Then sounds, which were even more frightening, came from the largest hut. Music and laughter - then gun fire.

CHAPTER THIRTY NINE

As they waited the noise outside grew louder and louder as the bandits sampled the travellers' duty free. There was the sound of scuffling followed by the strains of music and to their surprise the din of boisterous dancing. Then came a lull and with a roar a huge unkempt heavily bearded man brushed the sentry aside and burst into the hut followed by two equally rough looking characters one brandishing a large gleaming knife and the other a pistol.

Zuko glowered round. "Women. We want the women," he roared. John and Chuck moved towards the bandits. Torow tried to restrain them. "Perhaps just for dancing," he said.

"Perhaps," growled Chuck lunging forward.

One of the thugs stepped forward and hit Chuck on the head with the butt of his pistol then turned it round and pointed it at the others.

"Dance do they? Good. We need a little entertainment. They'd better dance good," said Zuko doing a clumsy, drunken pas de deux himself

The bandits, holding their knives between themselves and any would be rescuer, pulled Grace and Julia to their feet and marched them out as the men watched helplessly, hatred in their eyes.

"What can we do?" Chuck was holding his bleeding head.

"Keep quiet and watch for our chance," whispered Torow. The others growled their impatience and frustration.

"Even if he doesn't have any debauchery in mind now the girls dancing will get him going. I just hope he's had too much to drink." Chuck accepted a handkerchief from John and pressed it to his head.

John flexed his hands and his eyes narrowed. "If you want to have a go I'm game.

"We could take the sentry," suggested Chuck.

"What do you say, Jason?" asked John.

"Do not be foolish," interrupted Torow angrily. "They to ribbons would cut us. The sentry is changed every hour. They will not be caught napping." He stopped as a thought occurred to him. "Where is Hilary? I thought she is with us."

"She's outside - waiting," replied Jason.

"How come?" asked Chuck.

"When we stood up 1 told her to lie still and then follow us. I was terrified what might happen to her if the bandits got their hands on her. She's so--"

"That's a bit hard on the other two, don't you think?" protested Chuck. "Why should the prettiest one get the protection? They always get the best of it. I don't like it. The others are just as - as vulnerable."

"I wouldn't have thought of this if it hadn't been what we overheard Chuck --." He stopped abruptly and looked embarrassed.

"Overheard what?" asked John. "Come on. What?"

Jason drew a deep breath. "We heard the Mother Superior refer to one of the two girls as a prostitute - so it wouldn't matter to her. She'll know what to do."

"I don't believe this," said John. There was a long silence.

"It's true," said Chuck quietly. "I was with Jason when we overheard the Mother Superior saying something about it."

"Which one?" asked John.

"What does it matter," retorted Chuck angrily. There was another uncomfortable silence.

"Anyway," explained Jason. "I thought it would be useful to have someone outside. I told her to follow us and, if we didn't get out in twenty-four hours, to go for help.

"Can't we do anything?" Chuck paced about the hut. "We can't just sit here."

"We would not two steps get out there," warned Torow. "There are all around the yard some guards. Evil looking. And they know what Zuko would do to them if anyone escaped"

Torow told them that the sentry thought Zuko would not allow any of the other bandits to touch the women. The last time there had been women prisoners made available in the camp there had been a battle that even Zuko couldn't control. Anyway he liked to keep the perks to himself.

"That's a great comfort," retorted Chuck.

John started prowling around the hut again, more urgently now, examining all the doors and windows. He stood on a table and tested the wooden boards, which made up the ceiling. Chuck and Torow moved about in such a way that they were always between John and the sentry. Chuck continued to express great anxiety to do something about the girls. John tugged at a board in the ceiling, which had a little movement then he stopped, dropped to the floor, went to the windows and carefully examined the overhanging eaves. Outside it was getting darker.

As John was thus engaged a weeping Julia was thrust into the hut. Chuck rushed over and guided her gently onto a chair.

"Are you all right?" asked Chuck weakly.

"Grace. Oh Grace," sobbed Julia.

Julia was inconsolable so the others helped John examine the hut for weaknesses to give her time to recover.

"Would it help if you told us what happened?" asked Chuck presently.

"Grace. Oh Grace," she sobbed again.

"What happened?"

"He chose me but Grace insisted. She wouldn't let me – ," Julia choked.

"She must be mad," said John.

"Zuko liked her - spirit." Julia wept uncontrollably.

"Listen to me, Julia. Don't take it too hard. You won't know, but she's used to it." Chuck turned away in embarrassment.

She stared at him uncomprehendingly.

"We overheard the Mother Superior, Jason and I, she is, or was, a prostitute so it won't be so bad for her."

Julia pushed Chuck away.

"Don't do that, Julia." he exclaimed. "I don't think any the less of Grace. She is a lovely lady. The Mother Superior said so too. I'm just so pleased that it wasn't you that --," Chuck's voice trailed off.

Julia glared at him, sunk her head on her hands on the table and sobbed even more loudly. Chuck stood up and joined the others in looking for a weakness in the security. After a time John beckoned them around him and whispered. "We can get up through the ceiling. There is no attic but there must be just about enough room to crawl along to these overhanging eaves. We could drop down through them"

"Without being spotted?" asked Torow querulously.

"If Grace can keep Zuko occupied long enough so that the others get drunk we have a chance," said Torow.

"Steady on." Jason was anxious and feeling guilty now, thinking that he had perhaps contributed to Grace being in her present dreadful danger. "We can't just let Grace suffer for us. We must try to get her free. I'm not happy."

"I'm not ecstatic," said Torow looking absolutely miserable, "but we are trying to save her as well, remember. If they really get out of hand she is the most vulnerable of us all."

"Well, I've heard of her lot described as social workers, but this will be her most valuable - service ever, poor dear." John cringed as he said this.

"Stop it. Stop it all of you," shouted Julia. "Stop talking about Grace like that. She - she's - wonderful."

Chuck took her gently by the elbow and whispered to her "Why don't you pray?"

"Why don't you bugger off," said Julia and it wasn't a whisper.

CHAPTER FORTY

There was silence for some time during which John kept worrying at the ceiling, then came a happy grunt and he carefully folded a board over into the recess above. Jason pressed for immediate action but John would have none of it. "We don't move till the sentries relax. We wouldn't have a chance."

Jason paced about feeling anxious and guilty. Then the sentry opened the door and this sent them scurrying to their seats. In came two of the bandits followed by Zuko beaming all over his face and there, being pulled gently behind him in his huge hand, was Grace.

Zuko turned to Torow and spoke in Tyrnian. "You stay one more night. Then you go free."

He turned to Grace, bowed stiffly, beamed at her and left the hut followed by the two men. As he left, the large man who had struck Chuck, turned and gave a gloating leer. John stepped forward this time, his face a mask of fury, but the man was gone. There was a long silence as Grace still stood uncertain what to do, her face fixed in an artificial smile, then Julia rushed at her and threw her arms around her. The others stood about embarrassed. The sound of merriment outside got louder.

"Oh, Grace. Are you all right?" Julia hugged her tightly.

Grace nodded. She looked calm but detached as if she were thinking of something else but her lips were bruised and her cheeks and chin looked as if they had been sandpapered. She held close to Julia. Jason and Chuck hovered over them but did not speak or touch them.

Then Torow and Jason hoisted John up into the roof and he crawled out of sight.

Grace started to speak but only a squeak came out then she cleared her throat. She tried again and said to Torow. "Can we get away?"

Torow replied "We will try."

Grace shuddered. "Before tomorrow night?"

"I hope so," said Torow.

Grace sat down now and whispered something to herself. Julia sat down with her and took her hand but said nothing.

John's head re-appeared above them then he lowered himself into the room and drew the others around him. "It is touch and go out there. Zuko strode away in good humour but he has already hit one man who had drunk too much. There might be trouble."

"I will listen." Torow went over to the door just out of sight of the sentry.

"Good." John nodded approvingly. He carried on talking in a cool and business like manner although his soft eyes were on Grace. "I think we can drop through the eaves all right. There is a sentry back and front. We will have to take one of them out of the game. The noise outside will help but we don't want to have to fight."

"We could easily take the one at the front door but we would be seen. Let us make it the man at the back. We will have to drop on him while someone diverts this one," said Torow, nodding towards the front door.

"That sounds like me." Julia stood up with a defiant look in her face. "It's my turn now. Leave him to me."

"Right," said John. "I'll go back up and make an opening in the eaves. I can only work when there is a loud burst of noise. You can talk loudly or sing or something and when I give the nod whoever is going to do the sentry can come up. That's not my scene."

"We could have done with big Rory for this but I'll have a go," volunteered Chuck with a self-deprecating shrug.

They were glad to have something to do now if only to sing. They all joined in except Torow. He kept an ear by the front door. The sentry looked in from time to time but Torow engaged him in conversation.

"He is going to be relieved soon - probably both of them - to eat. We will see if the next men have been drinking - that would help," said Torow as he rejoined the others.

They could hear no sound from above as John worked away. The new sentries came and it was immediately apparent from their belligerence that they had supped of the wine. After what seemed an interminable time John beckoned to Julia from the hole in the ceiling.

Julia doffed her anorak, unbuttoned her blouse carefully and went to the door, fanning herself to suggest to the sentry that she was too hot. The sentry pulled the door further open and indicated that she should come out. She stood there gulping in the fresh air for a few minutes then turned to the sentry and fluttered her eyelids in a way the others had not seen before; it seemed so out of character. He came closer and smiled but looked wary and kept a firm grip on his gun. Julia reached out and grasped the sentry's bicep and squeezed the bulging muscle with a look of awe and admiration. The sentry preened himself and listened to what she was saying although he could not understand a word. The sentry now tried to do with his free hand the equivalent of what she had done to his bicep, but not to her bicep. Julia longed for the planned interruption. Inside the hut Chuck and Jason also waited impatiently for John's signal.

"Zuko looked happy," remarked Chuck.

"Well, he'll have had the best of service, won't he?" Jason hissed at him angrily.

John's head now appeared through the opening in the roof Jason reached up to him, scrambled through the opening and then pulled Chuck up behind him.

Then Torow peeped his head out of the hut and whispered loudly in Tyrnian, "Look there is Zuko coming."

The sentry looked alarmed, thrust Julia roughly back into the hut, shut the door and tried hard to look alert and watchful.

Torow pulled Julia quickly onto the table and pushed her up to the ceiling. John pulled her through, did the same for Grace then reached down for Torow and hauled him up. John directed them towards the hole in the eaves and set about replacing the ceiling boards. He followed them pulling the boards back into their place as he dropped through the eaves to the ground. The sentry lay limp on the ground, and as they were leaving, John thrust a bottle half-full of cognac into his hand and splashed some of the aromatic fluid over the body. He then dashed silently towards the largest hut and returned in two minutes with a full bottle. He slunk round the hut and placed it within easy sight and reach of the front sentry then rejoined the others.

They tiptoed silently towards the stockade gate. It was open but it was guarded. As they came closer they could see it was the big leering bandit who had hit Chuck earlier and dragged Grace out of the hut. Chuck's hand went to his injured face.

What happened next was so quickly started and over that the others took some time to grasp it. Before Chuck could move John had reached down for a large stone and leapt at the huge man who turned and saw John hurtle towards him. The first blow was struck before he had time to move. His knife clattered to the ground as he staggered. He looked at John and launched himself at the smaller man with a roar but before he could swing his massive fists John had hit him again, and again, and again. He slumped to the ground and John continued to rain blows on him. Blood spurted from his face. Jason and Chuck pulled him off.

"That's enough John. I think you've silenced him," whispered Jason.

John shuddered. "Sorry. I was angry. For Grace!"

CHAPTER FORTY ONE

John turned still shaking and they all crept silently for a hundred yards through the scrub until they came to a road. They stopped and looked for the sentry Torow had noticed on the way in but to their great relief they could see no one so they crept cautiously out onto the road then, just as they were ready to rush across it, a figure arose from the bushes opposite. Now also fully aroused and bursting for vengeance Chuck leapt at the silhouetted figure and seized it by the throat. The force of his attack threw them both to the ground.

A high-pitched half-throttled squeak came from the bundle beneath Chuck. "Chuck. Chuck. It's me."

Chuck rolled over and peered at the terrified face. It was Hilary.

"Sorry. Sorry Hilary. I thought ---" He helped her to her feet.

She caressed her throat for a few moments then still coughing and gurgling head bent down and picked up a rough walking stick, which she gave to Torow.

"For you. I made them to pass the time. I had two but I broke one on his head." She nodded towards another body slumped by the road. "When I saw you coming."

There were growls of appreciation all round.

Torow urged them to run the next stretch to put as much distance as possible between themselves and the bandits. Hilary pleaded to them to take it easy, as she was stiff having spent the night lying out in the cold and still shaken from Chuck's attack, but Grace was off like a shot and both Jason and Chuck told Hilary to keep up so sharply that it brooked no contradiction.

They loped quickly down the gentle slope following close to each other in the dark. The moon peeped out occasionally to make it easier so they ran until the sounds of the rollicking faded into silence and their own breathing was the only noise to be heard.

After about a mile Torow stopped them and listened, then said, "Right now we go over the hills. We will walk all through the night - if you can. We will hide during the day. I hope then to establish where we are. If I go too fast for any of you say so but do not fall behind." Torow strode off up the bill, his limp seeming not to affect the fast pace he set.

They were some miles away when they heard some shooting from far off. They could only guess what was happening but it increased the tempo of their strides.

"I don't hear the car. Are they not going to come after us?" asked Jason after some minutes.

"Not in the dark, I think." Torow quickened his pace slightly. "Let's keep this up. I would like to be fifteen miles away by dawn."

The weary escapers groaned but struggled on. Jason noticed that Grace was immediately behind Torow, striding hard. Torow's limp had become a sort of lop sided lope. It was difficult for them to judge how much distance they had covered when the first light streaked across the sky but they had come as far as they were able. The last few miles had been uphill which had been hard for all of them, but Grace, who looked the least athletic, was right up beside Torow all the way. They now had a wonderful commanding view of the valley. Eventually Torow stopped and they all collapsed under some trees except John and Chuck who gathered berries and Jason who brought cupped handfuls of cold water from a tiny stream for the exhausted girls to drink.

John took first stint as lookout but had not settled himself properly into his vantage point when he hissed to the others.

"The car. The black car. It's down there on the road. Coming this way."

"Damn," exploded Torow. "This country they know so well."

They watched hypnotised as the car crawled insect like up the winding road.

"Should we go on?" asked Jason.

"No." Torow lay still. "We are too tired. We must hide. It will be better. Get right down. And be still. Disturb one bird and they will be on us."

Grace began to shake and Julia went over to comfort her. They lay motionless as the car drew nearer and nearer. It was less than half a mile away and they were becoming increasingly aware that their cover was not too good, when there came a roar very familiar to some of them.

Swinging around from the shelter of a hillside came the helicopter. The hiding group desperately tried to creep under cover from the air. Now the bandit car did a very fast three-point turn and shot off downhill at a great speed. The helicopter, which must have been just on the point of spotting its real prey, swung and swooped after it. The car turned off the main road and disappeared up a heavily wooded track. The helicopter hovered over it for a few minutes shot an apparently speculative burst from a machine gun, circled wide over the area several times then turned back down the valley.

"The cavalry arrived just in time and we can't stand up and cheer," said Jason.

"John Wayne was never more welcome. I hope they don't spy the bus from the air," Chuck growled in alarm.

"I don't think it matters," Jason shrugged. "Damaged radiator and no petrol. Not much good to us now. No, we get to Spandek then contact the British Embassy. I've had enough of this."

"OK. Back to sleep." John turned away and resumed his vigil.

"Will you manage to stay awake?" asked Jason.

"I've stayed awake right through a Charlton - Watford no score draw. This is easy."

They slept soundly all morning. In the afternoon Torow climbed high into the hills to get a bearing. He was away a long time and when he climbed down over the rocks he was met with eager, expectant, upturned faces as if he were Moses.

"I do not think we are far off. We came the correct direction last night. Tonight I think we will have less far to go."

As the darkness crept in John whispered to Torow and then disappeared into the trees. He came back an hour later with a loaf of bread.

"I'm sorry I didn't have the heart to nick more but it was from a humble home. I left a pen-knife in exchange."

The loaf was shared out and then they were on their way. Again they walked through the night. They reached the outskirts of

Spandek while it was still dark so they sheltered by some haystacks to await the dawn.

"Now is the time for my drop dead" said Torow as the sky was lightening.

"Your what?" asked a startled Chuck.

"A message has been hidden for me. It will tell me where I meet Pyke if he has it made. Also the others will leave a message."

"A dead drop." Jason laughed. "At least I hope it is that way round"

When Torow returned his news was that there was no message. "So I have left a message for the others. I have described this road and said that we will be lying up in that wood there. There appears to be a deep cleft. We should hide well."

"I will go look for breakfast," said John and slipped off before anyone could contradict him.

They climbed to the wood and found the cleft Torow had noticed. It was deep and banked with ferns. A stream tumbled down alongside a path. Although the path looked little used they decided to stay well clear of it.

"Just give me time to bathe my feet in it before anyone stirs," pleaded Hilary.

She took off her shoes and socks and paddled in the cold water. Grace and Julia joined her, tucking up their skirts. Shortly they ran up barefoot, Hilary and Julia laughing, to where the men lay. What a lovely trio, thought Jason as he looked at the three very different girls. Very different, he thought with some disquiet. They shook their wet legs at the men who protested vigorously while enjoying seeing the girls happy -and enjoyed seeing the girls' legs.

The sun was getting warmer when John appeared in their midst without warning. With a start Jason said, "You know John, you would make a bloody good burglar."

John laughed and then produced some bread, cheese and carrots. He laid down some eggs and a can of milk. "The farm down there is so big they'll never notice this lot's gone," John assured them.

"And who can rub two Boy Scouts together?" asked Chuck holding up an egg. John tossed some matches down to him.

"Can we risk a fire?" Grace looked fearfully in the direction of the village.

"If we light it deep down there and use no grass or leaves we should be all right. Better make it now before the village comes to life." Torow started to gather twigs.

"A fried egg butty would go down a treat," said Chuck.

Within twenty minutes everything John had acquired had been consumed and they lay in the warming sun if not exactly replete much nearer to that happy state than they had been for some time.

"If only the bus were to come now all your problems could be over. You would be home in three days," said Torow.

"And you?" asked Grace.

"One day. I could be back at my desk on Monday. No one will have missed me.

"Well, I hope they've missed me." Chuck smiled as he thought of his colleagues painstakingly processing claim forms. He stopped gloating when he remembered what he was now involved in.

"You work in the prison service? You don't seem the type," said Julia looking questioningly at Torow.

"I do. I try to ameliorate conditions - with some success. And of course many people in prison deserve to be in prison. If you believe in prisons."

"And as everyone here now knows you work for Britain." said Jason.

"Not really. Not directly. I am a freelance."

"Well, thanks to you Larry's a free man." Jason looked with affection and admiration at the quiet unassuming man.

"You were wonderful," said Julia.

They now dispersed, found comfortable spots, snuggled in under the ferns and fell asleep. Chuck was on lookout at midday, and John and Torow were just discussing whether a further foray for food was advisable, when he heard a familiar sound and felt a surge of hope and expectation. He stood up and waved to the others. Then sat down again disappointed. "If we were waiting for the next bus we would be right. I thought it was Pyke - but no such luck."

Everyone sank back into the ferns as a bus toiled noisily up the hill.

"Pyke's bus didn't groan like that one." Chuck picked up a stone to throw angrily into the stream changed his mind and put it down.

"And our bus had a healthy belching sound," said John. "Except that a belch comes from the other end," quipped Chuck. Torow looked around. "If it stops we roll these boulders down on them." John dropped to the ground. "Down. It's coming straight for us." The advancing vehicle left the road and headed straight towards the cleft.

CHAPTER FORTY TWO

The sound of the grumbling engine stopped for a time, started up again more quietly then, bouncing and bumping towards them through the woods, came a little bus; a bright yellow bus. Nearer and nearer it came, Jason sure that no bus would be on a rough track like this unless it was coming for them. He shouted to the others to keep their heads down as he saw the bus heading right towards them. It turned up into the little cleft and stopped. John and Torow braced themselves against the boulders. Jason crept round a bush and peered at the bus. To his astonishment he saw it was Pyke at the wheel. He rushed over. The others also rose from their hiding places, scrambled down and clustered round the brightly coloured vehicle.

"Good old Pyke," shouted Chuck.

"Where did you get this heap?" asked Jason.

Pyke glared down at him, his face white and drawn, switched off the engine but did not climb out. Then it dawned on the group that it was THE bus. They had lived in it too long not to recognise its chubby shape, its large windows, its fat wheels and its high profile. The damaged bumper and patched up radiator only confirmed it. It was the little brown bus - but it was yellow. Not a quick repaint job - a smart yellow bus.

"How the face lift?" asked Grace.

"Good simile," grunted Pyke. "I just peeled off the old brown skin. Unclipped it really. Smart isn't it.

"A bit garish," said Hilary.

"Well, no one will think this bus is hiding from anyone." Grace nodded as she appreciated the purpose of the dramatic change.

"Exactly." agreed Jason as if he had been involved in some way.

Pyke explained tersely that he had only patched the radiator and fitted a sort of bypass and intended to go now and get a replacement at the next town. He asked that one of the others come with him, to leave as soon as Rory's party returned. He looked impatient and sounded irritable.

Jason stared in wonder at the bus. "How did you get here? I thought they had drained the petrol."

"I took a can with me when I hid. I'm not that daft." Pyke now looked hard at Jason. "I have had another dead drop. The passport for Larry is ready. Torow is to go to Dratoc for it." Torow nodded. Pyke went on, "Jason, you will go with him. It is only forty miles away by rail. I will drop you at the railway station."

Torow went off to gather his things together and Jason turned to Pyke to ask since when he was issuing the orders. Before he could say a word Pyke leaned close to him and with a grim look on his face said, "You will personally bring the passport back. It is a British passport. Torow must not have it."

"You sound as if you don't trust Torow?" protested Jason.

"That is an order."

"From whom?"

"From above - and it's important. Understood?"

Jason did not understand so he nodded and looked knowing. He had never heard Pyke speak so bad temperedly and sharply before. He seems to feel that he must take command, Jason thought. I wonder if Roger has been getting through to him? He knows something I don't, that's for sure.

He was about to try to assert himself when he noticed red stains on the door of the bus, that Pyke's left arm was hanging limply and that there was a large patch of blood on his shin. He leaned forward and saw that the floor of the bus and the seats were also spattered bright red. He called Hilary over. She surveyed the scene for a moment then quickly rolled up Pyke's shirtsleeve and took a look at the wound.

"It's broken. A bullet was it?"

Pyke nodded. Hilary rolled up her own sleeves, tore Pyke's shirt and revealed the extent of the nasty wound. Jason took one look and decided to leave her to it. Hilary shouted for Grace.

Rory came striding into the clearing with his party shortly before Jason and Torow set off on their train journey. They all looked fired but the interrogator looked most tired of all. He was laden with Lucy and Monica's remaining possessions and Larry was right behind him to ensure that he kept up with the party. He was blindfolded again before he saw the bus. Hubert had, as always, excelled in his map reading and brought them by a route, which was both reasonably easy and inconspicuous.

Rory volunteered to go with Pyke. He offered to drive in view of Pyke's injury, but the driver would not have it. He held the steering wheel with his injured hand only when he was changing gear. Hilary had washed and bound the wound and strapped on a rough splint. The injured man's face was white, and his eyes were sunk in dark caverns, but he would accept no further help. He dropped Jason and Torow at the station. His eyes narrowed as he nodded to Jason. Jason's eyes widened as he nodded back.

The interrogator had not eaten for about thirty hours so Larry approached him again, this time with a piece of chocolate.

"One spit and I'm off, pig," he growled.

The prisoner glowered then licked his lips and opened his mouth.

Larry broke off a segment and pushed it in roughly. "It's my turn to interrogate you now."

"Go ahead. I can answer all questions honestly. I have nothing to hide."

Larry pushed another piece of chocolate into the prisoner's mouth. "You don't deserve this. I don't know why I'm doing it."

"Because you are obeying instructions. As I was."

"I would let you starve."

"Then why you do not?" mumbled the interrogator through the half-chewed chocolate.

"Because there is much worse in store for you when we release you."

"Release me?"

"Yes. Let your own people deal with you."

The interrogator looked puzzled but said nothing. He opened his mouth expectantly.

"When they find a piece of your Shirley Temple mask in my cell and some other little clues you're for it. I might even send a letter of thanks to you when I get back to England. No, that's too unsubtle. I think we've done enough."

The interrogator's eyes swung about as if he were searching for inspiration. "If you release me I will be all right."

"Of course you will," said Larry. "I forgot. You'll get a fair trial."

The interrogator's brow furrowed as he contemplated his chance of that. For the first time he looked worried.

"Everyone in Britain gets a fair trial," said Larry, "Even murderers and pigs like you. But then Tyrnia is better."

The interrogator now looked confused and spoke in a slightly more conciliatory tone. "Tyrnia is building a fine country - for our children and our children's children. We will suffer a little in the meantime - suffer willingly."

"Well, I hope you are very willing." Larry loaded his words with menace but the interrogator shrugged. "And you have the gall to talk about children. What depraved horrors had you in mind for these children you were with? A children's party the same day as you were giving me the treatment. Are you a pervert as well or something?"

"I love children - our children." The interrogator responded angrily. "You would not understand. I want a better world for our children."

"I don't believe it - you love nothing but your stupid cause. You've obviously never had children of your own or you would realise that all your victims were children -perhaps sweet little children - once."

"I have a son."

"You're lying. You live alone."

"I do," said the interrogator. "His mother died - two years ago. His voice dropped. "Thankfully."

He's trying to engage me in conversation just like I did, thought Larry. No chance of a rapport with me, chum.

"Thankfully! You are a monster, aren't you?" Larry pulled back his foot to kick the man on the ground

"My son disappeared. I would not have liked my wife to have experienced that."   "What age was he?"

"He was eighteen when he left."

"And he was captured by the Tyrnians?"

"I don't know that."

"But I do," affirmed Larry. The interrogator shuddered. "They probably wanted information about you. They don't like you, do they? If you're still about it means he could not have given anything away."

The interrogator smiled proudly.

"I wonder what he had to go through to protect you?"

The interrogator kicked wildly at Larry who evaded the blow with a scoffing laugh.

"Probably what I was heading for. But you can comfort yourself that his tormentors will have been doing it for a cause."

The interrogator swore and kicked again. Larry dodged easily and swung the toe of his boot at the squirming sleeping bag.

"It is pointless to hurt me. You have everything you want."

Larry kicked again choosing his spot more carefully. "Some of the things that give me greatest pleasure are completely pointless."

Larry pulled up the head cover, zipped it closed and called on Alan to help him move the prisoner. They laid the bag in the middle of a flat clearing. The bundle writhed and twisted frantically. Larry bent down and whispered to the struggling man. "We have put you at the river's edge. If you move more than six inches you will fall in the river. So unless you can swim with your hands tied behind your back you had better be very still." The prisoner, trying hard to remember where the non-existent river was, slept not at all that night.

Larry told Torow of his brush with the interrogator. "How did you know about the son?" asked Torow.

Larry chuckled. "I didn't even know he had a son."

CHAPTER FORTY THREE

Jason and Torow had not long to wait at the little station. It was thronged with ill dressed but busy looking people as it was near the border and travellers from one country crossed over to the other on foot then took the train to their destination. This was a recently drawn boundary and many families and friends found themselves divided by this new barrier and, as cars were few, the train was packed most days. This suited the two men.

The train, shaped like a giant caterpillar with a big engine and small green carriages, climbed slowly through the steep hills. There were no stops on the way to Dratoc so they were there in just over an hour. They checked for returning trains and found that there was only one that day, but it gave them sufficient time. They strolled to the prearranged pick up point and, with Torow now amongst friends, had no difficulty in gaining possession of the precious document. They then stopped at one of the many small shops selling exquisite lace and Torow picked up a parcel for Larry. Jason looked anxiously at his watch as the pleasant old lady extolled the quality of her wares to the waiting Torow.

"He is a discriminating man. The best lace in Europe is made here. Who is the lucky woman, I wonder?" So saying Torow tucked the tiny parcel into his pocket. They hurried back to the station and boarded the train just in time. As they did Jason saw a young man in a leather jacket race frantically on to the platform as the train was drawing out. He did not board the train. Jason felt a strange sense of relief; his nerves were on edge now that they had a forged passport with them. This thought reminded him that he should have it, so he explained openly to Torow what Pyke had said. He liked this man and saw no reason to deceive him. Torow handed over the passport without demur. They both nodded off as the train jostled along.

Jason was awakened by an urgent whisper of "Mister Torow." He was startled that anyone else should know his companion~ s name. The train guard was shaking Torow. He spoke quietly and anxiously in Tyrnian and departed.

"A message for me." Torow tore open a slim package. "Handed on to the train just as we were leaving."

He looked at it closely and Jason could see, even at the narrow angle of the half-hidden paper, by the grouping of the letters that it was coded. Torow took a tiny scrap of paper and a paperback out of his inside pockets and started scribbling.

"That's a sheet from a code pad," blurted out Jason giving up the pretence of not looking.

"Yes," replied Torow without embarrassment. "1 always carry the next two sheets with me. So easy to destroy. Not so when you carry a whole one time pad."

"That always makes me think of a disposable nappy."

"This to swallow is easier," laughed Torow.

Torow struggled for a time then started to look harassed. It was the first time Jason had seen him showing signs of pressure. After a few foreign words, which Jason guessed were strongish, Torow thrust the sheets back into his pocket and brought out another two sheets. Jason could see that they were also code sheets from a one time pack but they were not of the British design. He tried to hide his surprise. Torow now took a different novel from his pocket and started to make sense of the short note almost right away. He shook his head and sank back in his seat.

"Bad news?" asked Jason.

Torow nodded grimly. "I am to be kidnapped as soon as I leave this train."

"What. By whom?"

"The Hornians I think. A gun in my back and they will across the border walk me. Probably have the border guards bribed or they have papers to cover my shipment. It would not be difficult. I with them go - or I die."

"Why do they want you?"

"I have an occasional job done in their country."

"I don't understand. I thought you worked for us."

Torow nodded. "I do. I work for you. I work for Tyrnia. I work for others also."

"A double agent?" Jason looked at Torow with growing apprehension.

"Not really - and yet I suppose, in a way, yes. I work for Damnesty."

"Damnesty. What's that? Never heard of it - them."

"Very little known. And that's the way we want to keep it."

"And what does it do? What do you do?" asked Jason. "And what does the name mean? Damnesty. It even sounds nefarious."

"Quite the reverse. The organisation has a long name. DAMNST is the Tyrnian acronym. We thought we would add a D to Amnesty and extend the meaning of the word - as you do turning evil to devil - in a way."

"So, a branch of Amnesty."

"No. No connection. Something similar, but no connection. We have a common concern for those imprisoned - but we do not bother ourselves with why they were imprisoned but how they are treated. We are an organisation totally opposed to torture whatever the prisoner has done." His voice now became intense. "If one person is tortured the whole human race it demeans." He paused and continued more quietly. "And we are active. We try to release any such person. But they are so many. We are so few. Larry was fortunate. I am in trouble because people who ask for our help think of me as an agent. If I help others they think of me as a double agent - as you did. I would help from the Tower of London free someone if he were being tortured. We owe loyalty to no one. We have done work - very little really - all over the world - but very little, sadly."

"That sounds wonderful."

"But governments only like us when we are working for them or in other countries."

"But Hornia? They're 0 K now surely?" queried Jason. Torow looked at him steadily then shrugged. "Intelligence services are a law unto themselves. It may be they want me in order to hand over to some other country in return for a favour past or future; it may be they think about them I know too much. This is a sensitive time. It may be they wish to cover up their tracks in Tyrnia. I do not know."

"I find this all absolutely revolting." Jason shook his head and turned and looked out at the passing mountains as if to take his mind off these horrors.

"I have come to understand," said Torow, "Particularly the hypocrisy. The nations who rail against this ill-treatment of prisoners often do the same - perhaps on a smaller scale - more selective - and of course for a far better cause. We have come only for the individuals to concern ourselves not for the nations." He paused. "I think is now ended my mission."

"Never." Jason spoke so loudly he looked around to reassure himself others were not hearing the conversation. All the other passengers seemed to be involved with their own discussions or were asleep. He continued more quietly as he observed the men and women occupying the seats nearest. "We must do something. We could gather enough for a fairly good disguise from this lot. I'll buy that silly hat over there for a start."

"They have instructions to pick up the man with the limp. The man who his left foot drags. I cannot disguise that. I have for years been trying to."

The train did not stop on the journey. Jason sat back and, looking at his anxious looking companion from time to time, screwed up his resolve. He pondered the significance of Pyke asking him to carry the passport. He didn't like it. He would do something.

In what seemed to Jason to be a very short time the train drew into the station with a squeal of steel on steel and with a last snort. He looked out of the window and searched the platform. It was crowded. That would suit the would-be assailants. No one would notice a brief skirmish in this lot. Then he saw, by a pillar, two large men obviously trying not to be obvious. As the train bumped to a standstill Jason was the first to swing open his door and step down.

He hesitated for a moment then limped slowly towards the waiting men. They straightened up, looked at him, nodded and separated a little so that he would have to walk between them. Jason continued to limp towards them. A man now swung out of a carriage in front of him and limped towards the waiting men. The man who had followed Jason out of the train now limped towards them. Jason saw the big men look perplexed. He glanced round and smiled; behind him came about thirty men all limping and all dragging their left foot. Torow was amongst them. A look of fright now appeared on the faces of the two thugs. They looked at each other for reassurance, got none, turned and scurried quickly out of the station, roughly pushing a genuinely crippled man, who was waiting on the platform, out of the way.

CHAPTER FORTY FOUR

To Jason's distress both Pyke and Larry looked surprised to see Torow with him when he returned to the bus although he thought he detected a look of relief in Larry's face. Jason now regretted that he had not shared his misgivings even more fully with Torow.

Pyke was busy, with the help of Rory and John, turning the bus back to brown again for the return through the border post. The thin panels which had been removed had been tucked under the chassis and the distortion which they had suffered, in the hurried one man removal and the subsequent bumping about, made the replacement difficult but Pyke found that in John he had a man who could use his hands. Pyke was grimacing in pain as he guided the work of his two assistants.

When the job was completed and the little bus looked like its old self again Jason was just bracing himself to confront Pyke and Larry about the attempted kidnapping when the two men came to him. Pyke looked to be in a foul temper. "Jason. Your train journey with Torow. Did you learn anything?"

Jason put the irritable tone down to the injured arm. "Not a lot. The country along the border is wild, very wild. I wouldn't like to have to cross these mountains."

"About Torow, Jason. About Torow." Pyke made to emphasise the point with a gesture and his face distorted in pain.

"I was not trying to learn anything about him. Why should I?" asked Jason.

"No, perhaps not, well, we have learned something of him. He is a double agent. Does that surprise you?"

Jason expressed his disgust at such a suggestion and told them, in some detail, of what he had learned about Damnesty and how impressed he was by the organisation and by Torow. On Pyke's retort that this was anarchy Jason really let rip. He told Pyke what he thought of the double standards, which allowed the organisation to be used, by their country, but regarded as evil when it applied the same high principles in other countries. He rounded off by pointing out that in his opinion they should be discussing how best to reward Torow for his magnificent services.

"Your opinion! We do not have the luxury of opinions. You should know that. We have our instructions. Torow is under arrest and will be taken with us."

"You mean to Britain I hope? We won't abandon him in Hornia will we? I wouldn't go along with that." Larry butted in looking anxious. His jaw tightened.

"We will get instructions in Hornia. We will then do precisely what we are ordered to do." Pyke stomped off displeased with the discussion.

Larry and Jason shared their disquiet over this outburst. "I protested, explained Larry." But Pyke told me about a friend of his who died because someone did not carry out his instructions to the letter."

This alarmed Jason and the two men agreed to keep a watch over Torow. Jason promised he would stay with the threatened man every step of the way from now on. They walked over to the group and found that Torow, who had not resisted arrest, was now in the bus bound by the wrists and ankles. Grace, Julia and Chuck were with him, all distressed by this treatment of the man who had, till now, been the hero of the expedition. Grace looked up furiously as Jason approached and expressed her disgust at what was being done to this man she had come to like so much.

"Don't concern yourself, dear lady," Torow entreated, his face which always looked crumpled into a smile now just looked crumpled. "When our members undertake the duties we the risks involved know. We do so willingly for those unfortunate persons who find themselves in the dreadful situation that Larry did. It is to help such people a privilege."

Jason, who had been feeling sick about the whole business now felt ten times worse. He knew that Larry's capture had been engineered and this gallant man had been put in great danger to rescue a man who had deliberately walked into a trap. Larry felt even more outraged. Pyke knows too, thought Jason, and yet can behave like this. He boiled with rage and frustration.

"You will be treated fairly in Britain. Won't he Jason?" Chuck turned to Torow. "Have you worked for Britain often?"

"Yes, and willingly when the objective is correct. Britain pays well which helps us to undertake unpaid work elsewhere. Many unfortunates have no one who cares. However to Britain I do not want to go, but even if I did, I am not sure you will get me through Hornia. They wish to discuss with me a certain missing person who could be very embarrassing to the present rulers when things change - as change they will."

"I will stay with you all the time from now on. Larry and I have undertaken to make sure that you are not left in Hornia." Jason looked over at Larry and felt a wave of pleasure to have such a man as an ally.

Torow shrugged from within his tight bonds. "We'll see."

Julia, who had been getting more and more red in the face now exploded, "I think this is disgraceful. We must do something whatever the cost. I am not going to take this lying down. None of us should stand for it."

Chuck smiled. "That sounds acrobatic but it is very Christian of you Julia - but then it would be - you being a nun."

"I am not a nun," retorted Julia sharply.

"A novice nun, then."

"I am not any kind of nun. I had never been in a convent in my life till this week."

Jason looked completely bemused and to break the awkward silence said softly, "Well, that should please you Chuck. You thought a nun would be inaccessible."

"And what did you wish access to Chuck?" asked Julia.

Chuck was now the one to look confused and embarrassed. "I don't understand. I thought Grace - I thought you - I don't understand."

Jason looked at Grace thoughtfully. "So you're not -". He stopped to chose his words carefully. "Are you the one from the convent, Grace?"

"I was brought up in a convent," replied Grace.

"Then - back with Zuko - why?" Jason stuttered.

Grace was silent for a time. Julia hung her head but it was she who answered. "Grace knew that I have just had a serious operation. She wouldn't let me be - ." Julia lapsed into silence.

"Oh, Grace!" exclaimed Jason.

"Zuko!" Torow spat out the name. "When I return, if I return, I will speak to Mantos. He will be punished."

"No, please don't. That would give substance to something insubstantial I wasn't really there. I was - meditating."

"Oh, Grace you're marvellous," said Jason.

"Julia is a good woman." Grace put her hand gently on the other woman's knee.

Julia had a tear in her eye but she laughed. "Good woman! Good pair we make. A lapsed nun and a prolapsed prostitute."

Grace broke in sharply. "Remember Julia, we agreed - I hadn't to call myself a nun and you weren't to call yourself a prostitute ever again. Remember what the Mother Superior said."

"Bless her, yes." Julia smiled. "Well, we were both just beginners - novices.

"I just didn't have the bent for it," said Grace.

"Me neither. In fact that describes my feelings precisely." She laughed. "I shouldn't laugh. It was laughing at a man in a gym slip that got me into this state."

The men looked embarrassed. To break the awkward silence Jason asked. "You don't wish to be a nun, Grace?"

"No. I don't think so. I'm confused. They don't like confusion. They like certainty. That's faith."

"Confused?"

"Yes. Growing inside me lately was the feeling that heaven was to have a home, a husband and a family. Some of them thought it was just a man - men - I was interested in. I had arguments. But the Mother Superior here understood. She helped me. I'm more sure of myself now - or I was --." She choked and broke off - her hands clamped tightly together and her arms thrust between her thighs.

There was another embarrassed silence which Grace herself broke this time. "But let's forget the true confessions bit and think about poor Torow. There must be something we can do to help." She looked at the other grim faces in turn. They all growled their assent.

"Do not put yourself at any risk for me," pleaded Torow. "I will be all right. I have friends everywhere."

"You have friends here," affirmed Grace emphatically.

CHAPTER FORTY FIVE

Pyke gathered some of the party together; those he thought already knew enough about what was happening to make superfluous any further attempts at secrecy. He anticipated he would need a lot of help in the days ahead; his injured arm was reducing his customary feeling of self-sufficiency. So he explained the current position as briefly as he could and stressed that any deviation from his instructions would put Larry in great danger. He spoke vehemently of the importance to Britain's security of Larry's speedy return.

"We must go through the border post with the same number as we entered. The plan was that Larry who is an accomplished mountaineer would cross over the border on foot and meet us at the other side. This is not now possible. He is not fit. I will obviously have to be on the bus so you, Jason, must go over the border."

"Over those mountains. You're crazy~" protested Jason. "I have vertigo. I couldn't go to the top of that little hill over there."

"Good, you won't take any foolish risks."

"I'm not taking any sensible risks either. You're not on."

"You will have a donkey."

"And you can find another donkey."

"We have another donkey. Torow will be on the other animal," explained Pyke.

"In that case you must go, Jason." Grace turned pleading eyes on Jason. "You said you would stay with him."

She thinks I can let him escape, thought Jason. He saw Pyke eyes narrow. And he thinks I might try.

Grace continued. "Give poor Torow as comfortable a journey as you can. See he comes to no harm. And I will come with you.'t

"No, you will not," barked Pyke. "We must have the same number on the bus. Now let's get on with it. We will now secure our two - prisoners into the sleeping bags. Do it here. I don't want the others to know what's happening. There has already been too much careless talk. Can any of you girls sew?"

"Of course we can. I've sewn habits and cassocks until my fingers were sore," said Grace.

"Right, sew the interrogator into that bag of his. Sew it lightly so that he can struggle out in a few minutes after we've departed. He will be released soon. Sew Torow in more securely so that he doesn't fall out on his donkey ride. Make sure he can breathe and pad his stomach. The donkey has a hard backbone."

"We will make him as comfortable as possible. Poor old Torow. Come on Julia let's see what we can do." Grace went off to find some sewing material.

"Help me lift him over here, Larry," asked Julia.

After a few moments Grace called over to Pyke. "Can we put the interrogator in the other sleeping bag. Torow's bag is torn and wouldn't be strong enough for the journey over the mountains. A lot of the stuffing has gone out of it."

"I know just how it feels," muttered Jason.

"Yes. Yes. Go ahead. Change the bags but be quick about it. Keep the blindfold on fill his head is inside. Make Torow as comfortable as you wish. It doesn't matter a damn for the interrogator he hasn't far to go." Pyke saw Hilary and turned to walk to her. He shouted as he went, "Remember pad the bag you are giving to Torow. It will be hard on that donkey's back. But don't take all day."

Larry helped Grace swap over the bodies and put Torow into a bag. They padded it and they could be heard discussing with him how to minimize his discomfort for the journey ahead. They covered his head but left one of the ties by his face loose so that he could breath. He now looked like a heap of merchandise being taken to the market, which was just what Pyke wanted. They put the cowering silent interrogator, who had not had a wink of sleep beside the phantom river, into the other bag and sewed it up more lightly. They took their time and when they were finished an impatient Pyke sent Larry to bring Torow over.

The two men bent the wrapped body over. "Right Hilary. Go to it," said Pyke.

Hilary drew back the cover of a ball-point pen and when she pressed it Jason could see a small globule of clear liquid apparently hanging in mid air, then a thin line of reflected light revealed a long needle. She screwed up her face and stuck the needle deep into the fabric drawn tight over the unfortunate man's buttocks. There was a squeal, followed by a brief struggle then the body in the bag went limp. Some of the party looked on with distaste as this was happening, but Hilary tossed her head and, with a defiant gesture, replaced the top of the pen.

"That will make it easier for him on the mountain crossing," said Pyke. And stop Jason trying any heroics, he thought to himself.

"I'll put in a word for him when we get home," said Larry. "Good chap."

"Double agent," hissed Hilary her head back and her blue eyes set hard.

That's a trick of the light, thought Jason, and she's had to brace herself. That was a tough thing to have to do. He patted her on the shoulder.

"This is thrilling. I could get used to this life of yours, Jason," she murmured.

Jason looked at her in perplexed admiration. He so wanted her to be the sort of woman he could love.

After they dispersed Jason saw Pyke go over to Torow's bag and stick an ordinary needle into him. There was no reaction. Pyke smiled grimly. Jason didn't see Grace pick up the needle and make to stick it into Hilary's thinly clad rear end - and then change her mind.

Pyke outlined the plan for the crossing. The bus was to go through the border post in the middle of the day when it was at its busiest with tourists. Larry was given instructions to release the interrogator before the bus set off towards the border. He was to be kept out of sight so that he could never link the bus with the rescue. Pyke repeated that the interrogator was not to be harmed as, with the fabricated clues pointing to his involvement, no one would believe a word if he went back and tried to explain what had happened. If he were injured, Pyke contended, it might just give his story some credibility. Pyke also emphasised that the vengeance would be sweeter if exacted at the hands of his own people.

"Right, let's go see Jason on his way," said Pyke with some relish.

Jason, mounted on a small but strong-looking donkey, with another donkey bearing the limp body on it tied behind him, looked decidedly uncertain how to get this caravan on the road.

Hilary approached him, gave him a warm kiss and whispered, "Have fun, darling. See you."

Grace and Julia both gave him a parting hug. Julia said, "Be careful." and Grace said sternly, "Look after yourself Jason and don't do anything daft, please." She started to say more then glanced at Hilary and added, "Everything will be all right."

Pyke smote the leading donkey on its rear and with an indignant bray off it shambled. "See you this evening, Jason. Or if you have to hide up - we will wait till tomorrow morning. Good luck."

The girls waved and Grace gave a thumbs up sign.

As the donkeys lurched up the slope the bus drove off and soon drew into a long queue of cars and coaches waiting at the border post. There was quite a delay and when Larry stepped out of the bus he was pleased to see that the harassed guards were not spending much time with each vehicle.

As Larry returned to his seat Rory beckoned. "That must have been quite a parting kick you gave your friend. He didn't take long to get free, but he was limping when I saw him going into the woods."

Larry shrugged. "I hope he gets what he deserves."

As they approached the barrier a soldier came on the bus, took a curious look at Larry who was not at all relaxed in Jason's bright purple uniform. He had hoped to be inconspicuous. How Jason could have picked such a uniform for himself he could not understand. But as Larry froze, the soldier just looked at the quaint, ill fitting jacket, laughed, and passed on. He only took a few minutes to clear the bus and it trundled on its way.

As soon as they were past the barrier Monica rose dramatically. "I have been uncomplaining long enough." There were gasps of disbelief. She shouted, directing her voice to Pyke. "Now that we are through the border you don't need the full number of passengers. I am getting off. I've had enough. I don't know what you are up to but I've had enough of it. I'm going to the police and get them to take me to the British Embassy. And I will not be reporting very favourably on this shambolic venture."

Pyke shook his head.

Monica's voice now rose an octave. "1 have this." She held up a large spanner. "And I'll break the window if you don't stop right now."

Rory piped up. "The glass is Monica proof remember Monica hit the window hard - with no effect. "I'll scream and scream until -"

"Until you get your throat cut. As you say we no longer need the full number of bodies. Now sit down and shut up." Pyke turned and gave his full attention to the road ahead."

Monica bristled for a moment then, sensing the power and the contempt in the turned back, collapsed and sobbed.

Most of the others were thinking the 'throat cut' a bit drastic but Larry's mind only took in the scene dimly. He was thinking about the ease with which they had been cleared through the border into Hornia; absolutely no delay at that barrier. The officer leaning by the door had looked pleased. Larry feared that the smirk was not a good sign.

CHAPTER FORTY SIX

It was hot as Jason set off but there were patches of cloud and the light wind puffed up just enough dust to give the rays of light a sort of translucent solidity. He dismounted and walked pulling on the rope, which brought the two donkeys in his wake. He could not have ridden out with his legs dangling, feet almost on the ground, in front of his friends, his party. This is more dignified, he thought, as he shuffled forth in the rags, which were his disguise; the reluctant donkeys stepping daintily behind him; much more dignified.

He padded up the narrow dusty slope until he was away above the dwindling landscape and his waving friends. His legs started to tremble and he stopped looking down. He stared stiffly ahead and into the rising slope on his right. The path bent away around the hill and he was soon out of sight of his more fortunate companions. He relaxed; free now to tremble as much as he wanted. He walked on until he came to a passing place. There he tied up the donkeys, took the sleeping bag off the other donkey and with a struggle laid the limp heavy body on the ground. Dead weight, he thought and shuddered as he made it as comfortable as he could. He then huddled well into the fern covered hillside having decided to stay here till it got dark. He just could not go on at this height. He peered nervously down - for the last time - and shrunk away. He realised it must be almost two hundred feet up the mountain. He shuddered. Only slithering lizards kept him company - and the donkeys.

Much later as the shadows of the great hills crept across the valley and softened the alarming perspective Jason slung the inert body gently on to the second donkey, secured it safely then climbed on the leading one himself; to hell with dignity now, and made a reluctant start slowly up the hill to a chorus of invisible frogs.

The uncertainty of what the darkness hid and the occasional stumble of the donkey was as nothing to Jason. He could not now see the height; the depth; the drop. He had sufficient lack of imagination not to visualise it. He was comparatively happy.

Thus he ascended to a great height, certainly thousands of feet, with no qualms. He was however suffering. The configuration of the donkey's back was in no way parallel to, or complementary to, his crotch. Each step brought its bump and rub.

Jason did try to walk for a few hundred yards leading the recalcitrant animals but he got the distinct impression that when he did this the beast handed over total responsibility for direction and even keeping on the path entirely to him. Not a good thing, he thought, and remounted.

It grew colder and he envied Torow snug in the sleeping bag slung behind him. The frog chorus stopped. More sense than to come up this high, he thought. As the mist crept in his already faint perception that they were going roughly in the right direction grew correspondingly dimmer.

"Faith," he said to himself, "Is what I need. Faith in a donkey."

They plodded on up and up till Jason felt his ears pop. Now, when a stone was dislodged from the path and fell over the edge, he could not hear it land. He shuddered and tried to persuade himself that the stones were falling on soft earth by the wayside. He kept hoping the path would start going downwards soon. It crossed his mind that he might have to descend in daylight. This troubled him so much he had to dismount and relieve himself, keeping as quiet as possible. The donkeys also took the opportunity to ease themselves but noisily and with such force that Jason feared they would start an avalanche.

However it was still as black as a coalhole when, hours on, they levelled out then, a little later, started descending. And as the donkey's body pointed downwards all the parts of Jason's body, which had become inured to the pain, were released to swell, burn and sting. Now new parts, delicate parts, took the strain of keeping his body from sliding on ahead. He groaned which startled the donkey and caused it to stumble. He groaned inwardly from then onwards and promised himself a good scream when his feet again touched the ground and his crotch touched nothing.

He was now trying to watch the terrain beneath him. As soon as grass started to grow high by the side of the path he had, he had been instructed, to leave the track and plunge westwards - by the sun. As he alternated between looking downwards and upwards this increased his discomfort. He checked to find out if Torow was awakening but there was no sign of life. The donkeys were now stumbling more often, partly because it was downhill and partly because they were becoming tired. Jason was also tiring and nodding off in a way which terrified him. He was unimaginative, but he did realise that a fall off this donkey at this time could be a long fall.

The sky was turning grey-blue away at the horizon behind him when the grass started brushing against his dangling legs. He turned the reluctant donkeys off the path on to what appeared to be rough grassy slopes. He hoped earnestly, nay desperately, that the advice that from now onwards it was gentle sloping ground was correct. He had been reassured - a bit - by Hubert's confirmation that it was likely to be so. Likely!

As the donkeys lurched on, through banks of cowslips and primroses, of one thing he was sure - at least fairly sure - he was out of Tyrnia. His adventure was over. He relaxed. It wasn't comfortable. He unrelaxed himself again.

He looked round to see if the slumped Torow looked comfortable. He didn't. He looked more limp than relaxed. This worried Jason. He struggled on downwards anxious that Torow might fall off with the change of gradient but the straps held him securely. In fact, he is probably more comfortable than I am, thought Jason.

At last he saw, away ahead and below, a flicker of fire and as instructed he headed towards it. Then as the ground levelled out he could no longer see the glow and was lost again but when the sky grew lighter he could detect, not so far away, a pall of smoke. When he arrived at the makeshift camp the group were all awake and getting ready.

"You took your time," growled Pyke.

Jason grunted.

"Did you really come over there? Good for you." asked Hubert, pointing to a track cut out of the side of a precipitous cliff, high up in the mountain.

Jason, who had just been wondering how he could dismount gracefully, took one look up to where Hubert was pointing, fainted clean away and fell in a bundle on the ground.

"And I didn't even mention the landmines," said Larry.

CHAPTER FORTY SEVEN

When Jason came to he was on the bus in his usual seat. Hilary, when she saw he was wakening, wiped his face with a wet cloth and whispered, "Was it tough?" and handed him a sandwich. He took a bite and put it down.

He looked around then got up and limped to the toilet. On his way back he saw that Larry looked worried and leant over him.

"Something wrong?" he asked

"Pyke has had instructions - but he won't tell me the details. I don't like it," whispered Larry.

Jason thought of the man fled up under the seat at the back of the bus and was alarmed. Larry went on, "But I gather that the Hornians have requested - backed with a threat - that we hand over our prisoner or I don't get through. 1 know that they've been watching you come down the hill. Guns trained on you. They must have thought you were Torow otherwise they would have searched for him at the border. So they have deduced, you having rejoined us, that Torow's with us now. Roger seems to have agreed to the hand over. He seems to be worried about Bruce too if we don't co-operate."

"Where and when?" asked Jason.

"I don't know. But I do know this isn't the road we would normally be on. I think someone will be waiting for us up ahead."

Jason shook his aching head. "Will they indeed."

With an involuntary Gary Cooper swagger he moved up the bus to Pyke, every step hurting.

"Pyke," he shouted. Pyke looked up.

"Turn off this road. At the next turning." instructed Jason gently.

"Sit down," barked Pyke.

"Turn off," hissed Jason, "or there will be some arm twisting. This arm."

Jason put his hand firmly on Pyke's wounded arm. Pyke squealed in anguish.

"Stop that. You'll have the bus over. Larry. Get him," ordered Pyke.

"One move and I'll take this arm apart." Jason shouted this time and gave the arm a twist. Pyke screamed in pain.

Chuck turned to Grace and Julia, "Travellers in trouble, the Mother Superior called us. She wasn't wrong."

Julia smiled weakly but Grace had her eyes on Jason.

"Next turning." Jason's eyes were now narrowed and his face set.

Grace came down the bus. "Don't Jason. Don't get yourself in trouble. It will be all right. Take my word for it."

Jason pushed Grace away roughly. "Go away. This is man's work."

He peered ahead for a turning. "If we pass one road and you don't turn this arm will end up in a tin of Chum." He gave the arm another twist. Pyke nodded grimly.

Then ahead Jason saw soldiers on each side of the road with arms up in a signal to stop. Jason renewed his pressure on Pyke's arm. "We're going through."

"You're mad. They've got guns."

"We're bullet-proof, remember?" growled Jason and gave the arm another twist.

Hilary was nodding enthusiastically, and her eyes were bright, as she looked at Jason. Pyke pressed hard on the accelerator and the bus shot past the surprised soldiers and was followed by a hail of bullets.

"I should have got off. I knew it," cried Monica at the same time shielding the tiny Lucy from the possible danger.

"From now onwards I am a devout coward," said Rory his gleaming eyes everywhere as he tried to take it all in.

As the bus steadied again Monica scrabbled about on the floor of the bus tidying up the fallen luggage and bits and pieces. Chuck huddled on the back seat with Grace and Julia. There were large signs ahead which meant nothing to any of them but at a prompting squeeze Pyke swung off the road at the turning. They could hear in the distance a siren starting to wail. It was a good broad new road and they shot along it as fast as the bus could go, which was very fast. The sound of the siren was getting fainter. They relaxed.

"We will release Torow as soon as we get clear." Jason growled to Pyke emphasising the point with some pressure.

"We might all have to abandon the bus. Split up and make a break for it. Better chance on our own," suggested Larry.

Then Pyke slammed on the brakes and Jason was about to tighten his grip on the injured arm when he looked up and saw that the road came to a complete end. The tools of roadwork were strewn about and heaps of rubble lay ahead and on both sides of them. The road was under construction. As always on such sites there was not a workman to be seen.

"Don't worry, things always get worse - before they get even worse." Alan picked himself up from the floor gingerly. "Bloody awful driving."

As they turned they could hear the siren coming slowly towards them. Monica started to tidy up again, changed her mind and abandoned the effort.

"Quick. We can pass them like last time. Go!" ordered Jason. The following car had stopped and swung across the road. Pyke drove towards it.

"OK, heads down. We'll rush them again." Jason felt for the tender spot on Pyke's arm. The bus accelerated.

"Look! Jason. Look!" shouted Larry.

There, lumbering up behind the car, was a tank. It stopped and turned across the road. Its turret rotated slowly towards them and its large gun, pointed upwards, fired a shot in the air, then it lowered and pointed straight at the little brown bus.

"If this were a Bond film the bus would sprout wings about now," shouted Rory.

"I know who's going to sprout wings," squeaked Julia.

Jason relaxed his grip on Pyke. "Slow down" he said softly, "and drive towards them - very - slowly."

He looked around the bus and sighed. All the fire had gone out of him as quickly as it had come. Hilary looked questioningly at him. Grace smiled reassuringly.

"Stop," ordered Jason. As they stopped, tyres squealing, he braced himself and stepped down from the bus.

"Anyone here speak English?" he shouted firmly.

"Over here. With your hands on your head"

Jason did not move. He would have had difficulty even if he had wished to. "Do you have identification?"

Someone in the army car laughed derisively. Someone in the bus laughed nervously. The gun turret seemed to twitch.

"You see," Jason went on, "We have been attacked by bandits just over the border. We thought this was another such attack. I am sure bandits don't have tanks but I would still like to see your identification. To be sure. If we are going to do business. ~

After a short time an officer left the car and came towards the bus. The other men in the car got out and pointed their rifles at him. The officer held out a card, which meant nothing to Jason.

"Ah! Good." Jason nodded knowingly.

Soldiers now boarded the bus and started to search without success then, as if they knew the design of the vehicle, they asked the passengers on the rear seat to stand while they swung the seat up on its hinges. The guard glanced inside nodded and passed on. He took a brief look at the luggage in the racks then left the bus and ordered that the boot be opened. He peered into the near empty boot and shook his head.

Jason winked at Larry.

"We know you have a prisoner? Taken from Tyrnia," said the officer gruffly, in good English. Jason hesitated and the officer now spoke sharply. "I am sure you have him well hidden. We have time to take the bus apart, piece by piece or perhaps better still we'll set it on fire." He nodded towards his troops.

One of the soldiers started to unscrew the petrol cap. Jason shook his head sadly and turned back to the bus. He felt totally and utterly defeated. He looked at no one as he re-entered the bus.

"Bring him out," shouted the officer. Several soldiers raised their rifles to their shoulders.

Jason pulled the lever and Rory and Chuck carried the sleeping bag out, Pyke and Jason, glaring at each other, followed.

"He is still alive?" The officer looked at the unmoving bundle. Jason nodded.

The officer took a knife from his belt and cut open the top of the sleeping bag and leant over the unconscious man. He put his hand on the clammy forehead and nodded. Another soldier came forward with a small flask and pressed it into the still man's mouth. There was a cough and a flicker of the eyes. Then a shake of the head and the eyes opened again, then a violent shudder, a tiny choked scream and a look of terror crossed the face.

Jason turned away not wishing to meet Torow's eyes but after a moment Chuck nudged him roughly and pointed. Jason reluctantly turned back and looked. He saw that the face twisted in fear - was not Torow's - but that of the interrogator.

"You!" hissed the officer. He turned to Jason. "We know him. Good. Well, well. Good. Not what I expected but good. So you were after him as well. I misunderstood. However I must insist that he accept our hospitality. This is even better. Very good. Thank you. The Tyrnians have asked us to look out for him but we have questions for him first. Then we will send him back. You may leave now. We will look after him better than you would have done. You will have a safe passage."

He signalled to his soldiers to take the sleeping bag and its shaking contents away then shouted after Jason, "Mind how you go." He looked down at the cowering interrogator and waved towards the bus smilingly gleefully. He was rubbing his hands as they lost sight of him. Jason had to use all his limited acting ability to look disappointed.

"If I ever find out –," Pyke drew his hand across his throat, the blood stained bandage making a red slash as if to emphasise the threat.

The little brown bus rang with song most of the rest of the day. Pyke did not join in the merry singing.

CHAPTER FORTY EIGHT

The first inclination of the bus party was to make a non-stop dash for home but it soon became apparent that neither Larry nor Pyke was up to it. They phoned ahead to a place recommended by the injured and unhappy driver.

I hope he doesn't have a domestic arrangement there too, thought Jason, or we'll never get home.

It turned out to be a small inn deep in the forest, well off the main road. They were the only guests and the innkeeper was delighted to have them. It was simple, almost primitive, but it was clean and comfortable.

The meal that evening was a jolly affair but quietly so. The mood was mainly of relief - and they were tired. Jason had slept in the bus but had still not recovered from his ordeal on the mountain.

The dish of the day was boiled head of ram covered with sunflower seeds. The cook proudly brought in a head for their approbation. It glared greasily, a tear of hot fat running from one eye.

Rory demurred. "I never could stand sunflower seeds."

Pyke, looking defeated, stayed at the table throughout the meal although obviously in great pain. His presence was inhibiting and Larry advised everyone to stay off the subject of the appearance of the interrogator instead of Torow.

"Never fear," said Rory. "I am a man of few words."

"Yes, but you use them over and over again," quipped Alan.

Monica chose to sit next to Jason, to his great chagrin, but he found that he was now a hero in her eyes.

"I like a man with fight in him. Too many Englishmen let everyone walk all over them. But not you. You were magnificent. A man of courage. We were the only two to stand up to Pyke. Weren't we?"

Jason sat timidly listening to her as his eyes wandered around the table, alighting on the others engaged in lively conversation. Pyke was doing the same, set faced and saying nothing. Hilary sat on the other side of the table in earnest conversation with John but she looked over occasionally and waved to Jason. She had berated him earlier for his stupidity on the bus but she had done so with a twinkle of admiration in her eyes.

"1 knew you were a fighter," she had said.

Grace and Julia were together, talking seriously but occasionally bursting into soft happy laughter. Chuck sat close to them and sometimes joined their conversation. In a relaxed moment his hand rested lightly on Julia's knee. She looked down with puckered brows, and then she smiled.

Alan and Rory were exchanging insults happily. "And what instant ruins are you going to put up when you get back?" asked Alan.

"I'll have to build a few bungalows to pay for this," said Rory.

"Why don't you settle down and build a few babies," Lucy, in good form, made cheeky faces at the two men.

"No chance, Lucy dear. You're preaching to the perverted. I think my wilds oats will continue to fall on stony ground for a while yet," said Rory. "I'm not the settling down type. Do I look it?"

"Well, with that grog blossomed belly - apologies to Dylan Thomas - you don't look exactly like a gay Lo-thar-io." Alan poked a fork towards Rory's stomach.

"Thank God for that," retorted Rory.

After a very heavy plum tart had been consumed with relish there was a lull in the conversation.

"No wonder that pig looked distressed. It was the thought of this tart coming after him." Rory folded his hands over his distended belly.

"Yes, the porker was just a warning shot across the bowels," groaned Alan.

"The bandits are probably water skiing behind the rubber boat now. I hope it sinks," declared Chuck.

"It will," mumbled Pyke; his only intervention of the evening. The others looked at him questioningly. "It has a slow puncture for anyone who uses it without the kitmaster's instructions."

"I hope Zuko is in it at the time," growled Jason. Grace flushed and looked down.

The silence settled in again so Lucy passed round some sketches Hubert had drawn on the journey. They were all admired;

buildings; landscapes and butterflies; birds and waterfalls; but the masterpiece, the one that drew gasps of delight was a drawing of the little chubby bus. Even Pyke smiled. The apparently haphazard sketching had done much more than catch a likeness; it seemed to distil the very nature of the bus and what it had meant to them.

Alan held the sketch up admiringly. "You've per-soni-fied it."

Hilary held the picture gingerly as if it were gold leaf.

"It's smiling." Grace was smiling broadly herself. "It looks so protective."

Julia almost hugged the picture.

"We must all have a copy," insisted Monica.

"I'll get copies made." offered Alan. "How many is that. Thirteen. Unlucky."

"Send one to Torow," suggested Grace.

Pyke scowled.

"But who is to have the original?" asked Alan.

All eyes turned on Hubert the man who had said so little. He thought for a few moments then stood up.

"I would do others but you can never catch quite the same impression again - at least 1 cannot." he paused and cleared his throat. "I have never wished to come on holiday since my wife died. Certainly not to the same places - nor to other places where I would have been among happy couples or happy families. This is my first holiday since then and it has been most interesting - and often enjoyable. I am not brave like most of you - and yet I have least to lose. I have been so impressed with the great good-humour throughout our hazardous journey that I would like to give my drawing to the member of this party who has made most light of our difficulties and added most to my personal enjoyment." Hubert paused again and looked around. "But I'm not going to. I'm going to give it to Larry. So that he can look at it in years to come and reflect that in his darkest hour - this is what was rushing to his aid."

Hubert sat down abruptly to a burst of laughter and applause.

As the piece of paper was passed to him the eyes set in Larry's tough and battered face filled.

Hilary kissed Jason warmly as the party broke up. "The hero of the day," she smiled.

"The zero hero. Amounted to nothing as always," he replied.

"It's the thought that counts - and the courage." Hilary reached up and caressed his nose. "You must be tired. I take it I'll be in no danger tonight." Jason nodded feebly. "Good. I'm exhausted too." She kissed him again, chucked him under the chin and went off to her bedroom.

Jason who was now completely exhausted was almost relieved. He felt too tired even for sleep. He went to the front door and climbed on to a low verandah. The night was still except for strange little noises coming from the dark forest. He didn't know what to make of the sounds- nor did he know why he was so bewildered? He felt as if he were in a trance. Now that Hilary was becoming friendly he was even more nervous of her. She liked adventure. He had had enough.

He was even more puzzled by Grace. She would abandon her calling for the family life. I don't know what a family life is, he reflected. She must have had one. He tried to think of his own mother and father and found it difficult to bring their faces to mind. He hadn't thought about it before but now he felt sad.

After a time Julia and Grace came to the doorway having walked round the inn. They were whispering happily.

"Lovely night, girls," Jason greeted them softly.

The three of them stood talking quietly for a few minutes then Julia excused herself.

"Don't tell me you're going for a bath," scoffed Jason.

Julia laughed "No, straight to bed tonight."

"She is a nice girl," Jason looked after the departing Julia.

"So the Mother Superior told you," asked Grace.

"No. I've made up my own mind."

"Good," said Grace.

"I'm sorry Grace. I was so mixed up. I said some dreadful things. I just couldn't think of - you - such a nice girl."

"But Julia is a nice girl. You just said so."

"Yes, but you - I like you I -. I am sorry. You have had a terrible time."

"Don't let's go over it. I don't intend to. It's past. Perhaps I can get some of my worries into perspective now. I think too much about myself. I realise that I am not really all that important."

"You are important - and I am really sorry. I would love to apologise to Julia but I wouldn't know where to start."

"Julia doesn't need an apology. She is a gracious lady. Remember?" A smile flickered on Grace's face.

"And you." said Jason. "And you are important. And I do like you."

"Thank you," murmured Grace and she stretched upwards and kissed him warmly. As Jason was about to respond she drew back and whispered, "Best of luck with Hilary." She turned and re-entered the Inn.

CHAPTER FORTY NINE

Pyke did not return to England with the bus. When they stopped over in France, at the Auberge Ballon, Pyke stayed on with Madam de Pre. She gave his wounded arm the tender loving care it needed.

For the first time in his career he had failed to fulfill orders. He could not face his colleagues. He resigned from the service pleading unfitness, and received a polite letter of acceptance and a modest pension. His former colleagues never saw him again although they continued to use the Auberge Ballon. Bruce told Jason later that Pyke hid whenever they called because he had told Madam de Pre that he was being sought for extradition. This, thought Bruce, added the ingredient of excitement, which he evidently found so necessary to his sex life and they loved happily ever after. But others did report that the large chef had gone and the cooking had improved.

The group parted with mixed feelings. They had grown very close. Rory as often on their journey took the pain out of the parting with his final quip. "Alan," he asked, "Don't move. I want to forget you just the way you are."

On debriefing all members were given a sum of money as compensation for their distress and any loss of or damage to property; instructions which made it plain they were bound to total secrecy on pain of dreadful retribution; and a choice of another holiday free of charge.

Rory asked for a mountaineering holiday in Holland.

On his return Alan found that he was scheduled to go with a party of teenage schoolchildren to Paris. He agreed to accept any other holiday on condition it coincided with the Paris trip.

Lucy and Hubert went off together to chart the route of a migratory butterfly in New Guinea; Lucy to write and Hubert to illustrate.

confirm it when he is fully recovered."

Monica started on a long list of complaints but abandoned them when in reponse to the first Roger replied without emotion, "If he had cut your throat, rest assured dear lady, he would have been reprimanded."

Her noisy neighbour's party was still going on when she arrived home to her flat. She slept through it.

One of Chuck's first actions when he returned to his office was to submit a claim for the camera taken by the bandits. The claim was rejected for lack of proof.

"Not even reported to the police," scoffed Mister Dunn.

Chuck then wrote a fictitious story of a bus party to Europe for the Company magazine which won him enough to pay for a new camera. His use of language so impressed management so much that he was appointed secretary to the Staff Consultative Committee. The minutes thence forward sometimes misquoted Mr Dunn but even worse reported accurately and at length any time he said something stupid.

Jason returned to the office expecting that all hell would be let loose and waited with mounting apprehension for the summons from on high. It didn't have long to mount, the bell rang and Roger's flat, giving nothing away, voice flatly invited Jason to his office.

To Jason's surprise Roger was smiling. To Jason's disgust a pair of flimsy silk, lace trimmed pants lay on the desk, but his mind was distracted from this by a piece of paper Roger was waving like a latter day Chamberlain.

"Well done," beamed Roger, "Listen to this. From the Hornian Ambassador. 'Parcel received. Absolutely delighted. We will take good care of it.' They're pleased, Jason. I'm pleased."

"I'm pleased that you're pleased that they're pleased," said Jason.

"That was a job well executed. And Larry's home. He's not well. We've put him in a nursing home for a few days. He'll be all right. We'll put him on light duties. Unarmed combat instructor or something."

"And the message?"

"Not well enough. Delirious. His version was muddled but I hope he can do better when he is fully recovered."

"You mean we might have been through all that for nothing?" Jason's face twisted in disgust.

"Not at all. We have it right here." Roger lifted and waved the silk pants like a latter day Brian Rix.

"I don't understand."

"Larry arranged to have the message recorded in case he forgot it or didn't get back."

Jason put on his - 'I am with you so far but please go on,' expression as he completely lost track of what he was being told.

"In code. In the lace - here. Very ingenious. The girl wore them through the border posts. I haven't seen the cipher boys take such an interest in their work for a long time. She - Hilary did you call her?" Jason nodded. Roger held up the gossamer garment and continued. "Hilary must be a brave girl to have worn this in those circumstances

Jason looked at the tiny scrap of cloth. A brave girl to wear them in any circumstances, he thought. "The message was important." Jason expressed this half way between being a question and implying that he knew all about it.

"We didn't think so to begin with; they want Lenci Dolitin; a man we didn't think was of any importance but it transpires that he is a high-ranking nuclear physicist. He came across last year but we paid little attention to him thinking he was a little fish which is evidently just how he wanted it. He was sick of what he was doing - what he was a part of."

"And what do you think now?"

"We reckoned if the Tyrnians were desperate for his return he must be important and that's how it is turning out; very important."

"And now?"

"We'll see. And you Jason do you wish to remain on the field staff now you have the scent of blood in your nostrils?"

"No. I'll stop now before it's the scent of my own blood, thank you. Perhaps you were right. No dedication. May I ask you Roger, with all the changes, to what are we now supposed to be dedicated?"

"Same as always, dear boy. To the service; to the section; to me - and not necessarily in that order. So you don't fancy action in the field."

"I think not. I'm definitely a paper man."

Roger nodded in agreement. "And you'll be pleased to hear that in view of your coup the Hornians are sending Bruce Dunlop back."

"Good," said Jason. "I know how much he likes to have Christmas at home."

"Emil has settled in well." Roger looked at Jason.

"So I see." Jason tried to keep all expression from his face.

A few days later Jason was transferred, not unwillingly to the Home Office. He was to join the staff, which prepared answers to parliamentary questions. "You," Roger had said, "Have just the turn of mind for that."

Later when Jason went round the department to say his farewells, he was surprised to see John, with his sleeves rolled up working away at a lock with the Kitmaster, looking more happy and relaxed than he could remember.

He was even more surprised to see Hilary sitting behind a desk.

"Hello, Jason. How nice to see you," she greeted him enthusiastically. "I have been asked to join the firm. Wonderful isn't it. We'll be working together. I'm going to like it here."

Jason explained about his transfer. Hilary said "Pity," then brightened up, "But I'm sure I'm going to like it."

The Home Office Ministers' answers were curt to the point of rudeness for the next few weeks. In fact a Junior Minister got promotion on the strength of one particularly aggressive and outrageous answer.

In the same week the Foreign Office received high praise for directing a U.N. team to a nuclear bombsite in Tyrnia which was then dismantled. This brought about a change of government in that country.

Lenci Dolitin and his wife settled in a village in the northern part of British Colombia - in an area not dissimilar to their beloved Tyrnian mountains. He was given a change of name and new documents. He had asked if he could be called Doulton but Roger had said that the would be a mug to take a name like that - so close to his own. He told everyone of his little pun for days. However, he never told anyone, ever, that the interrogator's son had a home in the next valley; a gift in return for some middle quality information brought with him when he defected some years previously.

A few weeks later Jason invited Hilary out for an evening at the most splendid restaurant he knew. He was determined to make absolutely sure that he was really in love. Hilary wore a low cut gown in a soft red, which set, off her own beautiful colouring. They had a jolly, happy evening. They supped well, they wined well and they reminisced. They held hands. He caressed her knee. She caressed his nose. They joked about the border guards, the convent, the passage, the little bus, the tank and Hilary's pants.

"I'm glad they didn't see through that," joked Hilary.

"Yes, that would have blown your cover," laughed Jason.

Hilary talked enthusiastically and at length about her new job in the department. She was happy. At the end of the evening Jason was quite sure he was in love, that he had thoroughly tested himself. The next day he proposed and was accepted.

Just two months later Jason stood waiting by the altar, and as the sound of the Wedding March swelled through the church, there walked down the aisle towards him the girl he loved, his beautiful bride - Grace.

They invited Chuck and Julia to be their best man and bridesmaid respectively but it was another four years before that pair walked down the aisle together.

As to the appearance of the interrogator in Hornia, when the powers wanted Torow, Grace said that she, with the help of Larry, had swapped the two bodies as instructed. Julia said that she, with the help of Chuck, had swapped the two bodies as instructed. No one could ever persuade them to say whether this duplication was deliberate.

"We have taken a vow of secrecy," they said.

THE END

This is Bob Adams first novel. He has written and had performed and published several plays. His first play won him an Alan Ayckbourne prize for short, short plays in 1989. Since then he has written plays on conservation, take over bids, cloning (before it became a fashionable subject) and a comedy in a transplant ward in a hospital. His latest plays have been comedies set in the farming community.

Bob has worked in the timber and furniture industries in Africa and Scotland and has served as an officer in the Parachute Regiment. He was awarded the OBE in 1980.

Printed in the United Kingdom
by Lightning Source UK Ltd.
136218UK00001B/292-309/P